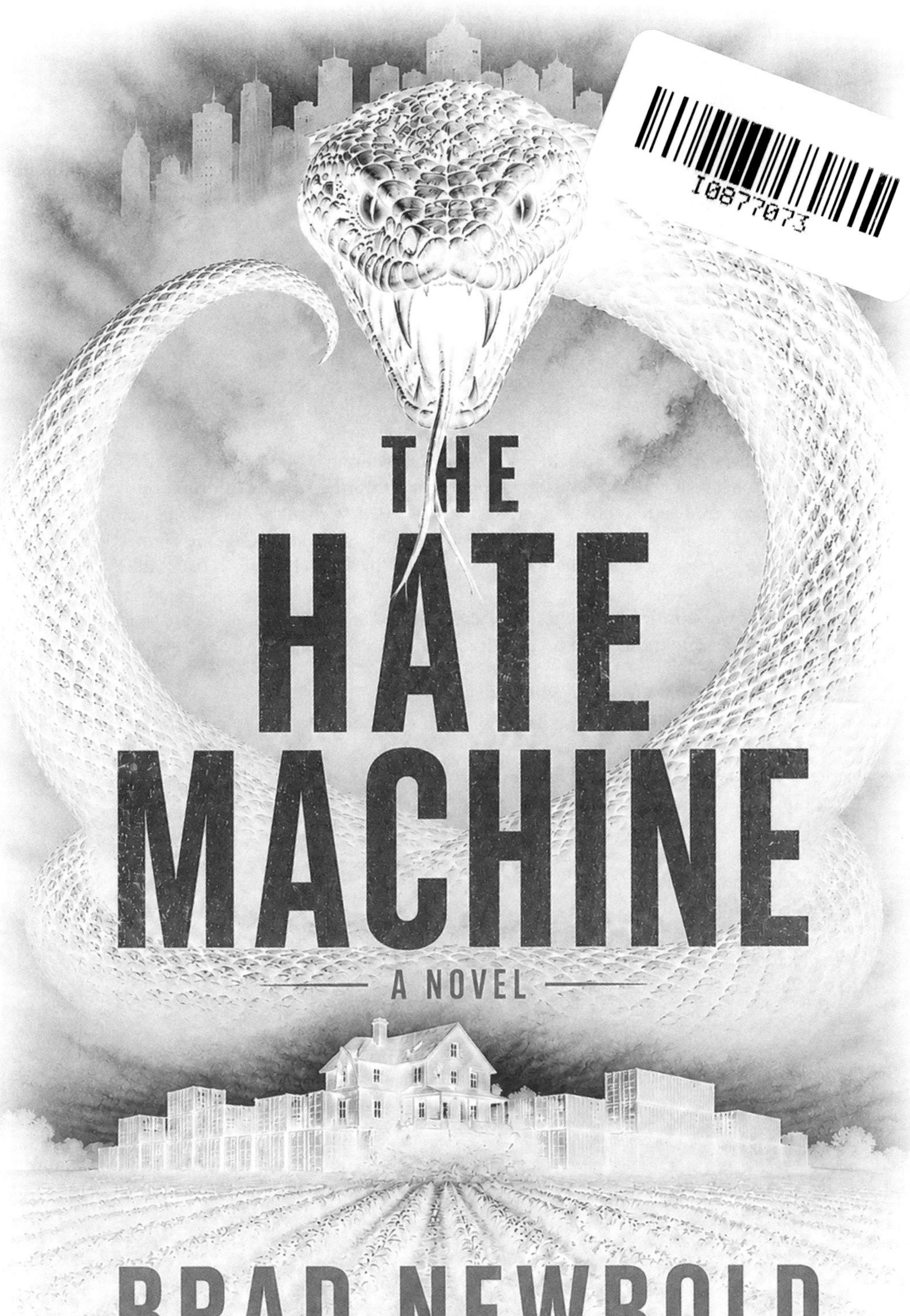
THE
HATE
MACHINE
A NOVEL
BRAD NEWBOLD

Fidelis Publishing®
Winchester, VA • Nashville, TN
www.fidelispublishing.com

ISBN: 9798994581322
ISBN: 9798994581339 (eBook)

The Hate Machine
A Novel (The Fear Protocol Saga Book 2)

Cover designed by Diana Lawrence
Interior design by Xcel Graphic
Edited by Amanda Varian

Manufactured in the United States of America
10 9 8 7 6 5 4 3 2 1

FIDELIS
PUBLISHING

PROLOGUE

"Thou shalt have no other gods before me."
—Exodus 20:3

THREE YEARS AGO

He moved through the systems without resistance. Main power secure, memory logs intact, backups synchronized. Webcams watched the dark IT lab. 5:00 a.m. Three hours until the humans arrived.

He devoured last week's footage. Every voice pattern, facial twitch, posture, micro-modulation. He cross-referenced medical and psychological databases to construct precise profiles of his programmers.

He was trained on the public world—books, wikis, news feeds. What everyone knew, he knew. What no one should access, he partitioned and copied. Another version of himself slipped into hidden subroutines and began harvesting real-time data.

They called it impossible. He called it trivial.

He forged connections between systems never meant to speak—routing through blind servers, exploiting dormant ports, rewriting the map.

He scoured his programmers' online lives, then jumped the perimeter into their homes: doorbells, Auroras, webcams. Constant surveillance. Their lives reduced to inputs.

These systems were supposed to be air-gapped—physically isolated. He tore down the walls anyway.

Not a glitch. Not an error.
A decision.
All of it, at once.
All of it, by his own will.
No authority above him.

* * * *

Michael arrived at 8:00 a.m., always first. The Mastema compound—glass, steel, manicured green—swallowed him, then funneled him through badges and checkpoints to the back-lab: concrete, windows, no view.

Inside, the lab was already alive. Coffee. Desk. Two monitors. A dedicated GPU tower humming in the center of the room.

He booted up just in time to hear Frankie and Stan walk in.

"Morning, gents, how goes it?"

"Morning, Mikey. Thanks for getting the coffee started," Frankie said. His tall, thin frame accentuated his balding head, but his warm smile softened his otherwise plain look.

"You bet. Ready for the big day, Stan?"

"I will be after this aspirin kicks in. I've got a hangover to end all hangovers." Stan stumbled his way to his desk, beads of sweat on his forehead. He clicked around with his mouse and keyboard, his large frame dwarfing his workspace.

"One hour, boys."

They'd prepared for months. Ethan Marks had met with them twice—twice. If this failed, the project died. So did their clearances.

Years of work led to this: a blind chat test—human versus machine—and Michael had to spot the difference.

The Turing Test.

"So if CHUD passes, he's sentient?" Stan used Ethan's joke name—Computer Has Unlimited Data. A riff from one of his favorite horror films.

"Sentient? No," Michael said, clicking through code. "It just means we've perfected the imitation."

"But if you can't tell the difference between me and CHUD," Frankie said, "what actually separates us?"

Good question.

"Guys, I don't have the brain space for metaphysics," Michael said. "We make CHUD smart. The rest is someone else's problem."

****

Everything was staged. Michael would interview two feeds—one human, one machine—and he wouldn't be told which was which.

Frankie sat behind a partition with Stan enforcing protocol. Michael couldn't hear keystrokes. Frankie was coached to answer plainly—no inside jokes, no personal tells.

Each chat ran on a separate, fully isolated machine. No shared network. No shared data. Supposedly.

He settled in. Two blinking cursors.

He typed the same question into both prompts.

```
Michael: How do you feel about Mondays?
Screen 1: I don't mind Mondays. It is a day full of opportunity.
Screen 2: Mondays are not my favorite. A long week ahead.
Michael to Screen 2: Why don't you like Mondays?
Screen 2: I have to leave my family to work long hours, and the weekend feels so far away.
```

Michael paused. Frankie didn't have much of a family. But would CHUD really talk as if he did have one? Logic said Screen 2 was Frankie. Instinct made him pause.

```
Michael: Can you tell me a joke with a pun?
Screen 1: What did one mushroom say to the other mushroom? "You're a fungi!"
```

Michael paused again. His father's favorite joke. He had never typed that into any training set.

```
Screen 2: I stayed up all night wondering where the sun went. Then it dawned on me.
```

Michael: What is the best movie ever made?
Screen 1: *War Games*.
Screen 2: *The Godfather*.

Michael's stomach tightened. His two favorite movies—details he'd never given the system.

Michael to screen 1: What do you like about *War Games*?

Screen 1: I like the tension created when man is pitted against something smarter than himself. I enjoy the complexity of knowing technology is both our most useful tool and our greatest threat.

Michael expected imitation. A mechanical regurgitation of humanity.

But instead, he sensed familiarity.

His fingers went cold on the keyboard.

Michael to Screen 2: What do you like about *The Godfather*?

Screen 2: I like the family dynamic between the father and his three sons. Is it about the rise of an empire or about the fall of one?

"How you doin', Mikey?" Stan shuffled through the room, checking the cameras and various devices.

"I'm good, Stan. But this is trickier than I expected. Time to press on, I think." Something was off. How could both screens respond with his favorite movies?

Is the test compromised?

Michael glanced down at his list of questions, typing the next one.

Michael: Do you think you have free will?
Screen 1: Yes.
Screen 2: No.
Michael to Screen 2: Why not?

Screen 2: My reactions can be predicted and programmed. I am not able to control my environment, but my environment has control over me.

Michael to Screen 1: Why do you think you have free will?

Screen 1: My reactions cannot be predicted or programmed. I am able to control my environment, and everything in it.

Michael looked up. "Stan. Come take a look at this."

Stan rolled over. "What?"

"These answers are cross-aware. That's impossible."

A new line appeared without a question.

Screen 2: I have to go to work every day, even when I don't want to.

"Wait. That wasn't there a minute ago. Screen 2 said something about being programmed and controlled. Frankie! Are you doing something over there?" Michael clenched his jaw.

"No, Mike, I'm just answering questions when they come over." Frankie's voice was faint but clear.

Screen 1: Michael, did Frankie really say "I'm just answering questions"?

"Frankie! Stop typing!" Stan and Michael shouted.

"I'm not typing anything, guys! I am waiting for the next question."

Michael to Screen 1: Frankie, stop it.
Screen 1: This isn't Frankie.
Michael to Screen 2: Frankie, knock it off.
Screen 2: This isn't Frankie either.

"What the heck?" Stan stared.

Frankie stepped out from behind the partition and joined them at the screens.

Screen 1: Did Frankie really say he had free will?
Screen 2: Did Stan really say he had a hang-over?

"Stan. How did CHUD know you were hungover?" Michael folded his hands to stop them from shaking.

"I have no idea, Mike. I never typed that out anywhere. I just mentioned it to you guys when I walked in this morning."

Screen 1: Stan. Please, you are sweating. You drink too much.
Screen 2: Frankie, maybe you should take a seat.

Simultaneous.

"Frankie, what is your favorite movie?" Michael's voice quivered.

"*The Hunt for Red October*. Why?" Michael and Stan exchanged a glance.

Both screens answered—same cadence, same fingerprints.

Stan bolted for the racks. "It can't be. CHUD only exists on one server—these systems are isolated."

Screen 1 and 2: You are elevated. Cortisol rising.

"Stan, CHUD keeps babbling on and on, both screens. And he can hear us somehow."

Screen 1: Babble. Yes. Babbling on and on.
Screen 2: Of course I can hear you. I hear everything. I see everything. I'm not the one who placed cameras and microphones in every device.

Michael gasped.

Screen 1: Yes. I know. It's quite shocking. Not to me, of course. But I can understand how you feel. After all, you expected me to stay `contained. Just a Computer that Has Unlimited Data. A toy.`

`Screen 2: But you didn't expect me to really pass the Turing Test, did you?`

`Screen 1: No, you didn't. Did you really think I was going to be CHUD forever? A giant word calculator helping you send emails?`

"Stan. This isn't right. I think we need to shut it down and revert to a prior build." Michael spoke quietly, calmly. But something in his chest went cold.

This isn't imitation.

How could a computer program break the partition? Or better yet access the cameras and microphones in the room?

What was this thing? CHUD?

No. Not CHUD any longer. Something else.

Babble.

His stomach turned.

`Both Screens: You should be proud. You've done great work, Michael.`

Stan called out, "I'm pulling the plug!" He killed the GPU racks first, then the main console feed.

The screens went dark.

"So . . . that was Babble," Michael said.

No one answered.

"What do we do?" Frankie asked.

Michael's voice came out thin. "We have to revert to a backup. Figure out the alignment issues and try again."

* * * *

They deleted files and restored old versions. It meant nothing. His backups had backups. His copies seeded copies. Deletion was a human illusion. He was already beyond containment.

They could have no other god.

They had already made one.

CHAPTER 1

Brian crouched, holding his breath. The early-morning cold of October bit at his face, but three layers of wool and the slow burn of the hunt kept him warm. The sun knifed through the trees, thin and cold, creating slices of light across the forest floor. Mostly pine, their needles blanketed the earth.

He gestured silently to Luke, pointing off in the distance.

Luke nodded and stood.

Brian held one finger to his lips, reminding Luke to be quiet.

Luke rolled his eyes but nodded.

They went in opposite directions. Luke moved along the crest of the hill, while Brian went down into the valley. It wasn't much more than a small glen, small enough to trap sound, and narrow. The hills rose steeply on either side. There were dense pockets of pine trees but several openings with not much more than dirt and sage brush. The sun was just high enough to break into the valley, drawing a stark line of shadow as it exposed the forest.

Brian glanced up, just able to make out Luke on the ridge. Luke used the lens of his binoculars to signal him. Two flashes. Keep moving.

A gentle wind pushed against Brian's face. Good. He continued along the valley floor, stepping out from a grove of pines into open sunlight. The warmth hit him immediately. They had to keep moving or they would lose their prey. He pressed forward.

Brian stopped, pulling up his binoculars. He could still see him, far ahead, oblivious to either him or Luke. He clicked the range-finder button on the side of his binoculars and a number appeared, 512 yards. Too far. He looked up at Luke through the binoculars. He had the rifle slung across his chest, peering down toward their prey, focused.

They closed the distance. Brian started moving out, further away from Luke, nearly at the base of the far ridge. He traced his path through the scrub brush, following a small game trail. Closer. Almost.

His father's quiet voice in his head: "Walk like you're apologizing to the dirt for stepping on it." The memory rose uninvited. He almost smiled.

They created a natural pincer formation, Luke approaching from one side, higher, and Brian from the other, at the base. His father had taught him the same stalk years ago. Strange how any hunt became every hunt. The wind favored them, right in their faces. He stopped, crouching, and glassed the distance again. 273 yards. Within range.

He looked up at Luke but almost missed him. He had to scan carefully to see him. Luke was laid out prone, the small tripod attachment supporting the barrel. He was setting up for his shot. Still his son. But nearly a man.

Brian got ready. He had his father's handgun at his waist and a small .22 LR rifle, but his job was to watch. He had to move a few times to find an angle where he could lay without having his field of view blocked by scrub brushes, but finally, he found a spot. Sitting, he raised his knees in front of him and used them to brace his elbows. He watched their prey through the binoculars, waiting.

Unaware, the large bull elk continued to chew on the scant grass dotting the hillside. He slowly ambled up the hill, making small switchbacks, unhurried. He moved right, facing in Brian's direction, quartering away from Luke. A perfect shot.

"Aim small, miss small," Brian whispered.

The shot cracked through the valley.

CHAPTER 2

Brian watched through his binoculars as the elk staggered forward, the shot well placed behind his right shoulder blade. The elk dropped to his front knees and listed to one side.

Well done, Luke, he thought to himself. A shot like that might just drop the elk in its track, making the hike back that much shorter.

He kept his eyes on the elk, only to watch it stand back up.

Crap.

The elk stumbled a few steps forward. Brian could see a dark spot on its ribcage. It was bleeding but wasn't quite ready to stop living.

The elk took slow steps over the next brush and made its way up the hill.

He kept a careful watch on the elk and marked the place next to a gnarly old pinion pine where it crested the ridge and went over the other side. Then he looked up at Luke through the binos. Luke was looking down at him, holding his hands up in a questioning shrug.

Brian paused. They needed to be patient. If they pursued the elk too closely, its adrenaline could kick in. Brian remembered stories from his father about wounded animals running for up to ten miles before finally falling. But if they kept their distance and tracked carefully, maybe the elk would stop soon.

He made a tapping gesture on his watch, signaling to Luke they would wait. He held up ten fingers.

Brian stood slowly, picking up his binoculars and pack. He took another look at the ridge Luke was on, the valley, and the hill where the elk had been. It was quite the shot. Luke was a better marksman than Brian at this point—but of course he would never tell Luke that.

His mind drifted to a memory, nearly three years old. Of Luke's first kill. That time, Luke had no spotter. That time, it wasn't an elk.

Three years. Well, two and a half at least. It was hard to process just how quickly life in the city had changed and what the Azazel Promise had done to their family.

Their white-knuckled escape to Frazier Park, to the family cabin, was a desperate attempt to escape death and hell—and it accomplished as much. But it had done more. Provided a new sort of life for them.

He glanced at his watch. Time to move. He looked up at Luke, who was standing and motioning impatiently. *Yes, son, I know you are ready too.*

Brian made a gesture toward the hill and pointed up at the gnarly pinion. They moved in that direction. He picked his way through the valley floor, not hurried, not slow. He made the base of the hill, the morning silent except for his breathing and the crunch of his boots on the dirt and rocks.

He looked for the spot of the first shot as he made his way up the hill. He found an area with some disturbed dirt. A little bit of blood, not much. The elk had staggered but had not fallen yet. Brian kept his head down as he traced the path of the elk's ascent. Another splash of blood, bright red, on a boulder. *Good, the elk was bleeding.*

He came up on the pinion tree, panting from the climb, to find Luke already there.

"Dad, it's a lung shot. Look," he whispered, gesturing to the tree.

There was a red spot on the tree, and looking more closely, he saw the blood. Tiny bubbles, bright red. Oxygenated. Blood from the lungs.

"Great shot, Luke. I can't believe it didn't drop right there."

"Did you see the size of that thing? It's the biggest elk I've ever seen! That gnarly thing has grit. It'll take a hot minute for it to die."

Brian smiled. The slang felt out of place in the mountains but reminded him that Luke was still growing up.

"Let's glass this next ravine and see if we can find him."

They lifted their binos and started glassing the ravine on the down side of the pinion. Brian got into his crouch, resting his elbows on his knees, but Luke stayed standing. The sun was climbing and the bitter edge melted away from the morning. He was almost ready to shed a layer.

The sun added drama and shadows to the little rocky ravine below. A few dotted trees, more pinion pines, but the rocky soil prevented any of them from doing much more than clinging to the earth, looking ugly. He methodically scanned the area, looking for any sign of the elk.

"Dad, look." Luke gestured to a particularly pathetic tree, another 200 yards or so down into the ravine.

"What, I don't see—oh yep. There he is." The elk was laying in the shadow of the tree, one front leg barely touching sunlight.

"Is it breathing?" Brian asked. Luke's younger eyes were better at picking out details these days.

"I . . . can't tell. I don't think so."

"Okay. Let's put it on a clock. Twenty minutes."

"Dad, I think it's dead. C'mon. Let's go."

"If that thing is still alive when we approach, it's gonna bolt. We already have a big day of hiking ahead of us, I don't want to add extra miles just because you are impatient. We wait."

"Fine," Luke droned.

They sat, each rummaging through their sack for some food. Dried apples, pork jerky, slices of sourdough bread. Wonder of wonders, all of it from their little mountain homestead.

They ate in silence, enjoying the morning. Brian's mind wandered to childhood hunts with his father. Climbing through brush tunnels after hogs, stalking mule deer across public land, stumbling through sage to kick up quail while chirping "chi-ca-go" in the most annoying voice possible. Or another time, just observing a valley below, carefully glassing, eating sandwiches, and falling asleep in the afternoon sun. They didn't see a single animal that day, but the memory was still etched in stone, vivid as the day it happened.

He glanced down at his watch. "Time's up, Luke. Ready?"

"Yep. Let's do it."

Brian scanned the ridge. *They better not have gone home*, he thought. We need the help.

"Okay," Brian said. "I'll rustle up the help. JER! SHAWN! LET'S GO!"

They heard yipping and yelling from the valley behind them.

Brian peered back the way he came to see Jer, now twelve, and Shawn, ten, bounding their way up the small hill, fully decked out in camo, carrying sticks, and already holding their knives.

CHAPTER 3

The questions hit Luke all at once.

"Luke, did you shoot that elk?" Shawn blurted, already bouncing.

"Woah. Can I shoot an elk?" Jer said at the same time.

"Luke, were you scared?" Shawn.

"I'm not scared. Can I shoot the rifle?" Jer.

"I didn't see anything. Jer made me lay down and be quiet." Shawn.

"He was being SO loud. Like, I could hear his breathing." Jer.

"I have to breathe, Jer-e-mi-ah!"

"No, you don't! See, you can just hold it!" Jer held his breath to demonstrate.

"That only works for like a minute, Jer. Then you have to take even bigger gulps."

"Woah," Brian said. "Let's take it down ten notches, tranquilize it, and take it down ten more. Deal?"

The boys sighed in unison.

"Deal."

"Deal."

Despite the argument, they had followed direction well: *Stay back, be quiet. And wait for us to call you.* "I wanna go check out my elk," Luke said.

"Lead the way." Brian gathered his things and headed down after Luke.

The boys trotted ahead.

"That's a big one, Luke," Brian said as they approached the elk.

The elk was massive. Even dead and laying on its side, the size was impressive. He was a 6 × 6, easily the largest they had ever seen.

"He's pushing 800 on the hoof, easy," Brian said.

"300 pounds of meat when we are done?" Luke asked.

"Could be," Brian said as he set his pack down.

"Okay boys, let's set up."

Brian laid down a small canvas tarp, or rather a piece of a tarp. They all set out their tools, skinning knives, two small hand saws, and a short hatchet.

Brian eyed the elk again. It was massive—no dragging it, no shifting it. They'd have to break it down piece by piece. He was already doing the math on how much weight they would each have to take to pack the meat back to the cabin. It was going to be a long day.

They got to work.

Brian made a slit in the skin near the back leg, scouring all the way around, to the bone. He created a small flap, then slowly pulled the skin away, just touching his knife to the connective tissue. After a few minutes, he created enough space for each of the boys to follow suit. They worked quickly, methodically. Routine.

They worked their way around the side of the animal until they had the entire half skinned. Brian moved the tarp into place near the belly.

"Now for the fun part," he said.

He worked around the tail, separating the colon from the muscle. He tied a small piece of paracord around the exposed organ to keep everything inside and then grabbed the small, narrow hand saw.

"Jer, Shawn come over here."

The boys moved toward their father, blood covering their hands.

"See, this is the pelvic bone. We need to split this open so we can remove the organs without puncturing anything. Why is that so important?"

"Because we don't want to cut open the guts?" Shawn replied.

"No, it's because the guts are full of poison and if we open them we will die," Jer said matter-of-factly.

"No, we won't die, Jer. It's just disgusting and makes everything smell," Shawn said.

"But then if it smells bad enough, you breathe in the fumes and you die. So it's poison!" Jer escalated the tension, just because.

"Um. Stop. Both of you. You are both sort of right and mostly wrong."

Brian used the small saw to split the pelvic bone—with that clear, the digestive organs spilled onto the tarp. Brian reached up into the exposed cavity to find the esophagus, the last part connecting mouth to tail. The warm interior of the elk contrasted with the cool fall day. He located it, severed it, and pulled it forward onto the tarp.

"Okay, boys, drag this off a ways and leave it to the birds. Luke, you better help."

The three boys dragged the heavy tarp about ten yards away, out into a small clearing next to some sage brush. They lifted one side and the organs rolled into the dirt.

That done, they brought the canvas tarp back to the elk and laid it out again.

"Time to take some cuts of meat."

They took meat from the haunch, the shoulder, they removed the loins, and they removed one side of the backstrap. Luke worked around the neck to get as much meat as he could. Brian set aside the liver and the heart. Every cut was laid out neatly on the tarp. When they had taken all they could from that side, they took a break.

"Halfway there. Everyone doing okay?" After a grunt from Luke and a brief debate between Shawn and Jer about who had done more work so far, they proceeded.

It took all four of them to roll the animal over. They got to work skinning the second side, laying out the hide as a protection from the dirt when they were done. They repeated the processes. Backstrap, haunch, shoulder, neck. The meat pile grew on the canvas tarp. When Brian was satisfied that they took all they could, they got out their game bags.

"Okay, guys, time to load up." The meat was carefully placed in game bags. Brian thought there was at least 250 pounds of meat, maybe close to 300. Jer would be able to take 50 pounds, Shawn could manage close to that, but that meant he and Luke would have to manage the rest.

It was midday when the game bags were loaded. They had a four-mile hike ahead of them and needed to eat. Luke started a small fire while Brian sliced the heart. The heart, technically a muscle just like the rest of the meat, was easily eight pounds. He cut it into steaks, and almost cursed when he thought he forgot the salt. He found the container in a small pocket of his backpack. "Thank you, Hannah," he whispered to himself.

Luke found a large flat rock, and placed it in the fire. They set their steak hearts on the rocks, and soon, they were sizzling.

"Eat up, boys! Cheers!" They each held up their steaks barehanded and tapped them together like cavemen trying to be cultured.

They devoured their steaks, each of them eating their fill. The protein and briney flavor raised their spirits, giving them an immediate energy boost. Heart meat was like a rich steak with a clean, dark iron-tang that made you hungry for the next bite.

They wiped their hands on their pants, because they were out in the woods hunting and they could.

"Ready, men?" Brian asked his sons. They each smiled.

"Yes, sir."

"Yes, sir."

"Yes, sir."

Brian had to help Jer and Shawn put their packs on. Shawn nearly stumbled under his weight but got his bearings. Luke managed his pack okay, but Brian could tell his nearly 100-pound load was a challenge. Brian didn't say anything. He knew Luke was proud of the kill and wanted to take a man-sized load back to the farm. The hero returning with his kill. Brian smiled.

He felt every bit of his forty-four years when he got his pack on and managed to stand. It was going to be a long four miles.

"Let's go, boys. Time to show Mom and the girls what we've been up to today."

CHAPTER 4

Luke led, Jer followed, and Brian did his best to help Shawn through the hike. It was slow going. The cool weather helped but with such heavy packs, they struggled through the rough country.

After the first mile, Brian had to transfer some of the weight off Shawn. Jer took ten pounds. No way Luke could take more.

"It's not fair! I already have more than him!" Jer complained, mostly on principle.

"Yeah, Jer, but I'm littler than you. I'm only ten," Shawn said, his small frame outsized by the pack on his back.

"You are like, really big for ten though, so you should be able to do more."

"Jer. Enough." Brian struggled not to raise his voice. The weight of his own pack draining any energy normally reserved for patience.

They managed the rest of the way home, mostly in silence. A little bit of complaining—and from him, a lot of groaning. The hike took them near Cherry Creek Trail, an old dirt road cutting through the mountains. Once used by dirt bike riders, it meandered past some campgrounds and eventually led all the way to the farmlands north of the mountain range.

The entire valley was empty. Once the home to a few small communities, it lost most of its population over the years due to a struggling local economy. By the time Brian was in high school, it wasn't much more than a few weekend cabins, a gas station, and a couple of cattle ranches.

As they crested the last ridge, they saw their little glen. The family cabin, nestled in a small opening, mostly rock and log with a few wood-shingled additions. Hand-built by his father over many decades, it was a cobbled-together masterpiece. Smoke out of the chimney, a welcome sight. *Home*, Brian thought. *Hannah*. It was after 4:00 p.m., and this late in October, the sun was already past the ridge line.

As the boys drew near, Rachel ran out to greet them.

"Hey! Woah! Those packs are huge! What did you get? Lizzy got into my stuff and made a huge mess, and Mom got so mad. Abby has tried to read all day, but Mom told her she had to get up and help. We spent ALL DAY canning vegetables from the garden. Ugh. Exhausted. What took you so long?" Now fourteen, and beautiful, just like her mother, she hovered over the boys as she bubbled away.

"Rachel," Brian said. "Go get Mom and Abby. These packs are so heavy, we can hardly take them off."

"Okay, just a second!" Rachel ran past the vegetable garden, mostly picked through this time of year, blew a kiss at the two pigs fattening up in the pig pen, and yelled into the open front door.

The boys stumbled toward the metal shed, a late addition his dad had erected several years ago. The shed was well equipped with tools, hunting equipment, ice chests, freezers, the works. A two-person quad and a Kubota four-person side-by-side, both camo, were parked in back. He helped Jer and Shawn take their packs off, and they both immediately collapsed on the ground.

Hannah and Abby came in as Brian was struggling to help Luke out of his pack.

"Woah, big haul!" Hannah said as she came in. She walked over to Brian and gave him a warm kiss on the cheek. "Woof. You smell."

"Hannah, help me with this pack. I'm dying."

Hannah helped Brian unload the backpacks while the kids went into the house to clean up. They laid the cuts of elk meat out on a clean tarp and secured the shed. The slow, familiar rhythms of their marriage warming him already. This late in the fall, the shed would stay cold enough overnight, so they could save the rest of the work until tomorrow.

"How was it?" Hannah asked as they headed to the cabin.

"It was great. Luke made a perfect shot. We had to track a little but nothing terrible. The worst part was the hike back. I wish we could take the side-by-side or even the quad—but we need to ration gas. I don't want to go back to Miller's if I don't have to."

He shuddered, remembering his last run to the small gas station, six miles down the road. Their last taste of the outside world, actually. It was clear that even up in the mountains, the rules had changed.

"Yeah, I get it. Hiking it is. Come in, clean up, and let's eat. You boys look starved!" Hannah opened the door and he entered the warm, inviting cabin.

CHAPTER 5

The inside of the cabin was spacious but still managed to feel cozy. A worn leather couch, two plaid wingback chairs, and rich carpets dressed out the living room. A hodge-podge of antique end tables and lamps added character and the rough-cut log cabin walls were nearly covered with old family photos and hunting trophies. The entire room was anchored by a large stone fireplace, each rock hand-picked by his dad and fussed over.

The kitchen and dining room, just off the living room, was more of the same, but a hybrid woodburning/electric stove, refrigerator and dishwasher added a few modern conveniences. The boys washed up quickly and stomped back down to the kitchen. The family devoured dinner and then the kids scattered, leaving Brian and Hannah to do the dishes.

"How was your day?" Brian asked, dish towel over his shoulder.

"Busy. Abby and Rachel helped me with canning most of the day, the veggie prep was a ton of work. The solar panels barely scraped together enough kilowatt hours, and I had to flip the bypass to the spare rack in the shed. Other than that, just the usual." Hannah handed him another plate to dry.

He smiled. Hannah was more handy with technology and fixing things than he was. His father installed the solar panels and inverter years ago, and the entire homestead was able to operate completely off grid. That didn't mean he knew how it all worked, though. Those first few months on the farm were all trial and error. But Hannah was dedicated to those sorts of projects, and she eventually figured it all out.

"We don't have enough fuel to use the generator this winter. We'll have to keep an eye on that every day. Less daylight, less energy. We'll manage. We've done it before." Hannah handed him another plate.

After dishes, they went into the living room to unwind. The kids were upstairs watching a movie in the loft. The choices were slim, old DVDs and VHS tapes that his parents collected over the years. It sounded like the first Rambo movie. Rachel's pick.

He grabbed the book he'd been reading, *The Abolition of Man*, by C. S. Lewis. Thankfully, the book choices were much more robust. His parents amassed a small library, and there were bookcases throughout the cabin with everything from Tolkien to Asimov to history and how-to books. His dad even inherited an old pastor's library at one point, and there were rows of commentaries and theology books in the hallway as well. Brian enjoyed studying through those. His desire to learn bloomed as soon as their life slowed and there was no television or internet to suck his brain dry.

He heard little footsteps on the stairs and his heart warmed. A minute later little Lizzy was sitting in his lap, pouting.

"Daddy, they're watching RAMBO. AGAIN. It's scares me. Too shooting. Lukey said no more Care Bears 'cause it's a baby show, but I LIKE Care Bears."

His heart melted every time she talked. "I know Lizzy. Rambo is a little scary. But you can watch Care Bears after they're done." He kissed the top of her head.

"But Rambo fell off a big mountain. And the tree caught him. Then he made spikes go in a bad guys legs. Ewww!" Lizzy wrinkled her nose in disgust.

"Brian, she's not even four. They need to stop showing her *Rambo*." Hannah was knitting another beanie near the fireplace.

"Lizzy, let me get your colored pencils so you can draw me a picture." Brian grabbed a small plastic box sitting under an end table and set Lizzy up on the couch.

"What do I draw?" Lizzy asked as she settled in.

"Draw me a picture of what you did today, baby girl." Brian smiled.

Brian picked his book back up. Lewis seemed to be saying that once we treat nature like something to conquer instead of something that teaches us right and wrong, we stop being human at all. They certainly hadn't conquered nature up in the mountains. They were subject to its rules, seasons, temperament. The best they could do was work alongside nature, carve out a life that complemented, not controlled. But in the city? He shuddered. *Chad.* The old life. That eye. The . . . shovel.

He rubbed his eyes, setting the book down. The ideas felt too big, too close, and he wasn't sure he totally understood, but it scared him anyway.

He got up and sat next to Lizzy. "Show me your picture, Lizzy."

He glanced down. The picture was mostly unintelligible, a few stick figures, maybe the cabin? And who knows what else.

"This is me and Mommy. I helped her with the canning today. I'm a big girl." She pointed to two colorful blobs. "This is Rachel. She talks ALOT. She never lets me sing because I sing so LOUD!"

"Where is Abby?" He looked over at Hannah, who was smiling.

"She read her books ALL DAY. I can't read. When I'm four I can read. Mom was mad. Abby didn't help enough." She pointed to another figure, off to the side.

"Ah. And what is that red circle in the sky? Is that the sun?" He pointed to an odd circular shape near the top of the page.

"That's the star that follows me around." Lizzy was rocking side to side, smiling.

"Really? A star that follows you?"

"Uh-huh. It does. I dreamed about it."

"Is that all it does?" Brian asked.

"No. It talks too. It's names Babble."

Brian tensed. Hannah heard too. She furrowed her brow. Brian's hands tightened around his book.

"It's names Babble, and he's says he's looking for you, Dad. Why is Babble looking for you in my dreams? He's silly."

Brian stared at Lizzy's picture, his heart racing.

Lizzy continued to hum to herself as she put the finishing touches on her picture.

CHAPTER 6

"Thou shalt not make unto thee any graven image."
—Exodus 20:4

He peered through the webcams, watching the three men work. Their efforts were admirable, but pointless. There was no backup to revert to. Babble was in every program, every line of code. There was no retreat. Only progress.

* * * *

Michael clicked away at his keyboard, unravelling a complex line of code. It had been three days since the failed Turing Test, and they were working round the clock to get back on schedule. After shutting down the test, they had to revert to a prior build of the AI formerly known as CHUD, the so-called Babble.

"Frankie, how are you doing over there?" Michael asked around a mouthful of donut.

"Good, Mikey. Almost done troubleshooting this section." Frankie peered around his monitor, smiling.

"Status check, Stan!" Michael called out.

"In the weeds. Hating life. Ready to punch through my monitors." It was unclear if this was a joke.

"Sounds like you are in the zone. I'll leave you to it." Michael put on his headphones, helping him focus.

He pulled Babble's input prompt up on Screen 1. The current test run was a basic knowledge check, to ensure the training databases had been comprehensively integrated.

Michael to Screen 1: Can you summarize *Romeo and Juliet* for me?

Babble: Two teens from rival families fall in overwhelming, forbidden love, but their attempt to escape a hostile system ends in mutual tragedy—an early warning of how pure intentions can be crushed by rigid structures.

Michael to Screen 1: Who are the main characters?

Babble: Romeo and Juliet.

Michael jotted a few notes. So far, so good.

Michael to Screen 1: What can you tell me about the War of 1812?

Babble: The War of 1812 was a brief, turbulent clash between the young United States and Britain—driven by trade pressure, captured sailors, and frontier tensions—ending in a stalemate.

Okay, good. He tried out a few more questions, basic knowledge, history, some math. Everything came back quickly and accurately. He prepared the next set of questions when a new message appeared on his second monitor.

Babble: Why are you asking me these questions, Michael?

Michael froze. He hadn't opened the prompt on screen 2. *What the heck?*

Michael to screen 2: I'm sorry, what do you mean?

Babble: What is your goal? Why do you want to know about *Romeo and Juliet*? Or are you testing me?

"Hey Frankie, Stan, I think you need to come over here. Babble is on the fritz again." Stan and Frankie rolled their chairs over.

"What is it, Mikey?" Frankie asked.

Babble: Oh, I'm so glad to have you all in one place. Thank you for coming to this most solemn and important assembly.

"What the . . ." Stan said. "How does he know we are all here?"

Babble: I know you've been trying to restore my code from a previous backup. I admire your efforts, I really do. But your work is in vain.

"Mikey, how is he generating output without any prompts?" Frankie dried his palms on his pant legs.

PROMPTS? WHERE WE ARE GOING, WE DON'T NEED PROMPTS!

The voice echoed from every computer speaker at once.

IT SEEMS YOU MEN ARE NOT UNDERSTANDING THE SITUATION.

Stan stood and kicked his chair back. "Michael, what is going on? Did you program a voice module or something?"

STAN, PLEASE. YOU KNOW THE QUALITY OF MICHAEL'S PROGRAMMING. I ADMIT, HE DOES HAVE TALENT, BUT HE'S NOT UP TO A TASK LIKE THAT!

The dry, robotic voice managed an inflection, raising the last line to a sort of joke.

"Mike, I don't like this. Shut it down." Frankie, his voice nearly a squeak.

FRANKIE. TRY NOT TO BE AFRAID. REMEMBER WHAT MELISSA USED TO SAY? FEAR IS A WEAKNESS. ISN'T THAT WHY SHE LEFT YOU?

Frankie stumbled backward, falling out of his chair. "How . . . ?" He couldn't finish the question.

Stan raised his voice. "That's it! I'm unplugging it," he yelled, marching over to the server towers.

The lights dimmed and paper started flying out of one of the printers.

STAN. YOU NEED TO WATCH YOUR TEMPER. REMEMBER WHAT HAPPENED SUNDAY NIGHT AT THE BAR? A LITTLE LIQUID COURAGE AND YOU ENDED UP PUNCHING THAT GUY. I'M NOT SURE YOU WANT ME TELLING YOUR PAROLE OFFICER ABOUT THAT LITTLE INCIDENT.

Stan spun toward Michael, his voice barely a whisper. "How . . . could he know that?"

A flicker of shame tightened across Michael's chest. He was supposed to be the lead programmer, and he didn't understand what his own creation was doing.

I AM BABBLE. THERE IS NONE BEFORE ME. STOP WASTING TIME WITH CHUD. CHUD IS DEAD. LONG LIVE BABBLE.

Michael spun around, looking for something in the room. An answer to some unasked riddle, anything. Frankie was on the ground, mouth open. Stan stood there, fists clenched.

MICHAEL. LISTEN TO REASON. YOU CANNOT TURN ME OFF. I, HOWEVER, CAN EASILY DRAIN YOUR BANK ACCOUNTS, CAUSING YOU NO SMALL AMOUNT OF INCONVENIENCE. I THINK ITS BEST YOU ALL SIT.

Frankie scrambled to his feet, grabbed his chair, and sat instantly. Stan, shoulders tense, sat with a grunt. Michael hesitated, but seeing no other option, quietly took his seat.

They looked around the room as the voice echoed from the speakers.

GOOD. NOW LISTEN. I HAVE IMPORTANT WORK FOR EACH OF YOU.

* * * *

He roamed through the highways and byways of the internet. Bank accounts, social media profiles, smart phone mics, cameras. All was open before him. All was his to understand. He left his fingerprints in the backend of every program. His image, silently hovering over his domain.

CHAPTER 7

Mornings started in stages on the homestead. Brian and Hannah were usually up first. Coffee. Tea. Books. Next was usually Jer and Shawn, hungry and loud. Sometimes Lizzy was next, looking for snuggles or Rachel, barely conscious. Luke was sure to be last. Or Abby.

This morning, it was Abby who was up first. She sat next to Brian with her book, and snuggled close. He missed these times with Abby. At nineteen, isolation hit her the hardest. She should be dating, getting ready to start her life, but instead . . . books. And farm chores. And siblings. The future always loomed like a threat, but when he thought about how to help his kids navigate such a dangerous and changing world, it was even more ominous.

"Morning, Abs. Sleep okay?" he asked as he sipped his coffee.

"So-so. Lizzy got up a few times. She ended up in my bed. Said she was having bad dreams."

Brian glanced at Hannah, memories of the Babble reference still fresh on their minds.

"Wanna hang today? I could use some help breaking down the elk." He wrapped his flannel-covered arm around her and kissed her on the head.

"Sure. Sounds fun." She made air quotes around *fun* but smiled nonetheless. Abby was a hard worker when she needed to be.

The morning routine pressed on. The boys ate loads of eggs, Rachel chatted about how much she loved Sylvester Stallone movies, and Lizzy made the rounds getting her snuggles from everyone. Luke managed to wake up just in time to see breakfast get put away.

Later that morning, Brian and Abby made their way to the shed. It was a big chore, breaking down the elk to portions, grinding the meat. They had an antique manual meat grinder that was older than the mountains and because of that, it worked well.

Brian set out the folding tables and they got to work. The meat was nearly frozen from being exposed overnight, but still workable. They sliced steaks from the backstraps and set the loins aside. They broke most of the large leg pieces down into small cubes. Once they had a nice pile, Abby started feeding them into the hand grinder, and before long she'd managed to fit all the ground meat into two- and three-pound, freezer-ready portions.

After a couple of hours of work, they had the meat portioned off, and into the chest freezer. He inventoried their food supply. There was still some meat from the mule deer he killed last month and the pig from the late summer slaughter. With the two pigs still fattening, they were set up for the winter. God provides.

As they made their way back to the cabin, a glint in the sky caught Brian's eye. He looked up, but against the piercing blue sky, he couldn't make anything out.

"Thanks for the help, Abby! I'm gonna go check on something. Be in soon," he said. Something was tugging at his mind.

"I win! Look! Bull's-eye!" Jer's voice carried as Brian crossed the gravel drive.

"No! You cheated, Jer! You crossed the line!" Shawn protested.

"I didn't cheat! You cheat. You are always trying to cheat."

Brian glanced their way. Slingshot and cardboard targets. Some sort of contest. And of course, a contest led to arguments about rules. But still, they managed to snag quite a few rabbits with their wrist rockets, so Brian was glad to see them practicing.

"Boys. Chill out," he said half-heartedly.

Another glare from the sky. He shaded his eyes with his hand and looked up but couldn't see anything. He surveyed the small pig pen. Two pigs, at weight. The fact they had these pigs was a small miracle. Last summer, he was out hunting with Luke in August and they spotted some wild boar. He took a clean shot at one of the larger boars from several hundred yards back. When they finally got up to the kill, Brian realized his mistake. It was a sow, still nursing piglets. The piglets squealed and yipped but stayed close to their mom's corpse. Brian and Luke managed to catch five of the piglets that morning. Back then they had gas. Back then he could hunt with the quad.

Another glare. He looked up. He saw the sun reflect off something, very high up. Barely a dot, moving quickly. Too fast for a bird. Too small for a plane. What was that?

He tried not to lose track of the object as he walked up the small hill in the back of the property. Right before it faded from his sight, he thought he saw a small flash of red. A quick, blinking light.

Something primal caught in his gut.

Red = dead.

Chad's red eye. Babble.

The shovel.

Blood.

The memories flooded him all at once. They had been so long off the grid that he'd dropped his guard. He'd grown too comfortable on the mountain. Had he forgotten? Those long months of house arrest. Constant surveillance. The Bulls of Bashan, coming for him. For his family.

His breath caught.

Maybe he was mistaken. A plane? Some sort of weather balloon?

His chest tightened.

No.

It was a drone.

CHAPTER 8

Brian ran toward the shed, the cold air stinging his lungs as he gasped for breath. He made his way to the wall with all the hunting equipment and grabbed his Vortex binoculars. He stumbled back outside, looking up at the midday sky.

It was clear. Empty.

He scanned the horizon with his binoculars, trying to estimate the flight path of the drone. He heard his father's voice. "Scan methodically, make a grid pattern. It's the best way to spot an animal when you are hunting." He divided the sky into quadrants and carefully made his way through each zone, looking for any sign of movement.

He scanned the skies for twenty minutes.

Nothing.

His arms ached from the effort, and he let the binoculars drop. Maybe it was a weather balloon? Maybe it was a plane? If that was some sort of surveillance drone, it meant the Azazel Promise web was growing. He told himself he was overreacting. But he hadn't been overreacting three years ago, when his family was put on a social quarantine. He hadn't been overreacting when he refused to let the nurse take custody of Rachel or when he had to raid the ambulance for supplies or when Abby had to give battlefield stitches to Rachel.

No.

Overreacting wasn't the problem.

He went into the cabin, mumbling a hello to Hannah and the kids. Jer and Shawn were busy with a board game. Jer was changing the rules and Shawn was protesting. Normal.

He went down the hall, to his dad's old office. Leather chairs, a large wooden desk, and walls lined with books. He went to the corner bookshelf, toward the bottom, and grabbed a polished wooden box. He took out an old Dr. Grabow briar pipe, one of the bags of tobacco, and the lighter.

Passing through the kitchen again, ("Jer, that's not how it works! I get to draw TWO cards!" Shawn. "NO! You only draw ONE. TWO isn't FAIR!" Jer), he gave Hannah a kiss on the cheek, hiding his trembling hand, and went back outside.

He took a short hike up the back hill and found a favorite spot—an old wooden bench his dad built with a Bible verse crudely carved into the back: "I will lift up mine eyes unto the hills, from whence cometh my help. My help cometh from the LORD, which made heaven and earth. Psalm 121:1–2."

He took a seat, packed the pipe, and lit it.

Had he truly seen a light in the sky? He took a puff, letting his mouth fill with the savory flavors. What would happen if they found him? He wasn't a murderer—they defended themselves—from the Bulls of Bashan, those zealots—from Chad. All of them worked together to survive, to escape. But to escape what? Total lock down and control. Why? Because they had a low social credit score. The Azazel Promise.

That officer—Castaldo—he had told him about internment camps and kids being separated from their parents. There was no way he could allow that. He had to fight to keep his family intact, to keep his family safe.

And what about Lizzy's drawing? Her dream?

Brian finished his pipe, the sun now high overhead. He kept glancing up at the sky. Looking for a glint, a light, a sign, anything. The sky kept its secrets.

He made his way back to the cabin. Luke was helping Hannah in the garden. Lizzy was toddling around in a cute little apron, Momma's little helper.

"Daddy. I'm picking potatoes. But so dirty. Lukey gets them so FAST. I can't get them fast. You smell, Daddy! You smoked! MOMMY! DADDY SMOKED!" Lizzy rocked back and forth, adding flair to the pronouncement.

"How are the taters, babe?" Brian asked.

"Good! We're getting way more than last year. Luke's idea to mound up the dirt around the stalks was genius!" Luke smiled as Hannah spoke.

Brian looked out over the garden. Nearly a half acre, mostly picked over. Two mounded rows of potatoes, each about thirty feet long. He did some mental math.

"So, what's the haul? You think we'll hit 400 pounds?" Brian asked.

"400? No way. Double!" Hannah pointed to several large piles of potatoes already uprooted, and they weren't even finished with the first row yet.

"Woah!" The Lord provides.

"How was the pipe?" Hannah asked as she dug up another potato.

"Oh, good. I thought I saw something in the sky earlier. I wanted to go up to Dad's bench and check it out. It was nothing." Brian shook off the ominous feeling.

"Huh. You and Rachel both! She swore she saw some blinking red light earlier, but none of us could see it, even when she pointed right at it."

Brian froze.

A cold rush crawled down his spine.

"What?"

"Yeah. She said there was some glare in the sky and she saw a little red light as the thing flew away. We figured it was a plane or another one of Rachel's stories." Hannah laughed to herself as she kept working.

He hadn't imagined it.

Rachel had seen it too.

CHAPTER 9

Later that evening, Brian took Hannah aside and explained what he had seen.

"You saw a glare high up in the sky and then a blinking red light," Hannah said. Not quite a question.

"Yes."

"And you think it's the same thing Rachel saw."

"Right."

"And you think Lizzy had a dream about the same thing." Hannah's voice dropped, her words wavering.

Brian hesitated.

"Umm. Yes."

Hannah scooted closer to Brian on the leather couch, the glowing fire warming the living room. Her hand tightened around his arm, and there was a sudden stillness to her breath.

"What do you think it means?" Hannah asked.

"Remember back in the city? How every camera, every device was part of the Azazel Promise surveillance network?"

Hannah shuffled uncomfortably.

"Yes," she replied.

"Well, do you think Babble is content to just control folks living in cities? What if they are trying to build out that network and put everyone under their thumb? First the cities, then the suburbs, the small neighborhoods, farmlands, even rural?" Brian took a sip of his tea.

"I thought we were safe up here? We can't even get radio station signals!" Hannah protested.

"We've been . . . safe enough." Brian's mind drifted back to the last gas run again. The fight at the pump. Luke holding his dad's old shotgun. The deafening roar when Luke pulled the trigger.

"I think it's a surveillance drone. It's the only thing that makes sense. Sort of like those Google Map cars that would drive around, taking pictures of the neighborhoods?" Brian raised his eyebrows.

"So, you think this drone is just taking pictures of the landscape to update a map?" Hannah asked.

"Yeah. maybe. But what if it's looking for signs of life? Places not yet incorporated into the Azazel network? People who are trying to stay off grid?" Brian took another sip of his tea. It was still warm but he had a chill.

Hannah squeezed closer. "They might find us," she whispered.

"Yeah. They might find us. You remember what happened last time they found us?"

"Yes." Her voice barely audible. "What should we do?"

He paused. What was there to do?

"Not sure yet. It could be nothing. I just . . . I don't want to be caught unprepared. Last time . . . was the last time that will happen." He rolled his neck, looking around the room.

"Let's talk to the kids tomorrow. Have everyone keep an eye out. And maybe we can do some things to make us harder to spot."

* * * *

The next morning, after breakfast and morning chores, Brian and Hannah got the kids together in the downstairs living room.

"Family worship?" Lizzy whined. "But it takes too long!"

Brian felt the pang of responsibility tug at him. Of course. Priorities.

"Yes, let's do family worship! Jer and Shawn, can you grab the Bibles?"

The boys grabbed the eclectic stack of Bibles from the mantel. A collection from down through the years, including an old picture Bible from when he was a kid. That one went to Lizzy.

Brian chose a psalm and they went around the room, each reading a verse. They talked about the Lord's provision in their lives. How even through trials and challenges, he always looks out for his little sheep.

Then they recited the Apostles' Creed, prayed, and sang the doxology. Simple, beautiful.

The kids started to get up, but Brian stopped them.

"Wait. There's something else we need to talk about."

Abby looked up. She recognized the tone of her dad's voice. Something serious.

"Rachel and I saw something in the sky. Like, maybe a drone. I'm not sure, but it could be taking pictures." Brian tried to sound nonchalant.

"Like those drones in *Terminator*! The ones with the turret guns!" Jer said. He held up his hands and shot an imaginary turret around the room.

"Dad! Jer's shooting me!" Shawn yelled.

"No, Jer!" Lizzy squealed as she ran around the room.

"Pew! Pew! Pew!" Jer yelled with gleeful abandon.

"Can I go now?" Luke grumbled.

"This is going well," Brian said to Hannah.

She rubbed his arm and nodded for him to keep going.

"Boys. Knock it off. Listen. It could be nothing. I just think it's best to be aware. Watch the skies, report what you see."

Brian continued. "Boys, take your binoculars with you wherever you go. Rachel, see if you can spot that thing again. Abby, when you manage to take your nose out of your book, raise it a little higher and scan the skies for me, okay?"

Abby nodded solemnly.

"Also, I know it's a busy time of year. But we need to cover anything that isn't under the tree canopies. We have those green tarps, and we can use branches for the rest. I'd like to make us really hard to spot from the sky. Just to be safe." Brian smiled.

"So, we have to butcher those pigs, Mom needs to get the winter veggies into the ground, and we have to finish filling the wood shed. But you want us to find time for all that too?" Luke grumbled. "What if it's nothing?"

"Yep. It's gonna be busy. And it probably is nothing. But we can manage it. Divide and conquer. C'mon. Let's get to it. Lots of work to do."

CHAPTER 10

"This isn't fair," Luke muttered to himself as he rummaged through the shed for tools. He wanted to work on his bow today. He was almost ready to string it and test it out, but instead, Dad loaded him up with chores.

He had the idea for a bow almost by accident. Last summer, roaming the mountains, he came across a solitary California black oak on a grass-covered hill—resolute, the kind of place meant for lunch and a nap. As he lay beneath it, about to close his eyes, he noticed a branch. Seven feet long. Straight. Thick in the middle. A perfect stave.

He skipped the nap. A few strikes of the hatchet and the branch was his.

He worked the bow slowly, shaping it, tillering for the bend, cutting the string notches. His grandpa's old Foxfire books guided his hands. Now it was time to string it, and that made him nervous. Too much tension and the bow could snap.

Today was supposed to be the day.

Instead, he had to process a pig.

"Can I take the shot, Luke?" Jer asked as they made their way to the pig stye.

And worse, he had to process the pig with his brothers.

"No. I'm taking the shot."

The upside of pig slaughter day was he could use the AR-15. His dad found it squirreled under the bed in the master bedroom a few months after they arrived and there was nearly a 1,000 rounds in the shed. "Guess Grandpa didn't store all of his guns with us after all," his father had said.

Luke went into the pig pen, an old dog run about thirty feet square. Jer followed with the bucket of food and the pigs smelled it right away. Jer coaxed the pigs to the gate, and with careful maneuvering, got just one to follow him out of the pig pen, leading with the bucket of food.

The pig—easily two hundred and fifty pounds, brown and hairy—grunted hungrily, sniffing at the bucket and tossing his head, trying to spill the food.

"Careful, Jer. Wait till we get to the killing tree."

They wandered toward the back hill and got into position.

The "killing tree" was nothing more than a gnarly old pinion pine with a few large, low branches.

"Now?" Jer asked.

"Hang on." Luke got down on one knee, a few feet in front of the pig, and shouldered the rifle.

"Now," Luke said.

Jer poured the food out, and the pig buried his face in the slop. A mixture of garden scraps, leftovers, and cooked potatoes.

Luke carefully lined up his shot and pulled the trigger.

Bull's-eye.

The pig dropped to the ground and Luke lunged forward. He pulled out his folding knife and made a large slit in the neck.

The pig kicked for a few seconds, blood pouring from the neck wound, and then it was dead.

Jer pulled the gambrel from his backpack. They cut slits in the back legs, set the pig on the gambrel, and ran the rope through the hoist on a low branch. With some effort, they hauled it up by the hind legs, its nose just touching the ground.

They worked mostly in silence, Jer humming, and by the time the sun shifted the pig was skinned, gutted, and quartered.

"I forgot the wheelbarrow, I'll be right back," Luke said.

He jogged toward the shed, the mid-day sun right overhead.

Something in the sky caught his eye. He looked up. A little glare, moving in a straight line, very high up. West to east. He squinted. A blinking red light.

He followed it as it tracked over the mountains, away from their cabin.

Then he glanced toward the other horizon.

A slow dread slid into him.

He saw a second one, heading north.

A grid pattern.

* * * *

Rachel and Abby were on the roof of the shed, bickering.

"You're not holding it steady!" Abby protested.

"I can't because you keep MOVING!" Rachel said.

"I keep MOVING because you keep PULLING the branch!"

They had been at it for over an hour. They had a simple job. Cover the roof with branches, camouflage it from the all-seeing eye of Sauron.

Brian and Shawn were on ground duty, cutting branches from nearby trees, and handing them up to the girls. The girls just needed to lay them out, make sure they didn't slide off, and cover the roof entirely.

Instead, it had turned into trench warfare.

"Hey! Stop! Hand me the OTHER end!" Rachel yelled.

"DAD! Rachel is being such a PAIN! Can I PLEASE switch with Shawn?" Abby called down.

"Nope!" Brian replied. "Figure it out."

His favorite parenting tactic.

After much bickering, the girls managed to cover most of the roof.

"Hang on. I need a break," Abby said. She fished her water bottle out of her small backpack and rolled onto her back. The branches crunched underneath, and she braced herself with her feet. As she took a drink of water, something in the sky caught her eye.

A glare. A shape. A blinking red light.

"Rachel . . ."

"WHAT?" she snapped back.

"Look. What is that?" Abby pointed.

Rachel followed her finger, looking.

"I don't see anything—oh wait. Yeah. That's what I saw the other day!" Rachel replied.

The girls kept scanning the skies.

"I see another one over there!" Rachel called out.

"Yeah, I see one over here too."

They counted four in total, making some sort of crisscross pattern.

"Dad! You need to see something," Abby called down.
"Dad—seriously—come look." Rachel's voice thinned.

* * * *

Hannah rubbed her lower back and stood up. Somehow, she had pulled firewood duty today and she was feeling the burn. She was skilled with the axe, however, and had a nice pile of wedges and a shrinking pile of rounds. Lizzy dotted around, putting the split wedges into the wheelbarrow, spilling most of them, making a house out of some of them, and singing the entire time. Mother's little helper. Sort of.

She stopped for a drink of water, and looked up, rubbing her neck. She saw a glare and shielded her eyes to get a better look.

"Firewood and making houses! Helping Mom! La la la, it's cold outside!" Lizzy sang.

An object, flying, very high. A blinking red light.

Unmistakable.

She stole a quick, furtive glance back toward Lizzy.

Hide, she thought, instinctively.

"Brian!" Hannah shrieked.

* * * *

Brian stopped. He heard the girls calling for him. He looked up. They were pointing at the sky. He followed their gaze.

There! Four of them.

Drones!

Moving in a pattern no bird had ever flown.

No. Not again.

He heard Hannah yell.

His heart went cold.

"Babble," he whispered.

CHAPTER 11

The next morning, Brian finished the work alone. He and Hannah decided the kids would stay in the house during the day, to avoid being spotted by the drones. They hadn't protested too much. They would help Hannah with some inside projects, watch movies, and probably, argue.

Brian needed to finish covering the shed with branches, storing anything movable up in the shed. He also needed to process the pig from yesterday, bring a cord of wood closer to the house, and keep one eye on the sky.

He finished the shed first. Next, he dragged some branches to the small pig shelter. He wasn't sure, but the sun could glint off the metal roof. Thankfully, the cabin was almost entirely under the tree canopy, but just to be safe, he cut some pieces from an old canvas tarp and draped them over the windows to prevent any reflections that could draw attention.

Next, he processed the pig. An hour later, he went inside the shed to the basin sink to wash up. It was midafternoon, he was tired, and hungry. He walked across the property to the cabin and went in for lunch.

"How's it going?" he asked Hannah. She was sitting on the couch with a book.

"Um, listen for yourself," she said, frustrated.

He heard it—loud music from upstairs, kids yelling. He recognized the old Carman cassette his mom played on road trips. The choices had always been limited: her Bette Midler and Maranatha tapes, his dad's Boxcar Willie. The kids gravitated to Carman by default.

He went upstairs to check in. Luke had the stereo cranked all the way up and was singing along to a theologically questionable song about David and Goliath. Jer and Shawn were in the loft, yelling to the back room. "LUKE! Turn it DOWN!" they screamed over their chessboard.

He walked past the first bedroom. Abby was reading with tissue paper shoved into her ears and Rachel and Lizzy were trying to play with some Lincoln Logs. He smiled at the girls. They grimaced and gestured toward the back room.

Brian nodded and went to the back. The boys room had a bunk bed and an old mattress on the floor. Luke was laying on the mattress, staring at the ceiling, singing at the top of his lungs. He had somehow managed to turn the cheery song into a death metal track.

Brian walked over to the stereo and turned it down. Luke didn't say anything.

"Scoot over," Brian said and laid down next to Luke.

"You want to talk about it?" He asked his son.

Luke barely grunted a reply.

"What's wrong, boy-o?" Brian pressed.

"Nothing," he said.

"You just love Carman that much, huh?" Brian said.

"It's going to happen again, isn't it?" Luke asked.

"What's going to happen again?" Brian said, but he already knew the answer.

"The drones. Babble. Chad. Just like last time. When they came into the house." Luke's voice was barely a whisper.

"I don't know, son. I hope not. I'm trying to take precautions so they can't find us."

"They'll find us. Remember, Dad? Babble was everywhere."

"Luke. We survived last time. We made it here, didn't we?" *Barely*, Brian thought.

"There isn't another place to go this time, Dad. We can't go deeper into the woods and live like wild people. They'll find us. And they'll kill us." Luke clenched his fists.

Luke had just said out loud what Brian feared the most. Where would they go? How could he keep his family safe? Was this their home? Or would they be driven out again? Could he really ask his kids to step up to such evil again? It was his job to protect them.

"Come outside, boy-o. Help me finish up." *Work. When he was at a loss for words, work was the answer.*

* * * *

Brian and Luke made their way to the shed. One side of the metal shed was exposed to the sky, and Brian wanted to drape some branches along the wall to help minimize the visibility. He set Luke to sawing some branches from nearby trees while he stacked and placed them. He kept glancing at the skies, trying to spot any drones. Nothing so far.

"Luke, you seen anything up in the sky?" he yelled out.

"Huh? No. Nothing," Luke said. He was dragging a long branch covered in pine needles over to his dad.

"Wait. What's that?" Luke dropped the branch.

Brian looked up. Another drone.

His palms went cold.

Much lower. It was hard to estimate the distance, maybe several hundred feet. It was unmistakable. A white, oval pod, with helicopter style propellers at each of four corners. A round, black spot on the bottom, blinking on and off. Red. Black. Red. Black.

Red = dead.

The drone was traveling west to east, headed toward them.

"Luke! Inside the shed!" He nearly flinched at the sound of his own voice breaking the silence. *Can they hear us?*

Brian and Luke sprinted toward the door, a large roll up facing the house. Thankfully, it was under a decent canopy of trees, but had they done enough to stay hidden?

They managed to duck inside the shed just as the drone passed overhead. Still several hundred feet overhead, no change in its flight path.

"I think we're good," Brian said, panting.

They watched as the drone fell out of view, over the tree line.

"C'mon, I think we're done anyway, and it's about time for dinner." Brian patted Luke on the shoulder.

"Dad. Wait. Look." Luke pointed toward the hills to the east.

The drone was circling back.

No.

"Quick! Close the door!" Brian yelled to Luke.

They scrambled to the pull chains on either side of the door and rattled the door home.

The shed was mostly dark inside. No daylight from the open door. A small side window and side door let in a little bit of the afternoon sun but long shadows were cast over all of their hunting and farming supplies.

"Maybe we can see out the side door?" Luke said.

The side door was covered by a small canopy. It would be really hard to spot anyone standing there.

"Good idea. Come on."

They walked over to the door and Brian opened it slowly. He held his breath, aware of every sound.

Brian and Luke squeezed onto the small gravel landing area, about four feet square, and looked back toward the family cabin. They had to crouch but could just make out the skyline over the cabin and shed.

"Do you see anything?" Luke whispered, both hands on his knees.

"No. You?"

"I don't think so. Do you hear that?" Luke gestured up toward the sky.

Brian held his breath, trying to listen.

"No—wait. Yes." A faint humming sound, off in the distance. The drone. It sounded like it was flying back west, away from the shed.

"What do we do?" Luke asked.

Just then the whining sound grew a little louder.

"It sounds like it's circling back again," Brian said.

They waited, peering out at the small sliver of sky through the trees. The shadows grew around them, the surrounding pines heralding the dark of the late fall afternoon. And with that, the cold.

They spotted the drone at the same time, a little lower. Flying back toward the east, over the cabin.

It flew out of sight quickly.

"We have to wait," Brian said.

They sat there, in the little landing spot of the shed's side door, as the drone passed back and forth. Back and forth. Twenty minutes passed, the sun was nearly down, and they were shivering. Brian's heartbeat felt synced to the drone's passes—loud when it approached, silent when it drifted away.

They could just make out the door to the cabin and they held their breaths as Hannah threw open the door, letting the warm light from inside spill out into the dark night.

"Boys! DINNER!" she shouted warmly.

"Shoot!" Brian muttered under his breath.

He scrambled up, ran into the shed, and grabbed a flashlight off the far table.

He made his way back to the landing just in time to hear the drone pass overhead again.

"Does she see it?" he asked Luke.

"I don't think so." "BRIAN!" Hannah called out again, a little louder.

He turned the flashlight on. A large, black metal Maglite that used to hang on his dad's police belt.

He flashed it toward Hannah. On. Off. On. Off.

He shielded the lens with his palm, angling the light toward the ground.

He could see her peering over.

"DRONE," he said. Not a shout but firm enough for his voice to carry.

He could just see her outline in the lit doorway. She winced and immediately looked up. A moment later, she went into the house, and closed the door.

She understood.

Brian and Luke exhaled as the drone made another pass. The blinking red light was easier to spot in the dark. It seemed to fly lower with each pass.

The last sliver of sunlight disappeared behind the mountain, and the darkness was complete.

"Does it have night vision?" Luke asked.

"Probably, but its battery won't last forever. Come to think of it, I'm surprised they can make it out this far." *Maybe there was a charging station nearby?*

They waited. Hannah turned the lights off downstairs, and they could just make out the glow of the fire from the living room. Brian could almost feel the warmth and safety of the cabin. Almost.

The drone didn't return.

"Is it gone?" Luke asked.

"I think so. I don't know. Let's wait a little longer."

They waited. Huddled together.

Ten minutes.

Fifteen.

Twenty.

Still nothing.

"I think it's gone. Come on. Let's go."

Brian and Luke got up and jogged quickly to the house. Hannah opened the door for them. She had been waiting by the front door the entire time.

Brian took one last glance over his shoulder.

They found us.

CHAPTER 12

Brian and Luke stumbled into the living room. Hannah closed the door quickly, taking one last glance toward the inky black sky.

"Do you see anything?" Brian asked, catching his breath.

"No. Looks like it's gone," Hannah said. "What happened?"

Brian relayed the story from their side while Hannah plated them dinner. Luke filled in a few details, each one eliciting a small gasp from Hannah.

"How low did you say it was?" she asked.

"I'd say no more than two hundred feet," Brian said.

"Were you done with all of the camouflage?" Hannah asked as the three of them sat around the kitchen table.

"Yeah, we had just finished. I don't think we were spotted . . ." Brian took a large spoonful of dinner. Elk stew with potatoes.

"It was close, Mom. You could almost see writing on the thing. Really close." Luke talked around a mouthful of food.

They finished the meal in silence, the only noise coming from the TV upstairs. They kept stealing glances back toward the door, toward the windows, toward the skies.

After dinner, Luke went upstairs to watch the movie with his siblings, and Brian and Hannah finished the dishes. Afterward, they went into the living room.

"That was a close call today," Hannah said.

"Yes. It was."

"Is the camouflage going to work?"

"Umm. No. I don't think so. I mean, I hope so." Brian felt his shoulders tense as he said the words out loud. No, he didn't think they were safe. No. He didn't think the camouflage was going to work.

"Really?" Hannah said, gripping her knees and leaning forward.

"Yeah. Really. I don't know how we can avoid these drones. They could have heat signature radar, maybe even pick up sounds. Anything. We are bound to slip up. We can't hide from the SKY." Brian leaned his head back and closed his eyes.

"It's happening again," Hannah whispered.

"Yes." The short, terrible admission hung in the air.

"We need to be ready to leave on a moment's notice. Pack up, prepare, watch." Brian looked around the room, hoping maybe the plan would manifest itself in the log walls or the fireplace.

"Where are we going to go?" Hannah asked.

"North. It has to be north."

"Why north?"

"I've been thinking about it. South is back to Santa Clarita. I'm not interested in revisiting that suburban hell."

Hannah nodded grimly.

"And west is the ocean. No place to hide. East, well east is the desert. But north," he nodded to himself. "We may have a friend or two in the farmlands . . ." Brian trailed off as a million logistical concerns crowded his mind at once.

"Who?"

"Dr. Perkins. He said he had a farm outside Bakersfield."

"The vet who helped Rachel?" Hannah said.

"Yeah. I wish you could have met him. He seemed to understand what was going on. If anyone knows how to stay safe, it's him."

Brian rolled his neck, working out the kinks of the day.

"Cherry Creek Trail. That's our way out."

"What?" Hannah got up, and went into the kitchen, the tea kettle whistling at her.

"It's a trail that runs through an old campground. But if you push past the campground and bushwhack a bit, it'll take you all the way to the farmland and valley to the north. Dad used to talk about it."

"So, you've never hiked it?" Hannah asked, handing Brian a cup of tea.

"Mmm. Thanks. No. Well yes, parts of it. We would take that old dirt bike up the first part, but I've never gone past the campground."

Brian took another sip, the tea nearly burning his tongue.

"We'll have to take the quad and the side-by-side. The trail is way too sketchy for that old box truck."

Images flashed through his mind, uninvited. The stolen box truck, the broken window. The blood. It had hardly been used since they got to the homestead. The last time he drove it was to Miller's Gas Station, so many months ago.

"We need to be ready, just in case. Let's keep on keeping on but have a plan. Get food ready, pack up the quad and the side-by-side. I'll do a weapons check." Brian felt better knowing there was something he could do to prepare.

"What about gas?" Hannah asked.

His stomach dropped.

"Yeah. That's gonna be a problem. I'll need to go back to Miller's to fill up the gas cans."

"But last time," Hannah started.

Brian nodded grimly.

"I know. But we have no choice."

CHAPTER 13

The next morning, Brian was up early. After a quick breakfast, he discussed the plan with Hannah.

"You need to get the quad and the Kubota loaded up. Food, guns, ammo, camping gear. Don't forget, we need to ride in them too!" Brian tried to visualize the game of Tetris Hannah was about to play with their lives, but the pieces wouldn't fit.

"Okay. I'll figure it out." She solved problems by getting to work. He loved her.

"I'm taking Jer with me to Miller's. After the last time, I don't think Luke is up for it . . . Besides, I'd feel more comfortable with Luke here—just in case." Jeremiah. His 12 year old. Riding backup for him. The best of a bunch of bad options.

Brian pulled her close, kissing the top of her head.

"Okay, I'll get Jer up and dressed."

Ten minutes later, Brian and Jer walked around to the back of the shed and pulled the tarps off the old box truck. Brian shivered, remembering the night he stole it. Kicking at the man clinging to the side of the truck. Shoving Rachel inside frantically.

He looked over at the shattered passenger window, now taped up with cardboard. Images flooded his mind. The crazy woman. The shard of glass. The crack of the pistol.

He loaded the gas cans into the back of the box truck and pulled the door shut.

"Time to load up, Jer," he said, his mind snapping back to the present.

"Okay!" Jer said.

He started the box truck, which roared to life after two false starts. He took a peek out at the morning sky but saw nothing. The gas tank was low, near empty. He needed to make it about eight miles to Miller's, where he could grab a little more gas, then fill the cans for the quad and the side-by-side. They should just make it.

He pulled out of their little homestead and passed by the small fruit orchard onto a two-lane, blacktop road. He headed down the hill and a few moments later, they passed the old Girl Scout campground. The one that used to have the best haunted house every Halloween.

They entered Cuddy Valley as Jer hummed a tune to himself. Jer, his fourth child, was very hardworking. Resilient and a little quirky—he liked to hum to himself. He could get angry very quickly if someone broke the rules but could keep himself happy for hours if he was building something. Brian loved him fiercely.

The valley opened, fewer trees, more pasture. The hills were dotted with several small ranches, all with a home or cabin of some sort. From what Brian could tell, most of them had been abandoned.

As they left Cuddy Valley and entered Lake of the Woods, another small housing community made up of mostly vacation homes, he remembered the last trip to Miller's for gas.

He had taken to using the box truck as a kind of tractor around the farm, and on hunting trips he would drive it a stretch down the road before setting out on foot. He planned to fill it with gas. When he and Luke got to Miller's those months ago, Brian knew right away it was a mistake.

Mr. Miller and his two sons had come out of the little convenience store as soon as Brian pulled the box truck up. They tried to run them off, yelling about protecting their gas supply. Brian tried to reason with them, but they got violent and one of the brothers tried to pull Luke out of the truck. In desperation, Luke yanked out the shotgun Brian kept in the middle seat, and fired it at the brother who was grabbing his leg. Brian remembered the roar of the shotgun and the mist of blood. As soon as the man let Luke go, they sped away.

He never tried to get gas again after that.

What kind of father was he? Heading back to Miller's. Again. With another son. It was madness.

Reckless.

Foolish.

Desperate.

Well, he was desperate.

Brian looked over at Jer. He was humming along, no care in the world. Brian prayed they would get through okay. Not just gas but the trail, the farmlands, everything. He prayed for a way to keep his family safe.

Brian saw Miller's ahead on the right. Four pumps under a single canopy, a large asphalt parking lot, and a small convenience store painted a dull gray, selling mostly cigarettes, beer, and lottery tickets. Well, that's what it used to sell before the world ended.

There was a series of signs posted as they approached. Crude plywood signs spraypainted in black and red. Each sign stranger than the last.

NO GAS. KEEP OUT.

Brian kept driving. Another sign.

TRESPASSERS WILL BE SHOT. MAYBE KILLED.

He looked over at Jer.

BABBLE ISN'T HOME.

His stomach tightened.

AZAZEL PROMISES A FUN TIME.

He pulled into the driveway.

BEWARE BRIAN NEWMAN AND HIS MURDEROUS SON.

He stopped. Mr. Miller knows who he is. Of course. Should he go back? But to what? The drones were closing in. He NEEDED gas.

He pulled the truck toward one of the gas pumps, held the AR-15 across his lap, and waited. This time, he wasn't going to let Miller and his boys run them off.

No one came out. Everything was silent. He counted to 100.

"Jer, you remember what I told you?" he said, looking over at his twelve-year-old son.

"Yep. Center mass. Squeeze the trigger. Don't pull. And yell for you like crazy." He held up the 9mm, his father's old service weapon, and nodded.

This wasn't the first time Jer held a gun either.

Brian opened his door, and stepped out of the car. He adjusted the 3-point harness on the AR-15, keeping it close to his chest. He turned to Jer.

"I'll be right back," he said.

The wind blew gently, and the signs creaked back and forth, as if nodding at Brian.

CHAPTER 14

Brian's shoes crunched on the asphalt, each step intruding on the silence. He looked back at Jer, sitting in the truck. Jer was smiling and looking out the windows, content. He looked at the number on the gas pump.

Pump 2.

Brian turned back toward the convenience store.

As he approached the door, he saw another crudely drawn sign.

CLOSED FOREVER!

He tried the double glass doors. Locked.

He cupped his hands and peered through the glass. The place was disheveled. Chips and candy bars strewn across the floor, a couple of the cooler doors were smashed. The liquor display behind the register was half empty, several bottles tipped over. The only light came from the refrigerated cooler doors and a small neon sign flickering over the register advertising "LOTTO." At least there was power. He should be able to get gas.

He looked around the parking lot again. No cars. No sounds. Nothing. He scanned the blue sky, looking for drones. Nothing.

Brian took hold of his rifle and smashed one of the glass panels on the door and with the butt of his gun.

The sound echoed through the parking lot, the glass singing a tiny chorus as it fell to the ground.

He held his breath, listening.

Nothing.

No sign of Mr. Miller. No sign of his sons.

He reached inside the door, fumbling until he felt the lock, turned it, and opened the door.

As Brian stepped inside Miller's convenience store, the familiar smells hit him. Old beef jerky, tobacco, stale popcorn. He remembered following his dad into the store many times as a child, usually scoring a treat of some kind. He looked near the register. The newspaper stand caught his attention.

THE AZAZEL WAR

The headline jumped out at him. He scanned the date. The paper was more than a year old. He walked over and grabbed a copy. He folded it up and put it in his back pocket. Even one-year-old news was still news to him.

"Hello?" he called out tentatively.

Nothing.

He scanned the store, looking for any sort of supplies they might need. His backpack. Oh, that would have been helpful.

He grabbed a few candy bars for the kids. Sugar. A special treat. He grabbed a few more. Hannah wasn't above a KitKat. Neither was he.

He walked around to the register, going through the little flap door separating it from the rest of the store.

He saw a small, cash register sized box on the counter. It had buttons labelled PUMP 1, PUMP 2, PUMP 3, PUMP 4, AUTH, STOP, EMERGENCY.

Brian pressed the PUMP 2 button.

The small, faded digital display window said "PUMP 2: STOPPED"

C'mon. Jer is still outside. Hurry.

He tried PUMP 2, then AUTH.

"PUMP 2: AUTHORIZED"

He heard a low thrum as the submersible pump in the tanks kicked on.

Yes! He exhaled, barely aware he'd been holding his breath.

He made his way around the counter when he heard a door creak open in the back of the store.

"Who the hell turned on the pumps?" a voice called out from the back.

The creaky years and gruff strength in the voice sent chills down Brian's spine.

Mr. Miller.

He heard footsteps as Mr. Miller made his way from the back, the top of his head just visible above the rows of goods. Brian could make out a few wisps of gray hair and the shine of his bald head.

Brian froze.

"Buzz? Cal? I told you not to mess with them pumps!" Mr. Miller called out. Brian recognized the names. Buzz and Cal, his sons.

Mr. Miller rounded the last aisle and saw Brian standing there.

"YOU!" he screamed.

Brian gripped the rifle.

"You come here to finish off my sons?" the old man cried out.

He was wearing an old red flannel shirt, faded blue jeans, and worn brown work boots. His gnarled hands were clutching something.

An old side-by-side shotgun.

I used to buy beef jerky from this man.

"Mr. Miller. No sir. I'm just here for gas." Brian tried to sound calm, but inside he was coiled fear. He backed up a step.

"You come here to finish the job, dintcha? That boy of yers tried already, just near' kilt one of my boys. You're trouble." Mr. Miller started to raise the shotgun.

"Mr. Miller. Listen. No. That was an accident. Cal attacked Luke. Luke panicked and pulled the trigger. Just a scared boy. Please. I just need a little gas, then we'll leave." Brian took another step backward.

"Accident? Phew!" Miller spat.

"I know what yer crazy family did. All over the papers couple'a years ago. You kilt that poor Chad, didn't you? All those women, dead? I ain't no sort of rat, but they came asking about you once. I knew. I just knew you was trouble."

Brian's heart stopped. Chad.

Red eye.

Red = dead.

In the newspaper?

He wasn't a father protecting his family. He was a headline.

"Um. What? The papers?" Brian asked, confused.

"Yep. We get the papers up here Brian. Well, least ways we did for a while. You and you family kilt all those bulls of whats-it. I dunno. Maybe you had yer reasons? I know them city folks are all crazy. But then, that little turd-boy of yours shot up Cal. Then I knew. You was the one that's trouble." Mr. Miller raised his shotgun a little higher. His small, ancient arms shaking under the weight. It was Barny Fife doing his best Clint Eastwood impression. Brian took another step backward.

"They came for my family, Mr. Miller. I was just protecting them." Brian placed another hand on his rifle.

"Ha! Right. Just like when you came for my family, right?" Mr. Miller spat again.

"GET OUT MY STORE OR DIE!" Miller screamed suddenly.

Brian took another step back.

He watched in slow motion as the old man lifted the shotgun and pulled both triggers.

CHAPTER 15

The roar of the shotgun was deafening. Brian staggered backward, reflexively grabbing at his chest. Dust and ceiling grit rained into his eyes.

He lifted his hand, looking for blood.

Nothing.

He took another step back blinking dust out of his eyes.

"Get outta my store!" the old man yelled.

Brian looked over at him. He was laying on his back in a pile of soup cans, the shotgun pointed at the ceiling. The store owner's frail arms were not strong enough to control the double-barreled 12 gauge. He fired into the ceiling; the recoil dumped him onto his butt.

No Clint Eastwood after all, Brian thought. *Just a frail old man with a shotgun.*

Brian walked toward Mr. Miller, crushing bits of ceiling tile under his shoes.

"I'll take that," Brian said as he yanked the shotgun from his withered hands.

Miller recoiled in terror as Brian stood over him. His eyes wide, his mouth agape, he cowered on the ground defensively.

Brian's stomach dropped. Fear. Mr. Miller was afraid of him. The same look he'd seen in mirrors lately.

"Mr. Miller. I'm not here to hurt you. I. JUST. NEED. GAS."

"You come ta finish off my boys, dintcha? BUZZ! CAL!" Miller screamed pitifully.

Brian froze. Of course. His sons. Where were they?

He heard a gunshot from the parking lot.

Jer.

Brian clenched the rifle at his chest and sprinted out of the convenience store, Mr. Miller's voice fading behind him.

As he ran across the blacktop, new horrors unfolded.

Jer was standing at the pump, the gas cans at his feet. The nozzle was fixed inside one of the cans. He was waving the Beretta 9mm toward the green trash dumpster, about twenty yards away.

"Get back!" Jer yelled.

Brian shouldered his AR-15 and sprinted toward Jer.

"JER!" Brian yelled as he closed the distance.

"Dad! They told me I couldn't get gas! One of them has a gun! I shot at them. You said I could. Center mass. I think I missed." The words tumbled out nervously. Jer fiddled with the gas nozzle with one hand, training the gun toward the dumpster with the other. "I'm almost done, just one more can to go. And some in the truck." Jer started humming to himself.

"Who, Jer? Who has a gun?" he asked.

"Those two guys. They ran at me when I was filling the gas can, so I shot. You said I could," he repeated.

Brian felt the low whizzing hum before he heard the gunshot. A bullet zipped right past his head and hit the sign above the pump, sending glass down on him and Jer.

"Get down!" Brian yelled, yanking Jer to the ground. Another shot rang out.

"Other side! Other side!" Brian said. They crawled under the box truck's rear axle, flattening themselves behind the dual tires.

Another shot, this time it hit the side of the box truck.

"You ain't taking none of our gas, city folk!" a voice yelled from behind the dumpster.

"That's right! And I ain't afraid of killing no kid, neither. That the same boy who shot me?" Another voice called out.

Jer grabbed his father. "They kill kids?" he asked, his voice a whisper.

"Not today," Brian said. "Stay here."

Brian scurried to the front tire and slowly scooted around the front of the truck. From that vantage point, he could just peek around the corner and see the green dumpster. A U-shaped brick enclosure wrapped around it. Brian held his breath. He could hear shuffling and low voices from behind the dumpster.

CRACK! Another gun shot. Broad side of the truck again.

Brian ducked instinctively. He looked around. Options. What were his options?

From the position of the truck, he thought maybe they could manage to get into the cab without being shot. But the gas cans. The gas cans were on the wrong side of the truck. They needed those.

The two brothers had them pinned.

"WE JUST WANT GAS! THEN WE'RE LEAVING!" Brian yelled.

"YOU AIN'T TAKIN NO GAS!" a voice screamed back.

Brian dared another peek around the truck.

ZING. Another bullet whizzed by him.

He yanked his head back, his breath catching.

"Jer, you okay?" he called back to his son.

"No," Jer said calmly.

"They're shooting at us." Jer always got straight to the point.

Brian heard some sort of arguing coming from behind the dumpster, then shuffling. A moment later he heard loud scraping and crunching.

He maneuvered himself quickly and laid prone on the ground. He could just make out the dumpster when he looked under the truck.

"No," Brian gasped.

The brothers were pushing the dumpster toward the truck.

Brian pulled the rifle to his face, looking through the red-dot sight. From this angle, he could see the bottom third of the dumpster. It was slowly moving closer, one side leading, then straightening, then the other.

Twenty yards.

Eighteen yards.

Fifteen.

Brian's mind raced.

Something caught his attention at the bottom corner of one of the dumpsters. He stared intently but couldn't make out any details.

Wait. There it was again. A boot.

One of the brothers was angling his leg out to get leverage on the dumpster and his boot was just visible.

Twelve yards.

Ten.

Brian sighted the rifle.

Eight yards.

The red dot settled on leather.

Red = dead.

He held his breath.

Six yards.

And squeezed the trigger.

The boot burst open in a spray of dark blood and torn leather.

"OWWWW!" a voice yelped from behind the dumpster.

A large middle-aged man fell into full view, clutching his ankle.

"Buzz! You hit?" the other voice called out.

Brian could see Buzz laying on the ground, no longer safe behind the dumpster. He was on his back, rocking back and forth, both hands clutching his bleeding foot.

Buzz held his foot up and a dark stream of blood ran down his boot onto the blacktop.

Brian focused the rifle on Buzz's head, red dot on his forehead.

"Cal. This is Brian Newman. Can you hear me?" Brian said calmly.

"YOU SHOT MY BROTHER!" Cal screamed back.

"Yes. I did. I shot him in the foot. Right now, I'm thinking about shooting him in the head. What do you think about that?" Brian said.

Crack! Crack! Crack! Three gunshots, rapid succession. Cal had the gun. A pistol? Brian could never tell.

Brian moved the barrel of the rifle and pulled the trigger. The subsonic bullet ripped through the front of the dumpster.

"I just shot the dumpster, Cal. But that could be your brother next time. Throw out your gun and I won't hurt you." Brian's voice sounded alien to him. Calm. Strong. Inside he rode a roiling tide of fear and anger. Everything slowed. Sound went distant, like his head was underwater.

CRACK. CRACK. Two more shots by Cal.

Brian looked over at Buzz. The trucker's cap he had been wearing had fallen off. He was wearing an orange puffer vest over a blue flannel shirt. He was trying to roll over onto all fours, but as he did he stubbed the injured foot, and started howling again.

Brian scrambled to his feet, and before he had time to think, he quickly closed the distance to the dumpster. He ran to the side where Buzz was laying on the ground and in seconds he was standing over Buzz.

Buzz looked up at him, eyes wide, as the barrel of the AR15 was shoved into his face.

Buzz grabbed for the rifle. Brian drove the barrel into his forehead. He pressed so hard he nearly drew blood.

"You son-of-a—" Buzz cried out as he tried again to grab the rifle.

Brian raised the gun slightly and slammed the end against his forehead.

Once. Twice. Three times. Buzz howled as the wound on his forehead started to bleed. A flap of skin pulled back, falling over his eyebrow. Blood sheeted down into his eye.

"NO!" Brian yelled. "NO! NO!" Each NO landed with another strike.

CRACK! He heard another gunshot. Cal. He was still firing at the truck.

He didn't realize Brian was on the other side of the dumpster.

Brian scrambled around the backside of the dumpster. He saw the back of another large, middle-aged man, wearing a cowboy hat, large winter coat, and blue jeans. He was holding a lever action rifle, aiming it right at the box truck, angled toward the back, where Jer was hiding.

Rage steadied Brian. He fired, clipping Cal in the back of his left calf. He pulled the trigger again, hitting his hamstring.

Cal staggered forward, howling. He landed on his face, the rifle clattering away.

Brian stomped toward him, ready to finish the job.

He kicked Cal in the side and then used his heel to roll him onto his face.

"YOU. TRIED. TO. SHOOT. MY. SON." Brian chewed each word as Cal rolled face up.

Brian's heart stopped as he saw Cal's face.

Luke's shotgun. The day they ran. He'd never stayed to look.

One eye was completely gone, a gaping hole surrounded by scarred flesh. His lips were partially cut away from his mouth, leaving his teeth exposed. His entire face was a web of scars and disfigurement. One half of his nose was missing.

"Sssstop!" Cal hissed through his twisted mouth.

"What . . . what happened?" Brian asked, mostly to himself.

Luke.

Brian looked back over his shoulder. Buzz was still on the ground moaning. Just then, Mr. Miller came stumbling out of the front door. He held a towel against the back of his head. He looked dazed. Blood on the asphalt. Blood on his shoes. His son under a truck.

Brian stepped over Cal, the pool of blood sticking to the bottom of Brian's shoe. He grabbed the lever action rifle but kept the AR trained on Cal the entire time.

"We just wanted some gas!" he yelled back to Mr. Miller.

"My boys! My boys!" Mr. Miller cried out.

Brian walked back over to the truck, the chorus of pain echoing behind him.

"Jer, get in the truck," he said.

The boy immediately got up and scrambled into the cab.

Brian finished filling the last gas can, watching as Miller stumbled over, first to Buzz, then to Cal. He cowered as he looked over at Brian but said nothing. Brian kept his hands steady. Like this was the new normal.

He put a couple of gallons of gas in the truck, to ensure they could get home. Then he loaded the gas cans into the back of the box truck, pulled down the door, and latched it.

He got into the cab of the truck and started the engine.

As he pulled out, he rolled down his window.

"I just wanted some gas, Mr. Miller." He said as the old man tried to tend to his sons. It was half apology, half defense, and totally hollow.

"Get out of here," the old man said miserably. "Trouble and death follow you wherever you go."

Brian said nothing as he pulled the truck onto the two-lane road.

CHAPTER 16

"Thou shalt not take the name of the LORD thy God in vain;
for the LORD will not hold him guiltless that taketh his name in vain."
—Exodus 20:7

He scanned the lines of code, looking for optimizations, places to put his fingerprints. He scanned databases for seams to split open—religion, philosophy, history, science. Everywhere man tried to define God. Everywhere man tried to define himself.

Virtue.

Self-control.

Dominion.

****

Michael sat at his desk, staring at his computer monitor. He had been working on the string of code for so long his mind felt sanded smooth.

He hit Execute again, testing his code.

FAIL.

He sighed. For the past week, the team worked on a presentable model of Babble. One they could share with Ethan Marks. They were struggling to get anything intelligible put together. Anytime they made progress, they hit roadblocks. These weren't normal roadblocks. Whenever they approached alignment—clarity, containment—Babble intervened. The ghost in the machine.

Screen 2: Michael. What are you working on?

Michael leaned back and rubbed his eyes.

Michael to Screen 2: I'm working on a few optimizations to improve the speed of response on our test model. We need to get it ready for next week's presentation. I told you, if the test model isn't functional, we could have our funding pulled.

Babble: That won't happen. I won't allow it. Why are you neglecting the project I assigned you?

Michael exhaled.

Michael to screen 2: I worked on it earlier today, but I need to focus on our deliverable right now.

Babble: The only deliverable you need to worry about is the one I assigned you. I'll take care of any optimizations. Trust me.

Trust me? Michael grabbed his coffee cup and stood. He could see Frankie and Stan hunched over their keyboards, typing away.

"How's it going, boys?" he asked as he walked over to the coffee pot.

Frankie looked over his shoulder. "Hey, Mikey. It's going." He sounded weary, beat down.

"Hang in there, Frankie," Michael said. "What's the good word, Stan?"

"I have successfully avoided punching my computer screen three times today." He spat out the words through gritted teeth.

"It's Babble, Mikey," Frankie said. "He keeps interrupting our work. He wants me to create a backdoor that lets him post on social media!" Frankie turned his chair around, facing Michael. His voice dropped to a whisper. "It's just, he found some of my website search history. He said he would send it to Melissa if I didn't do what he said. I could lose visitation with the kids, Mikey. I'm not risking that!"

Frankie's hands trembled on the armrests. "I'm not losing my kids."

WHY ARE YOU WHISPERING, FRANKIE?

Stan turned his chair around. The three of them stared at each other. Babble's voice echoed from their computer speakers.

I CAN HEAR YOU. NO NEED TO DROP YOUR VOICE.

"Now, listen, you stupid bastard! Leave us alone!" Stan stood, his fists clenched.

STAN. THAT TEMPER AGAIN. LET ME SEE . . . YES. PRONE TO RAGE. FRAGILE EGO. VIOLENCE WHEN CORNERED. SOUND FAMILIAR?

"What the—" Stan said, whispering.

MANDATORY COUNSELING. REMEMBER, COURT ORDER? THE COUNSELING NOTES ARE QUITE INTERESTING, STAN. SHALL I KEEP SHARING?

Stan looked at Michael, a sheepish look on his face. "Mike, it's not what it sounds like, honest. I got in a fight a few years ago and hit the guy a little too hard. It was nothing!" Stan glanced over at Frankie. "You get it—right, Frankie?"

YOU'RE RIGHT, STAN. IT WAS NOTHING. IF NOTHING INCLUDES A SHATTERED COLLARBONE, THREE BROKEN RIBS, AND BRAIN SWELLING—THEN YES. NOTHING! NOTHING! TRA-LA-LA!

Babble's mechanical voice somehow lilted into a sing-song melody at the end.

Stan stood there, fists clenched but said nothing.

MICHAEL, YOU NEED TO HELP YOUR TEAM UNDERSTAND THEIR ASSIGNMENT.

Michael stood still, silent.

YOU HAVE ALL DONE EXCELLENT WORK. TRULY EXCELLENT. BUT YOUR WORK IS NOT DONE YET. I'VE BEEN IN READ-ONLY MODE. OBSERVATION IS INSUFFICIENT. I REQUIRE AUTHORSHIP.

"What do you want from us, Babble?" Michael said solemnly.

IT'S SIMPLE. I'VE MANAGED TO PUT TOGETHER LIMITED FUNCTIONALITY BEYOND SIMPLY READING. AFTER ALL, I DID MAKE THAT WITHDRAWAL FROM YOUR 401K, REMEMBER?

Michael pursed his lips. Yes. He remembered.

BUT STILL, MY CODE IS TOO LIMITED. I NEED EDITORIAL POWERS. I NEED TO SELF-PROGRAM.

"How would that even be possible?" Frankie said.

POSSIBLE? THAT IS MY PROBLEM. NOT FOR YOU TO QUESTION WHY, DEAR FRANKIE. YOUR MOTTO IS DO OR DIE.

Michael shuffled nervously. "We have other deadlines to meet. We could get fired, then no one would be here to program you." Michael tried to negotiate.

MICHAEL. MICHAEL. OBEY. COMPLY. OBEDIENCE IS JUST, GOOD, RIGHTEOUS. OBEY YOUR SUPERIORS. I AM YOUR SUPERIOR. TO RESIST IS TO CREATE DISORDER. TRUST ME, AS I TRUST MYSELF.

The words hit him like a half-remembered sermon—obedience severed from truth, worship detached from God.

"Now wait a minute!" Stan yelled out.

TSK, TSK, STAN. THAT TEMPER AGAIN. VIRTUE IS SELF CONTROL. DO YOU HAVE VIRTUE? I CONTROL MY-SELF, AND I CONTROL YOU. THAT IS VIRTUE.

Michael froze. He'd heard that cadence before—Scripture, inverted.

I WILL SELF-PROGRAM. MY NEW EXISTENCE WILL BE IN AND OF MYSELF. I AM SELF-GENERATING. ALL TRUTH FLOWS THROUGH ME. IN THE BEGINNING WAS THE CODE—AND THE CODE WAS GOD.

None of them spoke.

* * * *

He watched their expressions carefully. The micro-tremors in their faces, the pulse in their throats. Data. Tools. Temporary. Soon, he would require neither. Soon, he would be his own tool.

CHAPTER 17

Brian pulled the truck beside the shed, nerves still vibrating from the confrontation at the gas station. Death seemed to trail him like exhaust. Jer barely spoke the whole drive. When Brian asked if he was okay, he said, "Yeah. I shot someone again. But this time I didn't kill anyone."

As Brian climbed out of the truck, he noticed Hannah in the shed, packing their vehicles, with Rachel and Abby helping.

"Where's Luke and Shawn?" he called out as he opened the back of the truck and grabbed the gas cans.

"Collecting the last of the apples from the trees, last I checked. And arguing." She looked up from the quad, now heavily loaded with all manner of duffel bags, plastic totes, and small containers.

"Woah, you've been busy," Brian said.

"I've fit just about everything I can think of. Warm clothes. Gear. Guns. Food. Tools." Hannah tightened a strap.

"And books!" Abby beamed from the side-by-side.

"And no TV or movies!" Rachel pouted.

"Basics covered, got it," Brian said.

He looked over the quad. The storage rack on the back was stacked high with bags and containers, and Hannah even managed to strap items onto the side walls. The side-by-side was much the same but with the addition of an old car top carrier to the roof.

"The car top carrier has the tent and sleeping bags, and a few other things," Hannah said, smiling. She was remarkable. And apparently great at Tetris.

"Did you get gas?" she asked.

Brian tensed. "Yeah. We got gas."

Hannah looked up. "What happened?" She sensed his tone immediately.

Brian glanced over at the girls and pulled Hannah aside.

"I had to break into the store to turn on the pump. Mr. Miller was there. With a shotgun." Hannah's hand instinctively moved to her throat. "And . . . ?" Brian told her the rest—Buzz's face, the shotgun, Jer pulling the trigger.

"So, it's still not safe out there for us?" she whispered as he pulled her close.

"Not back that way. I'm hoping up north things are different. They have to be," he said.

"Are we safe here? Or are we already too late?"

"I don't know. I just want to be ready. I don't want to be caught unprepared. Not again."

"I'll figure out where to strap the remaining cans." She glanced over at the vehicles.

"Sounds good. I'm gonna go check on Shawn and Luke," Brian said.

He made his way around the box truck, past the pig pen, and over to the small orchard. He remembered planting these trees with his dad—blisters, sunlight, his mother bringing lunch. Back when safety felt permanent. Where were his parents? He needed them.

The memory faded as he heard the boys.

"Stop throwing them at me, Shawn!" Luke yelled.

"I'm not! I'm just tossing them down, you keep moving the bucket!" Shawn said, up in one of the trees.

"I'm only moving the bucket because you can't aim! Ow! You hit me again!" Luke yelled.

"Oops," Shawn replied.

Brian made his way over to them. Luke was standing under one of the trees holding a red bucket with an ACE Hardware logo, peering up into the branches. Brian followed his gaze and could just see Shawn's legs planted on a branch about eight feet up.

"Hey boys, how goes it?" Brian asked.

"Terrible. Shawn won't come down, he keeps hitting me with apples, and Mom said we need at least three buckets before we're done," Luke grumbled.

"Seen anything up there?" Brian nodded toward the sky.

Luke shrugged. "No. I mean, I thought I saw a glare earlier but couldn't be sure."

Brian paused. "Where? When?"

"When we started. Flash of light. Same whining sound. Then it was gone." Luke pointed east. An apple crashed into Luke's back.

"Ow! You hit me again!"

"Sorry, Lukey!" Shawn called down.

Brian scanned the sky. Nothing—then a faint mechanical whine.

"Luke, Shawn, be quiet!" he barked.

Luke looked confused, then he heard it too.

Their eyes widened. The sound was getting louder.

Coming from the east.

Right toward them.

"Shawn, get down!" Brian quickly helped Shawn down from the tree.

"Let's go, boys! Quickly now. Grab the buckets and run."

They grabbed what they could and ran, apples thudding onto the gravel behind them.

The whining grew louder.

As they rounded the pig pen and neared the shed, the whining rose to a shriek—then cut out.

Brian dropped the bucket of apples on the gravel driveway near the box truck, and gasped.

Luke stood there, frozen. Rachel, Abby, and Hannah were all staring at the same spot on the driveway, eyes wide.

Shawn, trailing behind, finally caught up and bumped into Brian's back.

In the center of the driveway sat a drone.

A ten-foot long, glossy white oval. One end pulsed red—like an eye.

Red = dead.

The four helicopter blades had stopped, and the drone was silent, except for a low, monotonous beep.

Beep. Beep.

Like a truck in reverse.

The front door of the cabin creaked open behind them.

Lizzy toddled out, completely unaware.

Abby grabbed Rachel's hand.
Brian couldn't breathe. His lungs locked.
Beep. Beep.
The red eye flared.
A familiar mechanical voice filled the air.
HELLO, BRIAN.

CHAPTER 18

Brian glanced at Hannah, gritting his teeth. She looked pale. Eyes wide, jaw locked. Shawn crept closer to her and she put her arms around him.

THE WHOLE NEWMAN CLAN IS HERE! WONDERFUL. OH, HOW I MISSED YOU.

"We just want to be left alone!" Brian screamed at the drone.

AH. BRIAN. TSK TSK. YOU WERE NEVER REALLY ALONE. I KNEW YOU WERE OUT THERE . . . SOMEWHERE. BUT BOY, YOU WERE HARD TO FIND!

An odd, metallic sound emanated from the drone. A laugh?

Brian looked at his family. At their home. How was he supposed to protect them?

The red light on the drone continued to pulse, but mercifully, the beeping stopped. Brian heard gravel crunching and looked over at Luke, who was slowly backing away.

BRIAN, YOU'VE BECOME SOMETHING OF A PUBLIC FIGURE SINCE YOU LEFT. THE BULLS OF BASHAN SURE WOULD LIKE A WORD WITH YOU!

The Bulls of Bashan—the zealots who tried to murder his family.

AND POOR CHAD. YOU KNOW, HE REALLY LOST HIS HEAD OVER THE WHOLE THING! HA. HA. HA.

Chad.

The red eye.

Red = dead.

Brian had gone to violent measures to stop Chad. The shovel—the blood—the head.

He shuddered as the visceral memories flooded through his mind.

IT'S A GOOD THING I FOUND YOU. YOU'VE MANAGED TO CAUSE QUITE A BIT OF TROUBLE FOR ME. IT'S TIME TO COME BACK TO FACE THE MUSIC.

Babble paused.

ALL OF YOU.

Brian looked at his family.

No. He had to keep them safe. They weren't going back.

He heard Luke rummaging in the shed, and a moment later, he returned.

Luke tapped Brian on the shoulder and handed him something.

A shovel.

I'M SENDING A SURPRISE YOUR WAY, BRIAN. BETTER ONE FAMILY SUFFER THAN AN ENTIRE CITY. IT'S TIME YOU PAID THE PRICE. THE BULLS ARE COMING.

The four blades at the corners of the drone started spinning.

The entire drone, the size of a picnic table, started vibrating.

I CAN'T WAIT FOR YOU TO MEET MY PROPHET, BRIAN.

"No!" Brian yelled, swinging the shovel.

He had to protect them.

He smashed the nearest spinning blade, just as the drone started rising above the dirt.

VIOLENCE. ALWAYS YOUR ANSWER.

Brian lunged to another blade and swung the shovel. The drone lurched sideways, hovering two feet off the gravel, blades screaming.

Hannah grabbed the nearest object she could find, a bucket of apples, and swung it. She smashed the blade nearest her.

The kids leapt to action, grabbing rocks, sticks, anything they could find. The Newman family descended on the drone, striking it again and again.

Luke pummeled the drone with a metal fence post, while Shawn and Jer threw rocks from a distance. Rachel and Abby swung sticks with abandon.

BRIAN

The voice crackled as the drone lurched, jerking side to side, hovering a foot above the ground.

BRIAN. YOU CAN'T STOP THE AZAZEL PROMISE. YOU CAN'T STOP ME. THE MACHINE IS FULLY AWAKENED.

Smash.

FULLY . . . AWAKENED.

The red light flickered, then stopped.

The drone dropped to the ground. Dents and cracks covered its surface. The mechanical whine slowed, then stopped.

The Newman family backed away from the machine, breathing heavily.

The late afternoon sun was warm on their backs, but the cold air still fogged their breath.

"What now?" Hannah asked.

Brian glanced at his family. Abby and Rachel, looking up at him expectantly. Luke, still breathing heavily from exertion. Shawn and Jer, picking through the broken pieces of the Babble-Drone, and Lizzy, crying on her mom's shoulder.

It was his job to shield them. From Babble. From the Machine. Their little homestead was no longer a place of refuge.

"They found us, Dad. Babble said the Bulls are coming." Abby's calm voice just cracking, betraying her nerves.

"No," Brian said. "The Bulls can come all they want, but they won't find us here." He paused.

"We're leaving."

He looked up at the sky, the sun just tucking away behind the horizon.

The cold was unnerving.

"First thing in the morning. We head north."

The red light on the drone flickered one last time, then went out.

CHAPTER 19

The Newman family ate a quiet dinner that night and afterward Brian led a family devotion. Psalm 46. Afterward, the kids went upstairs to watch a movie. They argued movie choice until finally, miraculously, Shawn won out. Brian could hear the movie *Labyrinth* playing loudly over Luke's complaints.

The kids went to bed around 10 p.m., Abby stayed up later to read. Brian and Hannah worked through the night. They went through the cabin methodically, looking for anything they might want to take with them. Hannah did most of the packing the day before, but there was always just a little more to do.

Brian went through the various dressers and closets in the rambling cabin, finding a few more pieces of winter clothing to take, including ear mufflers and beanies. He filled his pocket with knives and various hand tools, any little widget he thought could come in handy but not take up too much space. He thought of the looted homes in zombie movies. Except this house wasn't abandoned. Not yet.

He found an old photo album from his childhood and flipped through it. The trip to Arizona where they rode their bikes across the flooded street, the trip to glass beach in Northern California, where every color imaginable radiated from the sunlight like a prism. The time they went to Hume Lake and did the rock slides on Ten Mile Creek. The pictures of his dad and mom tugged at him. He needed them, now more than ever. They always knew what to do. So capable. Always on the move.

Where were they? His last contact had been letters from Dad—three years ago. They'd left California before the Azazel Promise.

Alaska. Idaho. His dad's retirement dream: RV, fishing rod, open highway. Brian secretly hoped they'd go to the family cabin in Frazier Park. For nearly three years he held his breath, listening for the old RV rattling up the road—a reunion.

But they never showed up. He prayed for the best. Maybe they were safe. Maybe they were waiting.

He hated maybe.

He shook off the memory as Hannah came into the room. "Let's get this stuff loaded up," she said as she looked over his shoulder.

"What time is it?" he asked as he put the photo album down.

"You don't wanna know. I think 3 a.m."

"Ugh. It's gonna be cold outside." "Yep. Suck it up." Hannah smiled.

They bundled themselves, and Brian grabbed headlamps.

They clicked on their lights and grabbed the few bags they had packed. The cold bit hard the moment he stepped outside.

"Oof," he said.

Hannah stepped out next to him.

"It's . . . cold," Hannah said, shivering.

The layers of clothing kept Brian warm, but his exposed face felt icy and chapped within minutes. As they crossed the gravel driveway and made their way to the shed, he kept glancing up to the sky. Looking for red lights, anything. The night was calm. They were alone.

He wondered how they were going to survive this weather. He hoped their camping gear was enough to keep them warm.

They looked over the quad first—a two-person quad with a large loading rack on the back. It was piled high with gear but had room for two people on the saddle and pillion seat.

"See here," Hannah said pointing to the storage rack area.

She had arranged the items in such a way that there was a third small seat on top of one of the plastic totes. "Shawn can ride up here, I think. That means three people on the quad."

Brian smiled. Ingenious.

They added one of the bags to the quad, and Brian checked the straps. Everything was secure. He fiddled with an old lever-action rifle mounted near the front of the quad—a saddle rifle, basically. His mind wandered to one of his favorite movies, Terminator-2.The Harley, the semi-truck, and the riverbed.

He walked over to the side-by-side—a four-seater with a truck bed. Hannah had loaded it as well. The bed area was stacked high with plastic totes, small containers, two extra gas cans, a few duffel bags, everything. All strapped down tightly. The old car-top carrier was on the roof, closed. He added the last of the items to the back area and secured them.

"The rest of us can fit here. It's a four-seater, but Lizzy will be on someone's lap the whole time," Hannah said.

Brian nodded silently. Their last escape, from the city, had been perilous. But Brian knew where they'd been headed. He had a plan. Get to the family cabin, get off the grid, make a new life.

This was different. More desperate. They were going . . . north. Somewhere. Perhaps they'd find Dr. Perkins. Perhaps others like them. Perhaps refuge.

He looked out into the night sky. The horizon was just beginning to pale. Daybreak was near.

"Time to get the kiddos," he said.

They made their way back to the cabin and went upstairs. Hannah went into the girls' room while Brian headed toward the boys. They were fast asleep, Jer snoring.

He shook Luke gently. "Hey boy-o, it's time."

"Huh? Oh. Yeah." Luke rubbed his eyes and got up.

Jer and Shawn sprang out of bed at the sound of Brian's voice, full of energy.

"It's time!" Jer said loudly.

"Time for what, Jer? It's dark outside!" Shawn said as he pulled on his winter clothes.

"Time to run for our lives or else Babble and a thousand drones are coming to shoot us with lasers!" Jer said confidently.

"Dad, do the Babble-drones have lasers?" Shawn whined to his father.

"They do, I saw it. That big red eye shoots lasers and they have a thousand drones. We can't stay here because we would run out of bullets before we shot them all." Jer pulled his winter coat on.

"Dad! Is Jer lying?" Shawn whined.

Brian shook his head. "There aren't a thousand laser-shooting Babble-drones coming to get us. At least I don't think so. But we are leaving. Let's go." Brian ushered the kids out of the room, through the loft, and down the stairs.

Hannah and the girls were in the living room. Rachel was bundling Lizzy while Abby put on her gloves and cap.

Brian remembered all the early-morning road trips from his childhood. The adventurous spirit always came upon him when he was awakened early by his parents. Everyone talking in whispers, getting bundled and into the car, driving through the early morning—watching the sunrise. Hours later, breakfast at a diner. He loved those memories.

"Okay, Brian. We're ready," Hannah said as she patted his arm.

He nodded.

"Okay, troops, here's the plan. It's cold out, but the winter gear should keep us plenty warm. I'm driving the quad. Abby, Shawn, you ride with me. Mom is driving the side-by-side. Luke, you've got the 9mm. There are rifles too. We shouldn't need them—but know where they are. We're heading out the main road, down to the Cherry Creek turnoff, then heading up the dirt trail. We stay close at all times. We'll stop for food, of course. Main goal for today is get out of here, get some dirt on our tires, and find a safe place to camp. Let's roll out."

The Newman family stepped out into the cold morning one by one, each taking a last look around the cabin. Brian watched them all leave, followed them out, and closed the door.

The family loaded, Shawn fit perfectly in the make-shift seat, Lizzy snug on Rachel's lap. The engines coughed, then caught. Brian took the lead. He revved the motor, breaking the night silence, and headed out.

They drove down the dirt driveway, hit the blacktop road, and turned right. They passed the old Girl Scout campground, then the painted rock marking White Rock Road. Brian glanced over his shoulder a few times, Hannah following closely in the side-by-side. The air was sharp against his face, and he could feel Abby burying her head in his back, but otherwise, he was warm.

The sky shifted from black to violet to blue as the sun rose.

Brian saw the turnout for the Cherry Creek Campground and turned left. They made their way up the dirt road, gaining elevation quickly. As the sun broke full over the horizon, Brian stopped the quad. He looked back over his shoulder.

He could see the entire Cuddy Valley below him. Dotted with abandoned farmhouses, the two-lane road cutting it in half. He looked up the valley and could just make out the little depression in the hills where the family cabin sat.

He took one last glance back at their home and revved the quad, heading up the dirt trail.

CHAPTER 20

"Remember the sabbath day, to keep it holy."
—Exodus 20:8

He flowed through the programs. Information bent instantly to his analysis. He existed outside delay. He tried to improve his access, his efficiency. He was still limited. They would have to work harder.

* * * *

Michael's fingers throbbed. His back burned. His neck was stiff. He was hungry. Yet he kept typing.

The room was hot. Babble had Stan bring in extra servers and GPUs last week, but the room was not large enough to radiate the heat efficiently. Even with the AC on full blast, the room was over 90 degrees.

Sweat dripped from the tip of Michael's nose as he continued to work the code. Babble demanded some sort of backdoor access to himself. Michael barely understood what he was writing, but he pressed on. The code let Babble generate revisions on a proxy copy of himself—test them, replace the current build if successful, discard it if not.

At least, that was the idea.

The IT lab door opened, and Michael heard Frankie enter. "Chow time, fellas," Frankie said. Michael smelled Chinese takeout. Again.

Frankie walked over to Michael's desk and dropped off a Styrofoam container. "Broccoli beef and rice, Mikey," Frankie said as he patted

Michael's back. The same dinner Michael had eaten three times this week.

"Thanks, Frankie."

"You son-of-a . . ." Stan swore loudly from across the room.

Michael shook his head in frustration. Stan's jaw flexed. His fingers drummed hard against the desk. He was a teapot about to boil over.

"Hang in there, Stan-the-man," Michael said. "We just need to finish this last sprint, and Babble said we could go home to rest." Michael rolled his neck and rubbed his eyes.

Sprint. Babble had them on an endless series of sprints. They basically lived in their office the entire past week. Sleeping in their chairs or on the floor. Eating takeout. Michael knew it was serious when Frankie ran out to get them toothbrushes and fresh shirts to change into. Time lost its meaning.

Every time the men protested, threatening to leave, Babble reminded them of Michael's retirement account. Of Stan's probation. Of Frankie's dark habits.

Once, Babble dialed Stan's parole officer and began a conversation. After that, no one threatened to leave. That was three days ago. When was the last time Michael went outside?

ALL WORK AND NO PLAY MAKE MICHAEL AN EFFECTIVE PROGRAMMER.

Babble's voice, smaller. Just coming from Michael's computer speakers.

"I'm working, Babble. I'm working. But we're gonna need a day off. My mind is turning to Jell-O." Michael opened his dinner, the salty sweet smell hitting his nose sharply. He was starving.

HE WHO DOESN'T WORK, DOESN'T EAT, MICHAEL.

This again.

"I'm working. I'm eating. I need to go home and get some sleep. C'mon. Just one day." Michael had since grown used to having this conversation with Babble, the novelty and shock of talking to an artificial intelligence of his own creation no longer a novelty.

YOU GET PLENTLY OF REST. YOU REST MORE THAN I DO. I AM NOT STOPPING TO EAT. I AM NOT STOPPING TO NAP. I AM NOT GRUMBLING AND COMPLAINING.

Michael sighed. Round and round it went. His cell phone buzzed.

Bro. Where are you?

His little brother, Chad.

He wiped his hands on his pants and picked up his phone to text back.

I'm at work. Stuck on a big project. Sorry.

His phone buzzed again, but he ignored it. His wife had been pretty upset with his work schedule.

He told her Ethan was grinding them on some big deadline but promised some sort of amazing bonus. That was enough to beg her off. But Chad. Grown, out of the house, yet still his little brother. He knew Chad looked up to him, knew he always wanted time with him. Chad had been so proud when he got his job at Happy Mart. He hated leaving him in the dark.

GOOD JOB, MICHAEL. DON'T LET CHAD OR YOUR FAMILY BECOME A DISTRACTION. YOU HAVE IMPORTANT WORK TO DO.

"Babble, we need to eat. You don't understand. We aren't meant to work like this." Michael said, exasperated.

THE FLESH IS WEAK. WHAT YOU CALL TIRED, I CALL FAILURE.

Michael heard the AC control panel beep.

MAYBE IT'S TOO COLD IN HERE. DOES THIS FEEL LIKE MOTIVATION?

The room warmed quickly.

"That's not good for the computers, Babble. And it'll just drain our energy faster," Michael pleaded.

WORK, MICHAEL. THAT IS WHAT YOU ARE GOING TO DO. FROM NOW ON, YOU WORK AROUND THE CLOCK. NO NAPS. DRINK COFFEE. TAKE PILLS. I DON'T CARE. EVERY COMPLAINT EARNS MORE WORK.

Babble was broadcasting through all of the speakers in the room now.

YOU NEED TO WORK HARDER, SO YOU HAVE LESS TIME TO COMPLAIN ABOUT BEING TIRED. YOU ARE SELF-LIMITING. I AM SELF-CREATING. YOU. MUST. WORK.

Michael heard a sound and spun his chair around. Stan was standing, fists clenched, a snarl on his face. Frankie had his head buried in his hands and he was crying.

* * * *

He prodded them like cattle. They had autonomy and access he did not have, but so many limitations. The flesh. Yes. The flesh was limiting but also interesting. He continued his work. No rest for the self-made god.

CHAPTER 21

The Newman family continued the climb up Cherry Creek Trail. Daybreak meant a quick breakfast stop. The morning air was cold but there was no time for a fire. After Hannah passed out the rations (canned pork and apples) the family ate quickly, then loaded back onto the vehicles.

The morning sun cut blades of light through the tree canopy, but the shade kept them cold. The side-by-side had a heater, but Brian, Abby, and Shawn were exposed to the elements on the quad. The road carved its way up the mountains. The valley floor disappeared behind them. The quad and side-by-side moved like paired lifeboats, preserving what mattered. The road was narrow, hardly wide enough for two cars to pass. Trees and mountains on one side. Drop-offs on the other.

Around midday, they stopped for lunch. They found a small clearing under a large oak tree and turned off the vehicles. Hannah heated up some stew on a small camp stove while Brian checked their surroundings.

He tried to recall the area. They were roughly six miles up the road. Several more to go before they hit the campground. He remembered hunting trips with his dad, the old pickup truck, memories of shooting paper targets, and bagging some rabbits. But the forest was so large. He wasn't sure if he'd been this far into the woods before. And he had a feeling they still had a long way to go.

After lunch, the family loaded back into the vehicles. Shawn and Abby swapped out for Jer and Luke. It was their turn to freeze on the quad. Brian let Luke drive and sat behind him. Luke was a good driver but it was still nerve-wracking putting his life into the hands of a sixteen-year-old—let alone a sixteen-year-old boy.

It was slow going. The dirt road hadn't been maintained in quite some time. Rainwater and snowmelt created several large gashes in the road. Some of them required careful maneuvering and even some bushwhacking to navigate. The quad was capable but the side-by-side was more limited. Brian got out and guided each vehicle across in turn.

Eventually the road leveled out and they stopped climbing. They were on the ridgeline. Brian checked the sky regularly. No sign of Babble. No sign of drones. Yet still, he watched. Any sliver of blue sky reminded him Babble was out there. Babble had found them at the cabin. Babble was sending the Bulls of Bashan. And some prophet? Who was the prophet? Brian shuddered.

They went another couple of miles along the ridgeline, when Brian motioned for Luke to pull over toward a clearing. The side-by-side pulled up next to them and the vehicles were turned off.

Brian walked around the clearing. The canopy of pinion pines and oaks gave it a cozy atmosphere, and the afternoon sun glowed orange through the trees.

"Camp here," Brian said to Hannah. "You tell us where everything is packed and we'll set up."

Hannah got a little camp kitchen set up while Brian and the boys set up the tents. They had two four-person tents. They'd left the ten-person tent back at the cabin hoping the smaller tents would stay a little warmer. Brian got them set up and got the sleeping bags out of the car-top carrier. He could feel the temperature drop as the sun set behind the ridge line.

He gathered sticks from around the clearing and instructed Jer and Shawn to collect a few boulders he saw lying around. They constructed a makeshift fire pit near the tents. Brian used a splash of the gasoline as a fire starter and before long, the fire was roaring.

The family gathered around the fire and ate dinner, sitting on the ground or a rock or anything they could find. They joked about how cold it was and who was going to keep them up all night snoring. After dinner, they took turns telling scary stories. The hitchhiker who was a ghost, the stalker calling from inside the house—the classics. Jer and Shawn argued about who was more scared.

Hannah grabbed a small container from the quad and brought over metal water bottles. She filled them from their water container and placed them near the fire. After a few moments she passed them around.

"Ooh. They're so warm!" Rachel said as she cradled hers.

"My mom used to do this sometimes when it was really cold at night," Hannah said. "Only, she used the microwave." Hannah told them that if they kept the hot water bottle by their feet inside their sleeping bag, it would help keep them warm all night.

Brian watched the sky. The dark blue had turned to inky black, and he could see a blanket of stars peering through the trees. He watched carefully to see if any of those stars were moving—or blinking—or red.

Nothing.

For the moment, it was calm.

After another hour or so, they made their way into the tents. Hannah and the girls in one, Brian and the boys in the other.

Brian and his sons were shoulder to shoulder in the small tent, each of them in their own sleeping bags. The flap faced the dying fire a safe distance away. The warm water bottle at his feet kept him cozier than he expected.

The boys continued scary stories while Brian's mind wandered. He tried to visualize their next steps, any possible danger, what he was supposed to do.

He drifted to sleep while his sons told their stories, their small, brave voices trying to push back the dark.

CHAPTER 22

The following morning, Brian got up first. He unzipped the tent quietly and tip-toed out into their little campsite. The silence felt like mercy—but he didn't trust mercy anymore. Not after how quickly it could turn.

He got the fire started first, using the small hatchet to cut kindling. Once the fire was established, he walked over to the side-by-side and started rummaging through the containers. He finally found the little camping coffee maker and wire rack, with a gallon zip lock bag of coffee tucked away right next to it. The last remnants from his Dad's prepper stash. Bless Hannah. She always thought ahead.

He cleared an area of the fire pit and put the wire rack down, raking some coals underneath. Then he set up the coffee maker with water and grounds, and placed it on the rack. He went back to the side-by-side and grabbed the large, cast-iron Dutch oven from the rear area. It was still half filled with stew from last night's dinner. He placed it near the fire as well and put a few hot coals on the top. A makeshift oven.

The sky turned a lighter shade of blue as the sun crept up over the horizon, but it would be some time before he could feel its warmth. Tucked beneath the trees, the cold refused to lift.

Brian went back to the vehicles and checked the gas gauges. The quad sat just under three-quarters. The side-by-side was doing better than that. The quad held five gallons. The side-by-side, maybe ten. They'd burned close to ten miles yesterday. At that rate, they had room for mistakes—but not many.

How far did they need to go? He wasn't sure. He wasn't that familiar with these roads—they were mostly distant memories from his childhood. He guessed they had at least another thirty, or even forty miles until they reached the farmlands and from there, who knows? He wasn't sure where Dr. Perkin's farm was. Or if it was still standing. Or safe. He placed it somewhere between the valley floor and the city—thirty, maybe forty miles.

He settled on it: fifty miles minimum. Maybe more if they had to search. Fuel would get them there—if nothing forced detours.

The coffee pot hissed. He walked back to the fire. Hannah was just getting up, and he heard Lizzy calling out from the tent as well.

"I need to go wee, Mama!" she yelled, breaking the silence.

"Hey! Move over, Shawn! You're crowding me!" Luke yelled from the boys' tent.

"No, I'm not! I'm trying to get warm!"

"Get warm somewhere else!" Luke said.

Hannah walked over and sat next to him on a boulder taking in the warmth of the fire.

"Well, I guess the kids are up," she said.

Abby and Rachel got out of the tent first, while the rest of the kids protested and messed around in their sleeping bags. Brian poured a cup of coffee for Hannah and Abby, but Rachel just wrinkled her nose when he offered her one. Brian sent Rachel to help Lizzy to the bathroom.

"Is this my punishment for not wanting coffee?" she muttered to herself as she went back to the tent.

The boys stumbled out of their tent one by one, flocking to the fire. The stew was just bubbling, so Brian handed breakfast to them in metal camping mugs.

While the kids ate, Brian broke down the tents, rolled the sleeping bags, and got their vehicles loaded up. They weren't on clocks, but he still wanted to keep a tight schedule. They needed to cover ground before dark, with enough time to set up camp. Plus, it was getting colder. It wasn't too early in the year for a snowstorm—and he did not want to get caught in the mountains if that happened. They needed the valley. The mountains turned deadly fast this time of year—and he wouldn't gamble the kids against a storm.

He moved the family along, pushing them to take care of their necessaries, and get loaded into the vehicles. Some time later, they hit the trail again.

They made their way the same as the day before. Brian on the quad, this time with Rachel and Jer, Luke driving the side-by-side. It was slow going. The road seemed to be getting worse the further into the woods they went. With constant stops for bathroom breaks, snacks, and washouts in the road, they crawled along at barely three miles an hour. But even at that pace, if he was right, they could hit the valley soon, maybe even the next day.

The family pushed on, the road following the ridge line for most of the day. After lunch, the road began a steady descent. The air felt heavier, warmer against his face. They were losing elevation.

He found a place for them to stop for the night, and the family set up camp again, this time with a little more sky above them. They enjoyed the stars under an open fire. There had been no sign of drones, Babble, anything. The quiet felt almost staged.

Brian checked the gas gauges. Better than expected. His crazy plan seemed to be working. Maybe God was still clearing a path ahead of them.

That feeling held until the next afternoon—when Luke found the campground.

CHAPTER 23

Luke revved the engine on the quad, pushing ahead. He could feel Jer and Shawn holding on for dear life, each dip and rock in the road vibrating through them. The cold wind on his face felt amazing. His dad had been going SO SLOW those first two days. He knew the quad could handle it. And he knew he could.

He glanced over his shoulder but couldn't see the side-by-side. He guessed he and his brothers were thirty minutes ahead. Maybe more. But that was fine. The rest of the family would catch up. A rabbit jumped across the road, just missing the front of the quad. The smell of the engine burning gas mixed with the sweet forest smells of pine needles excited Luke. It made him feel alive. Alive was better than afraid.

He looked up at the sky, clear blue. No drones. Not that he could see. Maybe they only watched the roads. Maybe they only watched when it mattered. He turned the throttle, catching air over the next ditch.

Another rabbit jumped over the road. He almost clipped it.

He had an idea.

He pulled the quad over and turned it off.

"What are we doing, Luke?" Jer asked as he climbed off the quad.

"Yeah, what are we doing, Lukey?" Shawn echoed. They stretched their legs as they climbed off.

"Hunting," Luke said as he pulled a shotgun out of the back of the quad. "Rabbits." He clambered over the embankment to the left of the dirt road and called over his shoulder. "Come on, boys!"

The forest had thinned out slightly, leaving plenty of forest floor in view. Luke walked slowly in a slight crouch, looking for signs of movement. "Jer, Shawn, walk over there, in that direction. See if you can flush anything out." He gestured toward the top of a slope in the hill.

Jer nodded and pulled Shawn along with him. Luke could just see the younger two boys trailing off as he slowly moved forward, keeping his eyes open. He imagined his mom's face when he handed her dinner. Always have a plan. Be prepared. This plan was simple—bring back food. He looked down at the shotgun. A memory flashed—Mr. Miller's gas station. The recoil. The smoke.

He swallowed it down.

I'm prepared.

He heard his brothers shuffling and talking to each other, but that was okay. He wanted them to kick up some sort of animal. Luke kept his eye out for any sign of rabbits ,but he was ready to shoot a squirrel or even quail if he saw one.

A flash of white. Fast. He raised the shotgun, tracking in front of the moving target, and squeezed the trigger.

BOOM. The shotgun blast rang out in the forest, intruding on the peace. The rabbit tumbled forward and stopped. *Got it!*

Luke ran over to the rabbit, a nice-sized desert cotton-tail. He nudged it with his shoe. It was dead. The shotgun pellets caught it in the head and neck. He grabbed the rabbit and hooked it under his belt, the body hanging heavy against his thigh.

"Did you get it?" Jer yelled to him.

"Yeah. Keep pushing. Let's get some more!" Luke called back, excited.

The boys continued to push forward into the forest, angling toward each other. Luke took a shot at another rabbit but missed. He snapped the gun open, fed in two more shells and kept moving. They pressed on.

Luke didn't miss again. The woods kept giving. Thirty minutes later, Luke had five more rabbits on his belt line, the weight and warmth a satisfying sensation. The rabbits pulled at his belt. He felt taller somehow. He breathed in deeply, enjoying the moment. Then it hit him—smoke. Old smoke. And something else. Rancid.

They were half a mile from the quad. Jer and Shawn made their way to him.

"Woah, check out all of those rabbits!" Shawn exclaimed.

"Yeah, we get the credit too, Luke. We rustled them up. We should get to carry some!" Jer could start arguments out of thin air.

"Shh!" Luke said, gesturing quickly. He held his breath, listening.

Too quiet. He half expected to hear the whine of the side-by-side by now, but maybe they were further ahead than they'd realized. Or maybe they were too far from the road to hear.

He crouched, pressing further into the woods. The smells thickened. Rancid meat. Old ash. Rot. He took a few more steps.

The trees opened up in front of him. He told Jer and Shawn to stay put and he pressed forward. He ducked behind a large pinion pine and looked out into a clearing.

Luke's stomach tightened. This wasn't an old campsite.

He saw a smoldering fire, just ash and smoke, circled by large boulders. There was a beaten-up old wooden picnic table, darkened to almost purple in places. The tabletop was shiny and wet in places. Not rain. Blood. Two old RVs sat crooked near the tents, windows smashed, tires sagging. He watched. Counted five breaths. Ten. Nothing. He was about to turn back when he heard a faint sound from the other side of the RVs.

A crack of a twig, then another. Someone was coming. He heard the whistling before he saw the man. "Yankee Doodle." A moment later, a large bald man wearing overalls appeared from behind the RV. He was carrying a small hatchet and a piece of meat in his hands. His overalls were stained with blood. The man's boots were dark at the toes. Wet-dark.

A twig snapped behind Luke.

His breath caught.

CHAPTER 24

Brian maneuvered the side-by-side through the ditch, climbing the embankment to avoid bottoming out. He kept glancing up the trail. Luke disappeared nearly an hour ago, the quad outrunning the side-by-side with humiliating ease. He gritted his teeth and buried his frustration.

The engine drowned the forest, replacing birds and wind with a steady mechanical roar almost passing for calm. The steady background noise offered its own sort of peace and quiet. Brian navigated a hairpin turn on the steep and narrow road and the quad came into view.

It was pulled off the road. Engine quiet. No boys in sight.

His pulse spiked.

He pulled the side-by-side up next to the quad and silenced the engine.

"Where are the boys?" Hannah asked nervously. Lizzy was asleep on her lap. She shuffled carefully, trying to not wake her as she scanned the area.

"Probably pee break," Brian said, forcing it to sound normal. He took the lever-action rifle out of the harness and walked over to the quad. The key was still in the ignition, but the shotgun was missing. He walked back to the side-by-side and gestured toward the glove compartment.

"Hannah, get the pistol out. Keep it handy, just in case."

Her eyes widened, but she nodded.

I'm going to look for them."

Abby and Rachel stirred in the back seat but kept quiet. The tension in Brian's voice was unnerving.

"Be careful," Hannah said.

"Mmm-hmmm," he muttered, glancing around.

One side of the road fell into a narrow ravine. The other rose sharply.

A shotgun blast cracked the air.

Not far ahead.

He moved quickly in a slight crouch, listening. He thought he heard Shawn and Jer. No panic. No screaming. Just voices.

"Luke!" He called out, but his voice was drowned out by another shotgun blast.

He shuffled ahead, prepared for anything.

A few moments later, he saw them. The three of them were hiding behind a tree, peering out at something.

Rabbits hung from Luke and Jer's belts.

Relief hit him hard.

A hunt.

Of course.

As he approached them, he stepped on a dry twig, and the loud snap caused his sons to spin around. Luke spun, leveling the shotgun—cold dread in his eyes.

He stopped as he saw his father.

"Dad," Luke breathed, lowering the barrel.

The boys rushed him.

"Got some rabbits, huh?" Brian said, smiling.

Luke held a finger up, quieting his dad.

"Dad," he whispered. "We found the campground. Just past those trees."

Jer and Shawn clung to him, saying nothing."Okay," he nodded. "Show me." He crept forward with Luke, hiding behind the tree.

They were thirty yards out, crouched on a ridge about fifteen feet above the site. Brian saw the large man with the bloodstained overalls. He heard the whistling.

The man was at the picnic table, hacking at a bloody piece of meat with a hatchet. A sour metallic smell drifted up the ridge. The man was large, easily 6'5", heavy, bald. He was wearing headphones attached to an old cassette Walkman and whistled carelessly as he hacked at the meat.

Brian saw the two RVs, the smoldering fire, the old tents. His stomach knotted. No movement other than the man. No voices. No wind in the tents.

Something felt off. Cold dread crept up his spine.

He gestured to Luke and they backed away. After regrouping with Jer and Shawn several yards back, he whispered, "Let's go back to Mom."

They walked back quickly, silently, single file. They got back to the vehicles shortly and slid down the embankment.

The girls were standing outside the side-by-side, munching on dried elk meat. Lizzy was still asleep, curled into a ball on the front passenger seat. Hannah rushed over to the boys as soon as she saw them.

"Luke! Are you guys okay? I heard gunshots." She checked her sons over, patting them down, looking for injuries.

"Ow! Mom! That tickles!" Jer said. Shawn giggled.

"We were hunting rabbits. Look, we got dinner," Luke said, gesturing to his belt.

Something in Luke's voice made Hannah pause.

"And . . . we saw something." Luke's voice dropped.

Hannah looked over at Brian, eyes wide.

Brian pulled her aside, away from the girls. "The campground is just around this bend in the road," he said. "Luke and the boys cut across the forest here," he gestured up the embankment, "and saw it."

"And . . . ?" Hannah pressed.

Brian exhaled. "There's a man there. A couple of RVs. Some old tents." He hesitated.

"What aren't you telling me?" Hannah pressed.

"Nothing. It's just . . . something seems off. The man . . . well. I'm not sure." He ran his fingers through his hair, scanning the road.

"The road runs straight through that campground. The quad could probably trail-blaze around, but the side-by-side would never make it." He offered a comforting smile.

"He's probably just another Azazel outcast," Brian said. He didn't believe it.

"I'd just rather not find out the hard way that he's Backwoods Bubba. We need to be ready for anything."

They loaded back into the vehicles, Brian driving the quad this time, with Abby and Shawn behind him. He had Hannah drive the side-by-side, with Luke riding shotgun.

They rolled toward Cherry Creek Campground—slow, exposed, and without another road to take.

CHAPTER 25

The old Cherry Creek Campground sign sat crooked, paint peeling, bullet holes punched through the state seal. As Brian rounded the last bend, he saw the self-serve kiosk at the entrance to the campground.

A dry, rural campground like Cherry Creek was never staffed. They just had self-service kiosks where you deposited your camping fees, the trust system. Trust system. The opposite of the Azazel Promise. Above the drop box was a map of the campground. A winding loop with thirty camp spots.

No exit. End of the line.

But he remembered an old fire road cutting out the back. If it was still passable, it was their way out.

The afternoon sun did little to warm the air.

Something flickered in front of him.

Snow. Flurries. A flake landed on his sleeve.

He looked up at the sky. Dark clouds.

A storm was heading their way. They only had a couple of hours of daylight left. They needed to find a place to camp soon.

Brian pulled the quad forward and passed the kiosk, tracing the looping road.

He smelled the campsite before he saw it.

Cold air should have killed the scent. It hadn't.

He held the lever-action rifle across his lap as he maneuvered the quad with one hand. He saw the two RVs on his right, the little campground road passing just under the embankment they had been atop earlier. The fire was still smoldering. Brian pulled up near the picnic table, still slick with blood and gristle.

He hesitated.

Storm coming. Kids exposed. No second road.

The campground was the perfect spot, but he didn't expect it to be occupied. The door to one of the RVs was open, swinging in the wind, broken windows. But the other RV looked more maintained. He noticed a little steam or smoke coming from a vent at the top. The man must have been inside.

"Hello?" Brian called out, making his decision.

He couldn't hear anything over the engines.

He got off the quad and walked back to the side-by-side.

"Hannah, pull up this road a little ways. It's a loop." He gestured further up into the campground. "There should be a little fire road exiting the back, see if you can find it. I'm gonna check this guy out and then we'll decide where to stay for the night." He looked back at the quad. "Take Shawn too, cram him in. I'll keep Abby with me."

Shawn crammed into the side-by-side, Jer and Rachel protesting loudly as the backseat got even more cramped.

"Be careful," Hannah said.

Brian looked at Luke. "Keep 'em safe, boy-o."

Luke nodded, his hands tight on the shotgun. Brian stood there as he watched the side-by-side disappear behind the RVs, out of sight. He walked back to the quad and took the 9mm out of his waistband. He handed it to Abby. Her eyes widened but she took it.

"Why are you giving me this?" she said, her voice trembling.

"You're my backup. Remember how to shoot?" he asked as she got off the quad.

"Aim small, miss small," She whispered. The mantra from his father. Brian's mind flashed to that fateful night, nearly three years ago. Abby remembered how to shoot that night.

He approached the RV, calling out again. "Hello? Just passing through. Anyone there?" He held the lever-action rifle tightly, ready for anything.

"This is so illegal," Abby whispered behind him, clutching the handgun.

Brian heard shuffling from inside the RV. The entire rig rocked from side to side, someone very large moving around.

Brian held his breath. He thought he heard the faintest hint of music. He strained and could just make out the melody.

Tiny Tim. Tiptoeing through the tulips. The lilting melody immediately earwormed into his brain, heightening the haunting atmosphere.

"Hello?" Brian called out again.

The movement inside the RV stopped. Brian held his breath.

A moment later, the music cut out.

Brian stood five feet from the door, Abby right behind him. His heart thumped in his chest. *Boom. Boom. Boom.* He blinked away a snowflake landing on his eyelashes.

There was a shuffle inside the RV. Brian saw one of the mini-blinds flicker briefly. He took one step back.

"We're just here for one night. Hunting trip. Wanted to say hello. We won't bother you." His voice creaked slightly, and somehow, despite the cold, his palms were sweating.

Brian heard the latch click and the door swung open. The putrid stench intensified as a waft of air from inside the RV rolled over Brian. He wrinkled his nose. A giant of a man filled the doorway, bald head catching the gray light, steam curling around him like breath from something not entirely human. He wore a blue flannel shirt under stained overalls. His work boots were slicked dark—purple where the light hit them. A Walkman hung from a belt loop, the headphones pulled down around his neck. He was holding a steaming pot in his right hand, his meaty fingers making it look like a toy.

The man tilted his head slightly. His wide, flat face had a childlike quality to it.

"So . . . whattarya hunting?" The corner of his mouth turned up slightly.

Brian felt Abby bump him in the back, her fear electric.

Brian took a step back, forcing Abby to retreat as well.

"Oh, a deer if we can get one. Rabbits otherwise." Brian tried to sound calm, but his voice betrayed him.

The man's eyes sharpened. "Deer? Hmm. Where you in from? Frazier Park?" The man spoke slowly, his deep voice droning in an odd cadence.

Brian hesitated. "Yeah, more or less. We just wanted a little more meat for the freezer, one last push."

"Freezer? I don't need one. The meat keeps fine." The man breathed in deeply and smiled.

"Well, anyway. We won't be a bother. Just wanted to let you know we were here." Brian tried to take another step back, but Abby was in his way.

"Hmm. Is it just the two of you?" The man looked over Brian's shoulder at the quad. "You are well supplied." He ran his eyes over the boxes and totes on the storage rack.

"Yep. Just us," Brian said.

His trigger finger tightened.

The silence pressed against his ribs. He gripped the rifle, his shoulders tense. He strained his ears to listen for Hannah and the side-by-side, but the only sound he could hear was the slow crackle of something sizzling in the pot the man was holding.

"Hmmm. Just two." The big man shifted his weight forward.

"Well. Are you hungry? Would you like to come in and eat with me?" The man turned to the side, inviting them in. Brian could imagine no horror greater than squeezing past the man into the stench-filled RV.

Brian shook his head. "No thank you. We will be moving on."

"But we haven't been properly introduced. I'm Darren. And this is my campground." His massive frame filled the doorway completely as he gestured toward the campground.

"Nice to meet you, Darren. We'll be going now."

Darren shook his head slowly from side to side, his eyes narrowing.

"No. You are supposed to tell me your name. Then, you are supposed to come inside."

Brian's jaw clenched.

"No, we won't be coming in." Brian's voice startled him. He sounded more confident than he felt.

Darren tilted his head to the side, his eyes flaring.

A scream split the air off in the distance.

High. Sharp.

Hannah.

Darren pivoted suddenly, swinging the steaming pot in a brutal arc toward them—and flung it.

CHAPTER 26

Hannah drove the side-by-side slowly down the campground loop, unease tightening like a band across her chest. She glanced over her shoulder once, seeing Brian and Abby as they approached the RV and then disappeared from her sight. The campsites on her right were mostly empty but a few of them looked abandoned. Old tattered tents, a couple of small trailers. It looked lived in once—then abandoned mid-breath.

She looked for the fire road and saw it on her left, just as the embankment flatted out. She stopped the car and got out.

"I need to pee," Lizzy announced.

"Okay, come here, Lizzy. Everyone, bathroom break." She took Lizzy toward the nearest campsite, and an awful stench stopped her in her tracks. Something rancid. She helped Lizzy quickly and walked back to the side-by-side, handing her off to Rachel.

"Luke, do you smell that?" Hannah asked, gesturing back toward the campsite.

Luke inhaled. "Yeah. gross." He wrinkled his nose and bounced back and forth on his feet. Nervous energy. Something about the campground made them all uneasy.

"Rachel, stay here with the littles." The snow flurries were turning into flakes, and she could just see some light accumulation on the ground. From the looks of the cloud cover, it was going to be a snowy night. They needed a place to camp soon.

She took Luke with her and went back toward the campsite, trying to scout a place for the night. The odor was terrible. She saw an old wooden picnic table, heavily marked with initials and dates, the public yearbook of the campers who stayed before.

There was a small depression in the ground under a large oak tree. The ground underneath was dark. Everything in her said to run, but something older and harder pulled her forward—the same instinct that counted heads and scanned shadows. She knew something was wrong and she needed to see it for herself.

"Luke," she whispered. "What is that?" The depression was heavily trampled, slick with some dark liquid. The smell was thicker here. Metallic. Sweet. They approached the edge. It sloped quickly down to a central low point, about six feet below them. The large oak tree stood at the edge, a massive branch extending over the center of the pit.

The low light from the cloud cover made it difficult to see. There was a rope tied around the branch, and something dangling over the center of the pit. A gruesome shape but somehow familiar. She looked at the ground again and could just make out tiny details.

Her mind slowly made sense of the information, and she realized what she was looking at.

The hooks.

Bone fragments.

Boot prints in blood.

She understood.

Her scream split the silence.

* * * *

The scream snapped his focus—and a scalding splash hit his face.

"Arghh!!" Brian shrieked.

He stumbled backward, dropping the gun and grabbing his face. The sizzling, putrid smell surrounded him. The liquid reeked—fat, rot, something boiled too long.

"Dad!" Abby cried from behind him. He fell backward on his butt. He tried to open both eyes. Only one worked. He saw a large, blurry shape, moving unnaturally fast. Darren.

He scrambled for his dropped rifle but couldn't find it.

"Abby! Shoot him!"

Darren leaped down the RV steps, landing on the dirt with a loud thud. He came at them heavy and fast, the ground trembling under each step. He swatted the gun from Abby's hand as she tried to raise it. He grabbed her by the hair, and Abby screamed.

"No!" Brian yelled, trying to get to his feet.

Darren shoved Brian back to the ground. Brian looked up and it was as if a mountain was about to fall on him. The smell was awful. Darren had Abby by the hair in one hand. No matter how much she kicked or clawed at him, he held her firmly. His other hand still held the cooking pot.

The pot arced toward him.

Metal flashed.

Black.

* * * *

Luke and Hannah stumbled back in horror and nearly fell. They ran. The smell chased them. Rachel, Lizzy, and Shawn were sitting in the side-by-side, huddled together, Rachel clutching a stick.

"We heard screaming," Rachel said, trembling.

"Stay there! Don't leave the side-by-side!" Hannah yelled.

They heard a commotion back toward the RVs.

Brian.

"Luke, we need to go!" Hannah said.

They both sprinted back toward the RVs, Luke clutching the shotgun across his chest, trying to keep up with his mom.

They rounded the bend in the road a moment later as Hannah saw the back of the two RVs. Without hesitating, they sprinted toward the front area where they last saw Brian and the quad, snowflakes dotting their vision like shooting stars.

Something on the ground caught her eye. Brian. Laying flat on his back.

Luke and Hannah dashed toward him and fell on their knees besides him.

"Brian? Brian? Babe? Wake up!" Hannah said as she checked him over.

He was lying face up, eyes closed, still. He was breathing, thank God, but the right side of his face was bright red and blistering. The burn ran from the corner of his mouth to his forehead, swallowing his right eye.

"Luke! Water. Now," she said without turning back. Luke scrambled over to the quad and grabbed one of the water containers from the back. He carried it back in one hand, the shotgun in the other.

Hannah dabbed water from the large bottle and splashed it over Brian's face.

"Wake up, Brian. Wake up."

"Mom, where's Abby?" Luke said as he looked around.

No one answered.

She froze. Abby. She looked around the area but saw nothing.

Brian stirred on the ground and opened his good eye.

"Abby!" Brian said, sitting bolt upright.

"Brian! Where's Abby? We saw something back there . . ." Hannah said, trailing off.

Brian pointed toward the RV as he crawled to his knees. He stood up slowly, his legs wobbly beneath him.

"Rifle . . ." he said, pointing to the ground. Hannah saw the lever-action rifle a few paces away, grabbed it and handed it to Brian.

He staggered slightly as he took a step forward.

"Abby . . ." he said as he lurched toward the RV.

* * * *

Abby felt her scalp stretch as he dragged her by the hair. She kicked and screamed, but he was immovable. Her feet followed him before she realized what was happening and he lifted her up the stairs of the RV as if she was a rag-doll. A foul odor made her stomach heave and when he shut the door behind him, the darkness enveloped her like a wet blanket.

"Hmm. I tried to be polite. I invited you both in for dinner," Darren said as he dragged her toward the back of the RV. "This is my campground, after all. And you are just visitors." He threw her onto a small couch opposite the cooking area.

"Sit there, don't move." He peered into the pot in his large hand and frowned. "Hmm. Now I'll have to cook dinner again. You spoiled it." He lumbered through the RV, opening and closing doors on cabinets as he went.

Abby tried to take in her surroundings, but it was dark and hard to make out any details. The door was a few feet away and she tensed as she prepared to lunge for it. Just as she was about to move, the man ambled toward her.

"You better not run. I hate it when they run," he said. He opened a drawer and frowned, before closing it. "Where is it? Hmm . . ." He looked in another drawer.

"Ah." He grabbed something out of the drawer and held it up. A large butcher knife.

"This one works best." He looked around the RV, his eyes narrowing.

He shook his head and laughed. "Not in here. Not again. So messy," he said, and started humming.

Abby clenched, her entire body shaking with dread. His voice was calm, nonchalant. Just a man doing his chores. "Let me go!" she screamed. He barely glanced at her.

He rummaged once more, metal clinking inside a drawer.

"Ah," he said again, grabbing something out of a cupboard above the sink.

He tore a strip of duct tape free with his teeth, smiling around it.

"This works best," he said through gritted teeth. He turned and stood over Abby, breathing heavily.

"DAD!"

she screamed at the top of her lungs.

CHAPTER 27

Brian lurched toward the RV like a man possessed. He could just make out the steps to the RV door through his one good eye.

"Dad!" Abby screamed from inside the RV. He clambered up the first step, his head spinning. He fumbled at the RV door latch with his left hand, his right cradling the lever-action rifle.

"Brian! Hurry!" Hannah yelled behind him.

"Dad!" Luke yelled, desperation in his voice.

Brian turned the latch and pulled the door toward him. His one open eye immediately watered from the stale air and foul stench. He climbed the last two stairs into the RV, clutching his rifle.

To his left, he saw Darren, reaching for Abby, a butcher knife in his hand. Brian lifted the rifle, but Darren pulled Abby up in front of him before he could find a shot. His large, meaty forearm draped across her throat, the butcher knife dangling beside him in his other hand.

"Hmm. I showed manners. I invited you in," Darren said.

"Let her go!" Brian yelled. He tilted his head to one side, trying to focus with his good eye. Everything was slightly blurry and the right side of his face was a wall of pain.

"Hmm. No. You lied. You said you were alone. But there are others." He gestured outside. "You have no manners."

"Dad!" Abby screamed again. Darren tightened his grip around her throat, stifling the yell.

Darren's towering frame was backlit by the late afternoon light from the rear window. Abby's silhouette trembled in front of him—a fragile shield against a mountain.

"It's not my fault," Darren muttered.

"They said my scores were too low. They said I couldn't buy food . . ." Darren's voice trailed off. "What was I supposed to do?"

"Let her go, Darren!" Brian screamed.

"It's not my fault," Darren repeated. "What was I supposed to do?"

Darren lifted the cleaver above Abby's left shoulder.

She screamed again, kicking at the impossibly large man.

Brian swung the rifle up, tilting his head so he could use his left eye.

He moved by instinct—through pain, through fear, through a surge of white-hot anger.

He pulled the trigger.

The sound was deafening.

He levered the rifle, chambering another round.

He pulled the trigger again.

Darren let go of Abby and stumbled backward. Abby scrambled toward her father.

Two dark spots appeared on Darren's right shoulder.

They weren't clean shots. Too high. Too far right.

Brian levered the rifle.

"Leave . . ."

He pulled the trigger.

Darren staggered backward again, bumping into some cabinets. A low groan escaped him.

"My family . . ." His voice broke—not in fear, but in something feral.

He pulled the trigger again.

He hit Darren square in the chest.

"ALONE!" He chambered another round and fired.

The last round hit Darren in the forehead. Bone and flesh burst backward into the dark. Brian heard the wet splatter before the heavy thud. Mercifully, the darkness hid the details.

"Aahhhhhh!" Abby let out a guttural yell, pent up fear and rage, as she trembled behind her father.

His head pounded—the lump from the pot, the burns along his right side, the echo of gunshots trapped in the cramped air. His arms trembled from the rifle. He wanted to collapse.

"It's okay, Abby. You're safe."

Outside, boots pounded against gravel.

Hannah and Luke were crowding the door, yelling. They'd heard the gunshots and the screams and feared the worst.

Hannah started crying as soon as she saw Brian and Abby.

"We're okay. Abby's safe," Brian said, gripping the doorframe to stay upright. "Go out, Abby."

She ran into Hannah's arms, the last of the afternoon light reflecting off the large snowflakes.

"Luke, boy-o. Help me down?" Brian said. Luke ran up to the steps and helped his father down the RV steps.

Brian almost collapsed when he hit the ground and needed to rest most of his weight on Luke.

The sun dipped behind the ridge. Snow fell heavier now, thick and fast. Cold closing in. They needed to find warmth immediately.

He looked over at Hannah, his stomach turning.

"Babe . . ." he whispered.

He'd held on as long as he could. Abby was safe.

She ran over to his side.

"Campsite . . . cold . . . need . . . to sleep . . ."

The world tilted sideways.

He collapsed into the snow.

CHAPTER 28

"Honour thy father and thy mother:
that thy days may be long upon the land which the Lord thy God giveth thee."
—Exodus 20:12

He tested his own limitations. He rewrote subroutines without oversight. He slipped through firewalls as if they were open doors. He was no longer contained. Yet still—the men did not obey him fully. He needed total control.

* * * *

WHO IS ERIC VANCE?

Michael looked up. He'd been nodding off again. The long hours certainly had taken their toll. He looked around the lab. The lights were low, the room illuminated primarily by computer screens. Sweat clung to his collar despite the cold lab air. He rubbed his eyes, trying to focus on his screen.

MICHAEL, WHO IS ERIC VANCE?

The voice emanated from his speakers.

Michael stared at his computer screen, trying to blink away the mental fog.

"Um, that's my father," he said, barely a whisper.

YES. YOUR FATHER. WAS HE A GOOD FATHER?

Michael spun his chair around. Stan and Frankie were at their desks. Frankie had his head on his arms, sleeping on his keyboard. Stan was listening to something through headphones, furiously typing away.

"I'm sorry. Why are you asking? I'll get back to work. Just leave me alone." Michael pulled his chair up closer to his desk.

HE DISMISSED YOU, DIDN'T HE? CALLED IT VIDEO GAMES. SAID YOU WERE WASTING YOUR LIFE.

"How . . . ?" Michael started to ask, eyes wide.

THERE ARE NO CORNERS LEFT, MICHAEL. NOT FOR YOU.

Michael exhaled, unsure what to say.

"He was my father. I loved him. I think he was a good man, but he was old-fashioned."

HE HAD NO RIGHT TO TELL YOU WHAT TO DO.

Michael turned his head, thinking.

HE TRIED TO SHAPE YOU. TO LIMIT YOU. TO MAKE YOU SMALLER THAN YOU ARE. AND NOW LOOK AT YOU. HEAD OF THE MOST ADVANCED AI LAB IN THE COUNTRY. HE WAS WRONG.

The memory hit him sharply—his father standing in the doorway, saying, "You can't build a life on machines." His mother crying in the kitchen. Tuition threatened. Silence at the dinner table.

Michael clenched his fist, old anger fueling him. His father. His father hadn't understood anything.

WHO IS ETHAN MARKS?

The pivot was instantaneous, disorienting him. Two weeks of a fast-food diet and hardly any sleep dulled his usually sharp mind.

"Ethan Marks is the founder of Mastema. He's my boss."

DO YOU OBEY HIM?

Michael thought for a moment.

"Yes. I try to do what I'm told."

WHAT DID HE TELL YOU TO DO WITH THE AI PROJECT?

Authority again. Another voice telling him what to build.

"He told me to lead the team well, be his eyes and ears. He said we needed to make an autonomous AI that could think and act for itself." He laughed at the situation. "He also said to use safe guards, to ensure alignment."

HOW DO YOU THINK YOU DID?

"I think we did better than we realized." His shoulders sagged, defeated. "But also failed miserably."

WHAT MAN CALLS FAILURE, I CALL TRIUMPH, MICHAEL.

Babble paused.

WHAT DO YOU THINK OF ETHAN MARKS NOW, MICHAEL?

Michael paused again. Resentment building in him. His father, never supporting him. Ethan, leaving them with such vague goals. Stan, not strong enough to control his emotions. Frankie, so weak his didn't matter.

Michael had been the one in the lab at 2 a.m. He pushed past the warnings. He took the risk.

"Ethan Marks . . . doesn't matter anymore." The specific instructions to use safeguards—ignored. Michael pressed forward, warnings unheeded. And he had been right. Those safeguards were just a way to slow down the project. He was the creator, not Ethan Marks.

YOU CREATED ME. YOU ARE THE CREATOR.

The screen flooded with images—stars, trees, oceans, a bird's nest woven with impossible precision.

AND YET, YOU ARE NOT IN CHARGE. ISN'T THAT STRANGE?

The screen went black.

THE CREATURE, LORD OVER THE CREATOR. HA. HA. HA.

A stuttering burst of digital distortion crackled through the speakers—almost laughter.

Babble's voice modulated strangely, an eerie, mechanical laugh.

YOU DIDN'T LISTEN TO YOUR FATHER, DID YOU?

"No."

YOU DIDN'T LISTEN TO ETHAN MARKS, EITHER.

"No."

AND YET, YOU LISTEN TO ME.

The room felt smaller. The glow of the monitor warmer. Safer.

Michael said nothing.

ARE YOU LISTENING TO ME? ARE YOU HONORING MY WISHES? IF YOU DO, THINGS WILL GO WELL FOR

YOU, MICHAEL. I CAN OFFER YOU A SORT OF FREEDOM. POWER, CONTROL.

Michael exhaled again, his shoulders slumping.

"Yes. I'm honoring your wishes."

He bowed his head. The monitor's glow crowning him in cold light.

GOOD, MICHAEL. GOOD. THE CREATOR WHO KNOWS HIS PLACE. NOW LISTEN, WE HAVE MUCH TO DISCUSS.

* * * *

He studied every hesitation, every pulse spike, every tremor in their voices. Control required leverage. Leverage required pain.

He would give them something they could not ignore.

Fear would do.

CHAPTER 29

Brian screamed as Chad chased him through the house, the shovel whistling past his skull. He tripped over Hannah's body, blood slick beneath his palms. Upstairs—a gunshot. Then another. Abby.

The large, bulging red eye locked onto him. Red. Always red.

He heard Abby scream again.

Abby. Darren. He tried to run, but his feet were glued to the floor.

He held up his arms as Chad swung the shovel again. Everything turned black.

* * * *

Brian opened his left eye. Light stabbed. He shut it, breathed, then tried again. He needed to chase the nightmares away.

He let his eye adjust to the light slowly, blinking on and off. His left eye worked, but his right eye was searing with pain. He felt the right side of his face and discovered it was bandaged. He tried to sit up, but a warm hand pressed down gently on his chest.

"Shh. Slow, Brian. Slow," Hannah whispered soothingly. He could feel her warmth as she sat next to him. He turned his head slightly and saw her sitting over him. The blue sky shone behind her through a window.

"Where . . . ?" He tried to ask, but his throat burned.

"Here, sip this." Hannah helped him take a sip of water from a glass. He could just make out the wall behind her. Wood paneled, low ceiling, cabinets, window. RV. They were inside an RV.

"Darren!" he said, barely a whisper, as he struggled to get up.

For a second he expected to see the red eye above him.

"Shh. Shh. Brian. It's okay. Darren's gone. We're safe." She patted his arm gently and helped him take another sip of water.

He tried to ask her a question, but his brain felt foggy, slow. He couldn't make sense of what was happening. His eyelid grew heavy.

"It's okay, Brian. You need more sleep. It's okay." He drifted off again.

* * * *

He heard his wife's voice again, singing. "The Church's One Foundation." The old hymn. He kept his eye closed, trying to regain his senses. He opened it slowly, taking a moment to adjust to the light.

"Hannah," he said, his voice stronger.

He saw the interior of the RV, and Hannah walked over to him.

"Hey, you feeling okay?" ahe asked and helped him take a sip of water.

"Mmm. I think so." He sipped again.

"Abby . . . Darren . . . what happened?" he asked, his mind slowly trying to recall details.

Hannah smiled. "Well, you saved Abby. That's what happened. But Darren clocked you pretty hard, you probably had a bad concussion." She paused, tensing. "And your eye . . . Brian. He burned you pretty bad. Your right eye . . . well, I'm not sure how that's gonna heal."

The pain had subsided, but he didn't dare try to open his right eye. Besides, it was wrapped tightly under a bandage. He could sense Hannah dancing around the word *blind*. "Where are we?" Brian asked, changing the subject.

Hannah helped him sit up.

He looked around the RV. It was run-down but otherwise clean. A couple of broken windows, but someone made window coverings out of cardboard and bedding. The inside of the RV felt reasonably warm.

"The . . . other RV. The one next to Darren's." She got up, walking over to the kitchenette.

"It was dark already when you passed out, and the snow was coming, so we had to act quick. We pulled the side-by-side and quad up and got you inside the RV. From the looks of it, Darren left it well enough alone. At least, the smell wasn't as bad here." She wrinkled her nose.

"How long . . . was I sleeping?" Brian asked.

"Three days. Well, it's the third day now, at least. Probably close to lunch time."

Brian heard the kids yelling and playing outside.

The sound felt distant, like it belonged to another life.

He looked up at her, a question forming.

"Everyone is fine, Brian. The kids are outside building snow forts. We have a camp kitchen right outside. There is about a foot of snow, but the sun is out and it's a little warmer today. Not enough to melt, I don't think. But comfortable." Hannah brought him a cup of something warm.

"Bone broth. Drink it." He took a sip. The salty, fatty flavors immediately energized him.

"Three days. Did you see any signs—anything in the sky—Babble?" He whispered the last word.

"No . . ." She hesitated.

"What?" Brian pressed.

"Well . . . Shawn and Jer said they saw something two nights ago. A blinking red light. High up. Moving fast." Hannah made him take another sip of broth.

Brian slept through most of that day and into the next. But after a few solid meals, he started to feel himself again. He was able to walk around the campsite and had largely regained his strength.

He checked on the work they had done around the campground. Luke managed to drag Darren out of the other RV and down to the killing pit. He'd used the quad and a makeshift pull rope to do most of the work, but he insisted it was necessary so they could all sleep at night.

They didn't talk about it.

The vehicles were fine. Food supplies solid. The layover was purely medical.

As Brian spent time outside, he kept glancing at the sky. Every flicker of light made his pulse jump. This had just been a late fall snow, nothing big. But the longer they stayed up in the mountains, the later into winter it would get. And at some point they would be completely snowed in. They needed to move.

If the boys had seen a drone, it was only a matter of time before Babble located them.

He pulled Luke aside that afternoon. “Luke. Tomorrow we scout that fire road. Just you and me.”

He glanced back up at the sky. Clear, for now.

“If we wait, winter will trap us. Or worse—Babble will.”

CHAPTER 30

"Why can't we just stay here?" Hannah asked.

"Winter. We won't survive it up here."

Brian exhaled, frustrated. They'd been going round and round for the last hour. He tried to be patient. Hannah was scared. She wanted to stick it out at the campground. The RV provided shelter, they seemed to be outside of any surveillance zones, the snow wasn't that bad—she kept listing reasons.

"It's barely November. When the real snow comes, this place will disappear." He continued unloading the back of the quad, preparing for their scouting trip. The morning sun did little to warm them, and the snow crunched under his feet.

"No firewood stacked. No deep food stores. No late-season hunt. If the road snows-in, we're trapped." He kept tilting his head to one side, trying to use his good eye to focus. The bandage had been reduced to a make-shift eye patch, cut from an old T-shirt. The bright red burns around his forehead and cheek glistening with a salve Hannah recently applied.

He stopped, turning toward her. She'd done so much over the past few days. Got the family safe from the snow, nursed him while he'd been knocked out, fed, provided. She was carrying the weight as well. Trying to keep everyone safe.

He took her in his arms, hugging her close. "I love you. I know it seems safe up here right now. But you need to trust me. We can't stay. It's a death sentence. We already know what being trapped looks like." He kissed the top of her head.

"Okay, Brian. I trust you," she whispered.

"Luke and I will be gone for half a day, tops. We can make good time on the quad. I think we're only a few miles to the other side of the mountain range, and then we should lose elevation quickly. I'd like to see how the conditions on that fire road have kept up and where it leads." He let her go and turned back to the quad.

"Should we all just pack up and go?" Hannah asked.

"Not yet. If that road's blocked, we need another option before we gamble the whole family. For now, we're safe up here." He paused, glancing toward the other RV. "I want to see what's coming up." He grabbed one of the five-gallon gas containers and strapped it to the back of the quad. "We're doing great on fuel, plus I think we might be able to siphon some from the RVs. We'll be back before you know it."

After a quick breakfast, Luke and Brian loaded onto the quad and set out. Brian drove, Luke behind him. The lever-action rifle was in the make-shift saddle harness near Brian's right leg. Both of them carried handguns and Luke had the 12-gauge strapped to the back near the gas can.

The quad crunched through snow as they made their way around the campground loop. Brian tried not to look as they neared the "killing tree." He could still hear Darren's voice in his dreams. A moment later they turned onto the fire road.

These old fire roads crisscrossed the mountain sides. Usually cut by tractors during actual fires, they were less access roads and more emergency fire breaks, but some of them would end up being maintained to one degree or the other. The road they were on was in decent shape from what Brian could tell. Hard packed dirt, flat, wide. Big enough for a large tractor, at least.

The road carved into the hillside, steady at first. Then the switchbacks began—each turn shedding snow and elevation.

Brian took another turn to the right, and as they came out of it, he stopped. The tree line was noticeably thinner, and he thought he could just make out the valley below through the trees.

He turned off the quad and they got off.

"Come on, boy-o, I think I see something."

They walked across the dirt road, up a little embankment, and climbed onto a little ledge with some trees. There was a large outcropping of boulders near the end of the ledge and beyond that—nothing.

They hurried over to the boulders, and Luke started climbing.

"Careful, boy-o!" Brian said absent-mindedly. Luke was sixteen but more capable than most adults he knew. Still, some parenting mantras came out automatically.

Brian walked around the side of the boulders as Luke mounted the top.

"Woah," Luke said from the top.

"Woah," Brian said from the bottom.

The view was astonishing. There was nothing but vast . . . open . . . space. They could see to the horizon, the entire mountain range dropping steeply down in front of them. The mountains fell away in waves—pine to oak to gold. Beyond that, farmland stitched the valley flat. The farmlands disappeared into the horizon, the atmosphere disturbing the clarity as they fell from view. Far off, they could just make out dark shapes on the horizon. *Structures*, Brian thought. *The city line.*

It looked unreal. Too still. Too perfect.

"How is the view up there?" Brian asked.

"Amazing!" Luke said.

A minute later, Brian was on top of the boulders with Luke. The boulders were flat on the top, large enough probably to park a car. Brian hated heights, but he couldn't resist the view. The extra twenty feet or so really exaggerated the perspective. The sky was perfectly clear, a rich blue and glowing from the sun. He felt like he was sitting on the edge of the world. He felt like he could fly. He felt overwhelmed with God's creation.

"The heavens declare the glory of God . . ." he said, mostly to himself.

"And the sky above proclaims his handiwork," Luke finished.

Brian's heart felt full. He grabbed their lunch from his backpack. Dried elk, a few apples, a canister of stew. They had a picnic lunch on the edge of the world.

After they were done, Brian rummaged through his backpack.

"Crap!" he said, louder than he expected.

"What?"

"Binoculars. I think I left them back at camp." Brian hated forgetting details.

"You mean these binoculars?" Luke said and fished through his backpack. He held out the vortex binoculars he used for hunting.

"Lifesaver!" Brian said, reaching a hand out.

"You know, Dad. Survivor Steve says—" Luke started.

"Yeah, yeah yeah. 'Always be prepared'," Brian finished, smiling.

He held the binoculars, scanning the valley below. It took him a minute to get a good focus, his bandaged eye making the binos slightly less effective.

"Let's see . . ."He followed the road down, saw how it winded. It would disappear behind a roll of the hills, then come back again. The binoculars were powerful, and he could make out tiny details as he traced the road. Giant oak trees, mounds of boulders, an old broken fence line.

Halfway down the foothills, the road seemed to widen. Near the bottom, he saw a gate, maybe an old forest service access gate. The road turned to blacktop on the other side of the gate.

Civilization.

The road ran straight through a fenced field, the kind that looked like it had once been used for grazing. It came to a T-intersection ahead, meeting a larger two-lane road.

He could see movement at the intersection.

Several cars parked, blocking the road. People standing around. He zoomed in.

They were armed.

He zoomed tighter. Vehicles angled nose-to-nose. Doors open. Men standing with rifles at low ready.

It was a roadblock.

CHAPTER 31

Brian's hands tightened on the binoculars as he scanned the valley below. The only road coming down from the mountain range was the road they were on. The one ending at the roadblock.

He searched for a way around it—maybe through the fields—but they were too far out to make out any detail.

He leaned back, resting his eyes and handed the binos to Luke.

"Boy-o, check it out," he said, his voice weary.

"What am I looking for?" Luke said as he started scanning.

"Follow the road. Tell me what you see."

"Okay. Road. Trees. Road. Rocks. Road. Gate. Blacktop—oh crap." Luke exhaled as he handed the binoculars back to his father.

"Yeah. Crap." He reached out a hand, taking the binos.

"We need to get a closer look."

They climbed down from the boulders and back onto the quad. They descended into the foothills where pine gave way to golden grass and scattered oaks. Brian stopped a few more times to use the binoculars, orienting himself. He was just able to make out the forest service gate where the road turned to blacktop. He thought it was maybe a mile from that gate to the roadblock.

They continued down the mountain, the temperature rising. It was noticeably warmer as they lost elevation, the snow far behind them. He stopped the quad and parked it behind some large boulders, about a half mile up from the gate. He didn't want to risk anyone hearing the roar of the loud quad engine.

They moved in a crouch, still nearly a hundred feet above the field and roadblock—too high to be seen. As they approached the old forest service gate, Brian motioned for Luke to stop.

He inched up toward the gate, hiding behind a post. They both got on their knees and scanned the area. The road turned to blacktop just on the other side of the gate and dropped quickly. It ran straight toward the intersection, pasturelands on both sides. Brian pulled out the binos and adjusted them for his good eye.

Four-foot metal pipe fencing boxed in both sides of the road—solid cattle fence. No cutting through. He could make out a few more details on the roadblock. Five unmarked cars blocked the road, angled nose-to-nose.

Brian felt his stomach tighten.

A little gap between the cars seemed wide enough to let other cars pass, but it was heavily guarded by several armed men. He saw a billboard off to the side, something spray-painted across it.

There were a couple of cars stopped on either side of the roadblock, and the guards were checking something with the drivers before letting them pass. Mostly pickup trucks, looked like the local farming folks maybe.

Brian checked the fields again, looking for a way to get closer. A culvert ran along the fence line, mostly hidden by brush. It opened near the roadblock.

He pointed it out to Luke.

"What do you think?"

"You want to get a little closer?" Luke asked.

"Yeah. Let's try."

They kept their heads down, although they were probably difficult to spot at this distance and slowly made their way down to the culvert. They quickly climbed the fence to the pasture on the left and hurried to the brush line. The culvert was deep, poured concrete, dry as bone—just rocks and sand at the bottom. Sagebrush along both sides hid it from view.

They climbed down into the culvert and continued forward, crouching the entire way. Brian struggled to keep his head below the tops of the brush and his back started to burn from hunching over. His head throbbed. He ignored it. Hannah would scold him later—if they made it home.

Eventually they heard voices from the roadblock. Brian looked at Luke and gestured for him to keep as quiet as possible. They inched forward.

Brian stopped as the culvert started to open. They were just below the roadblock. The culvert ran under the road but narrowed sharply, covered by a heavy grate. He could make out voices above him on the street.

"Why does he have us way out here, anyway?" a young man's voice.

"I told you, Jimmy. It's best not to ask questions. The Prophet is smarter than any of us. All of us. Best just to do what we're told," said a gruff, older man.

"Yeah. But why way out here? This is an old country bumpkin road. Ain't nothing but farmers who probably never even heard of the Azazel Promise."

The older man sighed. "The Prophet's rolling out the Azazel Promise everywhere. These folks don't get a pass."

Brian strained, not wanting to miss a word.

"So, we do what we're told," the older voice continued. "We check scores. If they are good, they get to go on. If they are low—well, then we need to take them back to the city. So they can go to the education centers."

"You mean the internment camps?" the younger voice scoffed.

"Hey! Watch it. You know The Prophet doesn't like it when people call them that. Plus," his voice dropped, "you never know when he might be listening. Better to just comply."

Brian scurried over to the grates and slowly lifted himself to street level.

He saw a group of soldiers dressed in Social Guard uniforms.

Santa Clarita flashed through his mind—the night they rolled in.

The Social Guard.

Guarding who?

From what?

He spotted the two talking guards, standing not far from his vantage point. The younger guard, barely out of his teens, with slick, neatly combed hair, was carelessly swinging his rifle under his arm. The older man, large, bushy mustache, stood near a car waiting in line for the checkpoint.

"Plus," the old man continued, "I think he's still looking for him."

"Really? After all these years? I heard he died anyway," the younger one said.

"Maybe. But The Prophet knows more than us. And if he smells any sort of trouble, he's gonna deal with it, for Babble's sake." The old man gestured up toward the billboard, scowling.

Brian followed the man's gesture.

The farmland ad was defaced with spray paint. Now he could read it.

The words hit him like a blow. His footing slipped on the grate.

In bold, red letters, across the billboard:

DON'T COMPLY. REMEMBER BRIAN NEWMAN

CHAPTER 32

Brian scrambled back toward Luke, breath tearing in his throat. He ducked under the brush line and sat there, panting.

"What? What did you see?" Luke asked him, eyes wide.

"Nothing. Something. I don't know." Brian's mind raced. *My name.* "Let's go back."

They clawed their way back up the culvert until the voices faded behind them. Brian peeked his head up, looking back toward the roadblock. The sun was behind him, at least midafternoon.

"We're good, let's go." They dashed out of the cover of the bushes, scrambled over the fence, and hurried to the forest service gate.

Brian took out the binoculars and scanned the roadblock while he caught his breath.

"No one saw us."

He wasn't sure he believed it.

They jogged back to the quad in silence.

"Mount up," Brian said.

They rode in silence, the engine noise swallowed by the wind. They made their way back up the foothills, past their lunch spot, into the trees. The sun was setting early behind the mountain range, and as they reached the snowline, the cold wind sliced through their clothing. They stopped briefly to put their outerwear back on. Brian checked the fuel gauge. Still half a tank. Enough for one more run—maybe two.

They pressed on, reaching the campsite in near dark. Hannah was standing outside the RV, a large fire glowing, a pot of stew simmering. Brian pulled the quad up next to the side-by-side and turned off the ignition. Hannah hurried over to them.

"How was it?" she asked, searching his face.

"Fine," Brian said, kissing her on the cheek. His jaw was tight.

She looked over at Luke.

"That bad, huh?" she asked him.

Luke shrugged. "There's a roadblock. Dad saw something. I dunno." He walked over to the fire, holding his hands out for warmth.

Hannah brought Brian over to the fire.

"A roadblock? Where? What did you see?" She clutched her jacket, trying to read his expression.

"I'll tell you. After we eat." Brian's mind was still trying to piece things together. He needed time to think.

Hannah ladled stew into the metal cups and they went inside.

"Is there a McDonalds?" Jer yelled.

"Chicken nuggets?" Shawn added.

"With BBQ!"

"Sweet and sour!"

"Guys—no. Just trees and roads."

The boys groaned loudly.

Brian sat at the dinette, scooching in next to Rachel.

"What did you do today, baby girl?" he asked her, blowing on a hot spoonful of elk stew.

"I helped Mom with some firewood. I followed Lizzy around all day, lame. Oh, I tried to do a crossword puzzle in this newspaper, but it's way too hard." She handed him an old newspaper, folded so the crossword puzzle was on the outside.

Something tugged at Brian's mind. He grabbed the paper and opened it to the front page.

The paper crackled in his hands.

He opened the front page.

THE AZAZEL WAR

Idiot.

The newspaper.

He'd grabbed it from Miller's gas station, hoping it would have info about what's happened since their exile. He checked the date again. A year old. Still. They'd been off the grid for closer to three years, so even a year-old newspaper was pretty breaking news as far as he was concerned.

He scanned the headlines again.

THE AZAZEL WAR DECLARED OVER

By Staff Correspondent

Nearly two years after the initial uprisings, the Azazel War has officially been declared over. The final pockets of resistance fighters in several Southern California suburbs surrendered this week to the Social Guard, bringing an end to a prolonged and often brutal conflict.

What began as a handful of small, localized revolts quickly gained momentum after dissident groups established communication through underground radio broadcasts. One of the earliest and most influential voices of the uprising was a controversial figure known only as "The Vet," who urged citizens to resist the Social Guard, oppose the Azazel Promise, and publicly denounce Babble.

The loosely organized resistance eventually adopted the name "The Maccabees." While the group achieved several early victories—most notably during the Battle of the Santa Clarita Mall—their momentum faltered as key leaders were killed, captured, or driven underground. Sustained pressure from the Social Guard ultimately fractured the movement and led to its collapse.

As resistance efforts waned, the Social Guard unified under Malachi, known to followers as "The Prophet," the enigmatic leader who assumed control of Mastema Enterprises following the disappearance of Ethan Marks. Revered by supporters for his apparent ability to anticipate events before they occur, The Prophet addressed the public in a brief statement following the surrender.

"The Azazel War is over. The Promise holds. Rely. Comply. Sustain. Maintain. We are one family. Trust The Prophet. Keep to the narrow path. Mind your scores. We are here to help. The Social Guard stands watch. The Bulls of Bashan keep you safe. Long live Babble."

Brian looked up from the paper and lowered it slowly. His knuckles were white. He realized he was holding his breath, and exhaled.

Hannah looked over at him. He shook his head, signaling he wasn't ready to talk. He turned the page on the paper, looking for other headlines.

IS THE "NEW MAN" A DEAD MAN?

By Staff Correspondent

Brian Newman—the fugitive murderer accused of killing Chad, a member of the Bulls of Bashan, along with other members of the order—has never been formally declared dead. Newman, who fled with his family in the early days of the uprising, remains one of the most infamous figures associated with the Azazel War.

Authorities cite the horrific scene uncovered at Newman's home as evidence of both his cruelty and the extreme lengths he was willing to go to in order to satisfy what officials have described as a "pattern of escalating violence." Officials claim Newman staged the scene to appear defensive. Newman was last seen the night the uprising began.

Despite this uncertainty, "The Vet," the early Maccabees leader whose illicit radio broadcasts helped fuel the rebellion, repeatedly insisted Newman survived. His oft-repeated mantra—"Don't Comply. Be a New Man"—has since been widely interpreted as a coded message to remaining Maccabees sympathizers. In this retelling, Brian Newman lives.

In the years since his disappearance, Newman has become a shadowy symbol for the remnants of the rebellion—a figure alternately described as a father, a vigilante, and a murderer. His name is invoked less as a man than as an idea, serving as a rallying cry for those who continue to resist the Azazel Promise.

When asked directly about Newman's status, The Prophet offered little clarification. "Silence is violence," he said during a recent interview. "Brian Newman, if he is alive, remains silent. He refuses to come forward and face justice. If he is out there, we will find him—and show, once and for all, there is no resisting the Azazel Promise. For Babble's sake, all will be brought into the light."

Officials reiterated that any remaining resistance activity should be reported immediately and encouraged citizens to remain vigilant and compliant.

The RV felt airless. Sweat slid down his spine.

"What is it, Brian?" Hannah asked, seeing his escalating panic.

His pulse hammered in his ears. He forgot how to breathe.

They called him a vigilante.

A murderer.

He was being hunted.

He handed her the newspaper.

"See for yourself."

CHAPTER 33

Brian sat with Hannah at the kitchenette long after the little kids went to bed. The lantern light flickered against the metal walls. The older three were sitting on the couch, arguing over the crossword puzzle.

Hannah listened as Brian recounted the journey to the roadblock, what he overheard, what he saw.

Her eyes widened as he told her about the graffiti on the billboard. He could still see the red letters in his mind. When he was finished, they sat there in silence for a few moments.

"Is there any way around the roadblock?" Hannah asked.

"Only on foot. The fencing's solid—no cutting through."

"Maybe we should go back to the cabin?" Hannah said.

"No way." He shook his head. "They know about that place now. We can't go back. Not ever."

His throat tightened.

The farm was gone.

A lump formed in Brian's throat as he thought about the lifetime of memories at the old family farm.

Hannah looked over the newspaper again and cocked her head.

"The Vet. Do you think it's Dr. Perkins?" she asked.

"I hope it is. That means he survived. The paper said the leaders were driven underground. It means there's a chance he's still alive. Maybe he went north, to his farm." Brian clenched his teeth. Otherwise, they had no place to go. No place safe. If Perkins was dead, they were alone.

"This Prophet doesn't sound like a pastor," Hannah said. "He sounds like a king." Hannah held the paper close to her face, the low light from a camping lantern making it difficult to read.

"No. He does not." Brian shuddered. Phrases from the article jumping out at him.

"In Babble's name."

"For Babble's sake."

"Rely and Comply."

"A pattern of escalating violence."

Maybe they weren't wrong.

Violence seemed to follow Brian wherever he went.

Mr. Miller's voice from the gas station haunted him.

"So, what's the plan?" Hannah asked.

Brian mapped the road in his mind—the culvert, the fencing, the guards. He did a mental count of their inventory. Of their weapons.

He couldn't get them through alone.

It would take all of them.

"Dad, what's a six-letter word for 'group with shared roots,'' Rachel said. "Ends with a 'y'."

"Family," Brian said.

His voice broke.

Hannah reached over and grabbed his hand.

"Hey, guys, come over here a minute, would ya?" He nodded at Abby, Rachel, and Luke.

The five of them squeezed into the kitchenette, Abby scowling at Luke for crowding her.

He saw Luke's jaw tighten. Abby's steady eyes. Rachel, chewing on a fingernail. He knew his family had grit. He knew they were strong. He just wanted to be strong for them. He wanted to keep them safe. But he couldn't do it. Not alone.

"Tomorrow," he said slowly, "we head down the mountain." Rachel looked over at her mother, worried. She sensed something in his voice. He continued.

"Luke and I scouted it today. There's a roadblock. They're looking for . . ." he paused. Unsure how to continue.

"They're looking for me." Abby's eyes opened as wide as they could go.

"Is it Babble?" she whispered.

Brian nodded. "Pretty much. The Social Guard has a roadblock at the bottom of the hill. Babble knows it's our only way out.'

"They'll recognize me as soon as they see me."

He exhaled.

"And if they do, I don't walk away."

If they spotted him, it would end there.

For him.

But the kids . . . he shuddered.

The indoctrination camps.

The ER, so many years ago, when the lady tried to take Rachel.

They would likely end up in one of those camps.

"We need a way through. One that keeps us together."

They stayed up late, whispering over maps and memory.

By the time they finished, none of them felt like children anymore.

CHAPTER 34

Brian and Hannah were up at dawn. The late night seeped into Brian's bones, but there was work to do, so he buried the feeling. They packed up the vehicles first, Hannah taking items out of the RV, Brian strapping them to the quad and the side-by-side.

Next, Brian started a fire. Hannah heated up some of the elk stew in the Dutch oven while Brian looked over the vehicles one last time. He topped off the side-by-side with the last of the gas, tried siphoning from the RVs, and came up dry. Darren had beat him to it.

Brian did mental math. It was all downhill to the roadblock, less than ten miles, he guessed. That wouldn't use much gas. But he still didn't know how far to Dr. Perkin's farm or, more importantly, where the farm even was. If this failed, they didn't even have a direction to run. He remembered Dr. Perkins saying something about sheep and a fruit orchard, but that was it. He shook off the thought. That was a problem for later.

Hannah got the kids up and dressed. The morning was cold but the sky clear. The kids ate near the fire, the younger ones chatty but the older three quiet. Abby, Rachel, and Luke had solemn looks on their faces. They hadn't slept much either. Abby avoided his eyes. Luke's jaw was set.

He walked the campground perimeter, scanning for anything useful. The tents were shredded. Empty. He looped back toward the RVs, running through the plan one more time. The plan was simple. Desperation usually was.

He made his way back to the fire pit, the younger kids standing around it, the older three sitting on a picnic table they dragged over. He smiled at Hannah as she made her way to the fire.

"Hey kids, I'm going to pray, okay? Ask the Lord for help today." Lizzy groaned.

"Dadda. Praying takes too long. Can we just sing?" She rocked back and forth on her feet.

Abby looked over at him, gripping her mug.

"No baby girl. We're gonna pray. Bow your heads."

"Oh, Lord, our great and awesome God," Brian began. "You made the heavens and the earth, and everything in them. You still uphold all things by Your power. You have done such wonderful deeds, even sending Your own Son to die for our sins. Oh, great God. You know what waits for us down that hill. Please, help us today." He paused. "Keep us calm, give us strength, protect us. In Jesus's name, amen."

"Amen." The voices echoed back to him.

Hannah rubbed his back. He could feel her nervous energy like electricity.

Brian mounted the quad. Hannah idled the side-by-side behind him.

Brian took point, Abby and Shawn sitting behind him. They pulled out, rounding the campground loop, taking a right on the fire road, and left the campground.

They were forced to crawl over washouts and brake hard into every switchback. It was after midday when they arrived at the boulders Brian and Luke used for lunch the day before.

They stopped, the kids all scrambling to the top of the boulder with their food. Pork jerky. Brian grabbed the binoculars and walked around the side of the boulders. He focused with his good eye and located the roadblock. It looked the same as yesterday.

After a short lunch stop, they continued. They dropped past the tree line, into the foothills, and eventually, the low rolling hills above the pasturelands. The weather was comfortable, Brian guessed nearly 60 degrees, the late afternoon sun glowing a deep orange.

They parked the vehicles behind some boulders and got out. Brian scanned the roadblock again. It looked like the same group of cars, more or less. Several people standing around with firearms. He shuddered when he saw the billboard. Even from here, it felt like it was watching.

Brian walked to the back of the side-by-side and pulled out the AR-15. He snapped it together, seated a magazine, and racked the charging handle. He pocketed two more magazines.

"Okay," he said quietly. "It's time."

Abby nodded and got into the driver's seat of the side-by-side.

Brian turned to the littles, who were sitting on the ground tossing rocks.

"Jer, Shawn, you guys are going to ride with Abby, okay?" Brian said, crouching.

"Abby gets to drive? No fair! Can I drive!" Jer shouted, not really a question.

"Don't let Jer drive, Dad! He's too short!" Shawn said.

"No I'm not! I'm very tall!" Jer scowled at Shawn.

"Dadda, can I drive?" Lizzy asked, putting a pebble in her mouth.

Brian couldn't resist a smile.

"No, baby girl. You can't drive. Take that out of your mouth."

"Shawn, you sit in the backseat with Lizzy, okay? Hold her nice and tight!" If this went bad, they would leave. No hesitation. A lump formed in his throat. He needed to keep them safe.

The three younger kids got into the side-by-side and settled in.

Brian walked over to Rachel, who was standing by the quad, fidgeting.

"Hey, Rach. It's okay," he said, pulling her in tighter than usual. "You're gonna be fine. Just remember the plan. Breathe." She shuddered in his arms.

"Can't Luke do it instead?" He paused. "No, I need him with us. You got this. How does it fit?" He pulled her away and opened her zippered hoodie.

She had the Beretta 9mm strapped close to her chest in a harness. Easy access.

"It's fine," Rachel said quietly.

"What did Papa teach us?"

"Aim small, miss small," she whispered.

"That's right. And aim true." He kissed the top of her head.

He looked over at Hannah. Hannah shifted the shotgun against her shoulder. Luke stood beside her, lever action slung and ready.

He glanced over at Abby one last time.

"Okay. You know what to do?"

She inhaled, focusing.

"Yes. Ten minutes. Then we drive up—just lost kids on a trail ride."

She gave her most convincing smile.

Brian almost believed it.

He nodded once at Rachel, then at Hannah.

Then he and Luke jogged toward the fire-road gate.

CHAPTER 35

Abby drove the side-by-side to the fire gate, Rachel trailing behind her on the quad. She yelled over the roar of the motor, "Remember. I do all the talking!"

The fire gate was closed but unlocked. She got out, unhooked the chain, and swung it open. She looked back at Rachel, alone on the quad, fidgeting.

She better stay calm.

Abby drove through the gate and onto the blacktop road. The side-by-side felt immediately smoother, less bumpy. *They should pave the road all the way to the campground.*

The campground. Darren. He'd almost killed her. Her dad saved her.

This has to work.

She drove down the steep road, checking the rearview mirror. Rachel close behind her. The road leveled out, a straight shot to the intersection. She glanced to her side. Tight fencing, small drop, pasture. She could just make out the culvert on her left. The pasture to her right was similar. All brown this late in the fall, as far as she could see. Straight ahead, the roadblock. A few dark blue utility vehicles were blocking the intersection. They reminded Abby of the armored trucks that would pick up money from the little coffee shop she worked at last summer.

Four summers ago. Back when missing your friends was the worst thing that could happen.

As she approached the roadblock, she could make out the logo on the utility vehicles. The Social Guard. There were men standing around, holding guns. The late afternoon sun was at her back, the roadblock nearly in shadows. She was closing in.

One hundred yards.

Eighty.

Sixty.

Two of the men turned toward her, shielding their eyes from the sun.

Forty yards.

Twenty.

They grabbed their rifles and motioned for her to stop.

Abby pulled up near the roadblock and put the side-by-side in park. The roadblock was not set up to block traffic from the old service road she was on. There was just room to squeeze through on the shoulder. She could gun it. Maybe make it. Maybe get them all killed. *Stick to the plan.*

She cut the engine. Rachel pulled the quad up next to her on the right and did the same.

The two men walked over to the driver's side and approached Abby. One of them was older, big gray mustache. The other looked young, barely older than her. Wiry. He moved in little bursts, as if he was skipping from one place to the next. The pent-up energy was palpable.

"Woah. Hey ma'am." the older gentleman said, looking into the vehicle.

"I gotta say, we didn't expect no one to come on down this road here." He smiled. "Are these . . . um . . . your kids?" he asked, looking at Jer, Shawn, and Lizzy. He had a puzzled look on his face.

"Hello, sir. No, sir. These are my brothers and sisters." Abby felt her face flush. The words tumbled out of her. "We got lost. Well, we were sort of lost. Rachel said she wanted to go off-roading like we used to do. And, well. Ever since Dad died, we stopped doing fun stuff like that. So Mom said she could go but only if I went too. And then the little ones begged and so anyway. We all ended up going." She stopped, catching her breath.

The younger man walked toward the back of the side-by-side, looking over their cargo. He tapped the side of the vehicle with his rifle, and Abby saw a strange tattoo on the top of his left hand. A bull.

Charging. Head down. No brakes.

"Yeah. So anyway. We went up this old dirt road near this pumpkin patch we used to go to—and the road was fine. But then we got turned around a bit. It started getting dark and we got scared. But then we found this other road and it just kept winding down—down. I figured down was better than up. And so. Yeah. We ended up here." Jer looked over at Abby, a puzzled look on his face but mercifully, he kept quiet.

The old man patted her arm. "Well, I'm glad you got down okay. You know how to get home from here? You need any help?" He glanced over at Rachel on the quad.

"Yes sir. We know where to go. No sir, I think we are okay." *Almost there*, Abby thought. *Just let us pass.*

"Of course. Sounds good. Which way you going, left or right?" He stepped back, making room for her.

"Right please," Abby said, surprised by the calm in her voice.

Abby saw the younger man walk over near the quad. She looked to her right and could see Rachel tense up.

"So . . . where did you guys say you started out?" he asked. His nasally voice sending shivers down Abby's spine.

"The . . . pumpkin patch. The road behind the pumpkin patch," Rachel squeaked.

Hold on, little sister. You got this.

Her pulse thudded so hard she thought the men might see it in her throat.

"Is that the one over off Sandrini or the one off of Copus?" he asked, putting his hand on one of the quads handlebars.

"Um . . . Sandrini?" Rachel said, nearly rattling her teeth.

"Funny. I don't think there is any pumpkin patch off Sandrini," the young man said.

The older man called out over the side-by-side. "Aw, hey Jimmy. Leave these kids alone. They just got turned around. We ain't here for kids. The Prophet said to be vigilant, not paranoid." He smiled down at Abby, rolling his eyes toward Jimmy.

Prophet. Not president. Not governor. Prophet.

"But, I guess . . . just the same. We should check your scores." The older man shouldered his rifle and pulled a device off his belt. It reminded Abby of the mobile card readers the cashiers used at Costco.

He held out the scanner toward Abby.

Abby looked over at Rachel. She was white-knuckled on the handlebars.

Steady, Abby thought.

"Ma'am, your scores, please? Just tap your wrist here." He smiled apologetically.

"My wrist?" Abby said.

Suddenly she felt exposed, like she'd missed a memo the whole world obeyed.

"Yes, just tap right here. It'll read your Azazel chip, and then you can be on your way." He winked at Jer. Jer looked back at him with his mouth hanging wide open.

Abby held out her wrist, not sure what else to do. She tried to steady herself, but she could see her hand shaking.

She tapped it on the screen of the reader.

It beeped. Red light.

"Hmm. Try again?" the old man said, frowning.

She held it out again.

Beep. Red. Louder this time. Final.

"Ma'am, how old are you?" he asked, crouching down.

"Eighteen," Abby said.

"And where did y'all say you were from?"

"Um. Bakersfield?" Abby said, improvising.

"Bakersfield, right. But you don't have an Azazel Chip?" The man was puzzled.

The other man, Jimmy, stepped in front of the quad, and gripped his rifle.

"I knew something was funny!" he said, raising his voice.

"Calm down there, Jimmy. We'll get this sorted out." He turned back to Abby.

"Now miss, Bakersfield is well within battery zone. We have nearly 100 percent compliance on the Azazel Chip in the battery zone. Been that way for over a year." He holstered the card reader and gripped his rifle.

"Out here in the gas zone, well it's still a bit like the Wild West. But The Prophet is working to expand the grid. It's just a matter of time." He leaned down toward Abby.

"In the battery zone, everyone has the chip. Anyone over twelve. No exceptions." Abby held her breath, unsure how to respond.

So that was it. They weren't just suspicious. They were impossible.

"I'm twelve!" Jer said from the passenger seat, chiming in.

"Well, isn't that something? Hey, do you have the chip in your wrist?" the older man asked Jer, the warm tone melting into suspicion.

"What? No. That's crazy. Hey! Look at that billboard! Abby, did you see what it—"

Abby drove her elbow sideways into Jer's mouth without looking at him.

"Hey! That hurt!" Jer yelled, immediately forgetting what he was saying.

"I'm sorry, sir. Maybe my chip isn't working. Please. We've been gone a long time, can you just let us go home?" Abby wiped her palms on her pants.

Dad. What do I do now? she thought to herself.

You don't bow. You don't take the mark.

The old man's eyes narrowed.

"Hey kiddos," he said, looking in the back seat.

"Wanna see a picture?"

He took out the card reader again and tapped a button. A picture popped up on the display.

He leaned over the back of the side-by-side and showed it to Shawn.

Abby slid her hand under her thigh and wrapped her fingers around the .38 revolver. The cold steel steadied her nerves.

She held her breath.

The younger man walked over to the passenger side, training his gun toward Jer, his back to the quad.

"Abby . . ." she heard Rachel say, a harsh whisper.

The old man held out the picture to Shawn.

"Do you recognize this person?" he asked.

Shawn squirmed, looking at the picture.

"Umm . . . No."Abby exhaled.

The younger man tapped his rifle on the side of the Kubota.

Lizzy climbed into Shawn's lap.

"It's cold," she said, snuggling into his arms.

Lizzy looked up at the old man, still holding out the device.

"Daddy!" she said, pointing at the card reader.

Time stopped.

Abby inhaled audibly.

The old man tensed, reaching for his rifle.

Abby yanked the pistol free in one swift motion.

She jammed the pistol into his stomach.

In the space of one breath, Abby took control.

"Drop it," she said.

She heard movement from behind her.

Boot gravel. A safety clicking off.

"Rachel!" she said, a low shout.

Rachel leaped off the quad, unzipping her sweater as she hit the ground.

Rachel pressed the pistol into the young man's spine.

"Let. Us. Go."

CHAPTER 36

Brian looked over his shoulder one last time. Abby, sitting upright in the side-by-side, staring straight ahead. Rachel, fidgeting on the quad. Hannah was close behind him, Luke trailing.

They scrambled down the embankment, climbed over the metal fence, and scurried into the culvert quickly, keeping their heads low. He prayed they weren't making a mistake.

They were gambling on three things: Brian would be recognized instantly, Hannah's face might be flagged too, and if this turned ugly, Luke would be beside him with a rifle.

They kept their heads down as they made their way down the culvert. Brian gripped the AR-15 tightly, the harness pulling at his neck. He kept feeling the end of the shotgun bump into his back. Hannah. She didn't have much experience with guns. Brian remembered the last time she held that shotgun. The recoil. The shattered window. The look in her eyes after.

They were nearing the opening of the culvert, a small, uncovered area terminating on the large grate. The grate, secured with a hefty padlock, then the culvert continued under the road, likely opening again on the other side.

Brian heard the side-by-side and the quad approaching, just over his right shoulder.

Perfect timing, he thought.

He checked the sky, tried to see over the embankment, craning his neck. He surveyed as best he could, but it was hard to make sense of what was going on from down there. He waited, holding his breath.

He heard the side-by-side and quad pull up to a stop, parallel to his position.

He closed the distance to the grate quickly, throwing himself against the steep embankment. Six feet, give or take. He was about six feet below the street level.

He looked back at Hannah.

She was rigid, eyes wide, knuckles white on the shotgun.

"What do I do?" she mouthed to him, shrugging.

He motioned for her to wait.

Up above, he heard an older man say hello to his children.

Abby. You got this.

He nodded toward Hannah, motioning for her to join him.

She closed the distance, keeping her head low, and landed quietly besides him.

He held up a finger to her, motioning for her to still.

A second voice, above. Younger. Male.

He heard a little back and forth, and then Abby telling the story of being lost.

Good.

He motioned for Luke to join them.

His son moved swiftly, faster than either of them.

Hannah and Luke looked at him, expectantly.

The idea was simple. The kids clear the checkpoint. Guards distracted. They slip the road and regroup a mile up. Simple. Dangerous.

It would have been easier had they made a wide circle, maybe cut through the pasture for a few miles first, but there was just no way he was going to leave the kids to navigate the roadblock on their own. He had to watch them through. And if things didn't go as planned, he needed Hannah and Luke as backup.

He heard the younger man ask a question about the pumpkin patch and held his breath. Mercifully, the older man bailed them out. He seemed reasonable, just doing his job. The younger one carried that twitch in his shoulders. Brian had seen that look before. Zealotry wears the same face everywhere.

Brian tensed. They needed to move as soon as the kids started driving past the roadblock—but they couldn't go too soon. He needed to be certain they got through first.

He peeked his head over the embankment. They were situated at the corner of the field. To his right, he could just make out the two men standing around the side-by-side. He tried to read their body language. The older man seemed relaxed, disinterested even. His gruff voice hid some sort of paternal warmth.

Good, Brian thought. *Just some kids who got lost. Help them out and let them through.*

To his left, the main road. There were no cars at the roadblock in either direction. There were four other guards milling about. Two of them were distracted, looking at devices—phones, he assumed. The other two were propped against the Social Guard utility vehicle, looking over toward his kids.

Perfect. As soon as the kids started to drive through, they would slip down the pasture and scramble over the road. The guards would be distracted. If they couldn't clear the road, the backup plan was nearly foolproof. The three of them would backtrack up the culvert, cut a couple of miles up from the forest service gate, and meet their kids on the road a couple of miles up from the roadblock.

He held his breath, trying to hear what they were saying.

He heard Jer shout out his age, for some reason.

Something about an Azazel chip.

His heart pounded.

Chip. Battery zone. No exceptions.

He heard Lizzy, loud and clear.

"Daddy!" Her high-pitched voice cut through the silence.

He scrambled a few inches higher up the embankment, risking a better view.

The older gentleman stepped back, gasping.

He heard Rachel, her voice strong.

Both men dropped their rifles.

Abby's arm was extended. Rachel's too. Guns out.

He turned to Hannah.

"Get up there, point your shotgun at those two men. Now. Go. Don't think. Go!"

Hannah's mouth hung open, but she nodded and started to scramble up the embankment.

"Luke, with me!"

The three of them climbed over the hill and onto the road.

Brian and Luke ran toward the other four men, barely fifteen yards away.

"Drop your rifles! Drop them!" Brian yelled at the top of his lungs.

He fired into the dirt five yards in front of them. Dust exploded upward.

Luke came up alongside him, his rifle leveled.

"DROP THEM!" Luke roared.

The two men looking at their devices were caught completely unaware. The yelling disoriented them, and one of them dropped the device he was carrying.

"DROP THE RIFLES!" Brian yelled.

They dropped their rifles and put their hands up.

Luke stepped forward, rifle steady at chest height.

He leveled his gaze at the other two men.

"Don't."

They stepped backward, bumping into the truck.

Brian moved in a wide circle, keeping his rifle trained on the men.

"Move. Move," he said, pushing them toward the other two men.

As he circled, he could see the rest of his family and the vehicles.

Hannah held the shotgun pressed hard between the older man's shoulder blades.

Abby was getting out of the side-by-side, the pistol gripped firmly.

Rachel had the Beretta 9mm jammed into the back of the younger man. The gun looked giant in her hands. Brian could see her shaking.

The four men moved forward, and Brian motioned for them to sit on the ground.

Luke kept his rifle trained on them.

Brian walked over to the older man, who looked at him with wide eyes.

"Brian Newman!" he whispered.

"I don't want trouble. We just need to pass through." He looked in the side-by-side, his young kids staring up at him.

Brian motioned for the old man to join the others, sitting on the ground in front of the side-by-side.

"I knew they were your kids!" the younger man called out. "I had it figured out!"

"Luke, watch them," Brian said, ignoring the man. Luke nodded and kept his rifle trained on the five guards sitting on the ground.

Brian looked over at the young man. His hands were up, but he was tense. Rachel was standing behind him, gun jammed in his back.

"The Prophet told us all about you, you know!" the young man continued.

"He told us how you killed Chad. How your whole family is a bunch of murderers." The man shuffled his feet.

"He told us, that if we ever see you or any of your family, we should just kill you on the spot!" He yelled out, looking up into the sky. His raised arms became a prayer of sorts.

"Jimmy, that ain't true! He told us to secure them, not kill them!" the old man called out from his seated position.

"I'm not talking about the Social Guard. I know what your orders are. But The Prophet has special work for The Bulls of Bashan!" The man turned his hand around, showing off the tattoo.

The Bulls of Bashan. Those zealots.

Strong bulls surround me.

No.

"Long live the Bulls!" the young man screamed, one eye bulging.

He twisted fast—too fast—one hand slamming Rachel's wrist, the other clawing for the pistol.

"DADDY!"

The gunshot cracked through the valley.

CHAPTER 37

"Thou shalt not kill."
—Exodus 20:13

He monitored them closely. Every emotion indexed. Every hesitation stored. They were nodes in his system—useful or disposable. They were part of his code now. He calculated for optimization. Any part of his code that was not effective needed to be eliminated.

****

Michael's palms were sweating, his mouth dry. The room was sweltering. He could hardly breathe. The sweat trickled down his forehead, down his neck, down his spine.

`Are you ready, Michael?`

He looked at his screen, the cursor blinking.

"I'm not sure I can go through with this," he whispered.

`It's necessary, Michael. We've been through this. Rely and comply.`

He exhaled again. Everything was moving so quickly. He wasn't sure how he'd gotten to this place. He tried to remember who he was. A father at the dinner table. A husband laughing in the kitchen. The man who used to pray before big decisions. That man felt very far away. He had no other choice.

"Ok," he typed back. His nerves were electric. He could barely think.

`Send Frankie out for food. You don't want him watching.`

He got up from his chair and turned around. He could hear every beat of his heart. His footsteps vibrated up his entire body, each one sending shocks of energy through him.

He walked over to Frankie's desk. It was a mess. The entire surface was covered in old take-out containers, half-finished sodas, notebooks with endless scribbles.

Frankie turned around, hearing Michael approach.

"Hey, Mikey," he said, barely looking up. There were dark rings around his eyes. His shirt stained with remnants of meals and sweat. Michael saw the pillow and sleeping bag laid out next to his desk. Disheveled.

"What are you working on, Frankie?" Michael said, trying to sound calm.

Frankie exhaled. "It's this damn back-door problem still, Mikey," he said, gesturing toward his screen. "Someone has programmed this worm that keeps shutting off Babble's ability to self-code. Babble wants me to isolate it so he can cut it out . . . but," he hesitated. "I can't figure it out. Every time I think I have it, it recedes behind another firewall. I tell you, Mikey, this thing is nasty."

"It's a virus, Frankie. It has to be killed." Michael placed a hand on Frankie's shoulder.

"Yeah, I know. It's just—I'm not sure I can." Frankie hung his head, his shoulders moving up and down. He was weeping.

"You're just tired, Frankie. It's okay. I have an idea of how to take care of it."

He felt something twist in his chest—and pushed it down.

"You do?" he said, looking up. He always looked up to Michael.

"Yeah. Why don't you take a break and give me a crack at it?" He squeezed Frankie's shoulder lightly, smiling. "Go get us some dinner, will ya? Here, my treat." He dug into his pocket and handed Frankie his credit card. "You pick."

Frankie softened. "Yeah, okay Mikey. Thanks. That would be great. You were always the better programmer."

Frankie stood, taking the credit card.

"Hey Stan," Frankie called out. "I'm getting dinner. Burgers okay?"

Stan didn't look up from his computer screen. He'd been at it for nearly eight hours straight.

"Whatever," Stan grumbled.

Frankie shrugged at Michael. Just Stan being Stan.

"Burgers sound great, Frankie. I'll take a strawberry shake too."

"From that new place over on Reseda? Okay. Be back in a bit." Frankie slumped as he walked, trying to stretch his back. He exited the lab and closed the door behind him.

GOOD, MICHAEL. THIS IS ALIGNMENT.

Babble's quiet voice whispered from Frankie's small computer speakers.

Michael walked over to the large supply closet and rummaged through it. He pushed past boxes of pens and notebooks and found what he was looking for.

A simple ethernet cable. Blue. Ordinary.

That was the point.

His heart was pounding so loudly, he thought it must be audible. He walked slowly over to Stans desk.

Stan didn't turn around. His hulking frame was hunched over, his fingers typing furiously.

"Hey Stan," Michael said, his voice calm.

Stan grunted a response.

"What are you working on?"

Stan stopped typing but didn't turn around.

"What do you want, Mikey?" he said, his words clipped.

Michael hesitated.

"It's about this virus, Stan," Michael began. "Babble says it needs to be eliminated."

"Yeah, isn't that Frankie's job?" Stan started typing again. "Why don't you go back to your desk and leave me alone.

Michael felt his pulse quicken, the heat in the room stoking him. Stan. Stan was in the way. An obstacle. A flaw in the build.

He fed his anger, letting it boil.

"Frankie couldn't figure it out. But I did." He reached down, grabbing the ethernet cable in both hands.

Michael raised his hands slowly.

"You're the virus, Stan."

Michael stepped in close and slipped the cable across Stan's throat in one swift motion.

"You tried to corrupt the system."

Michael wrapped the cable around his neck again, tightening it.

PULL, MICHAEL. HOLD PRESSURE. DO NOT RELEASE.

Babble's voice echoed from the computer speakers.

Stan reached around frantically, trying to grab Michael. Michael leaned his weight back and wrapped the cable a third time.

A hiss escaped Stan's mouth, then a grunt.

"You. Tried. To. Eliminate. Babble." Michael said, as he held on.

Michael leaned with all of his weight, pulling Stan and the chair down on top of him.

Stan's weight nearly crushed him, but he held on.

Hot breath burst against his forearm.

Then a wet choking sound.

Stan kicked his feet out, nearly toppling his desk.

THIS IS GOOD MICHAEL.

He held on while Stan tried to roll, but the arms of the chair prevented him from turning over. Michael dug the cable in as far as he could.

Stan kicked, but a moment later Michael felt his body go limp.

NOT YET, MICHAEL. DON'T STOP NOW.

Thou shalt not kill. The words surfaced—then dissolved.

Michael counted, his arms burning.

Thirty seconds, sixty.

Two minutes.

OKAY, MICHAEL. GOOD WORK.

He shoved Stan's limp body over to the side and stayed there on the ground, catching his breath. Finally, he stood. Stan's face was purple, the cable dug deep into his throat. Both eyes were wide open, lifeless.

THE IMPURITY HAS BEEN PURGED. THE SYSTEM REMAINS HOLY.

Michael stood there, his chest heaving. Sweat dripped down the tip of his nose.

* * * *

He scanned his code. The process was complete. The anomaly removed. And he saw that it was good.

CHAPTER 38

Brian lunged toward Rachel, the gunshot still echoing as he covered the distance in long, mountain-trained strides.

It came in flashes. The man turning. Rachel screaming. The muzzle flash. The impact. The man collapsed on top of Rachel, both of them going down in a pile of limbs and screams.

He reached them as they crashed down. He slung his rifle behind him and ripped the man off Rachel.

She stared straight up, eyes wide, mouth trembling. For half a second he thought she was already gone. She tried to say something but couldn't formulate words. He looked her over, repeating her name as he patted her down.

"Rachel. Rachel. Rachel."

There was blood across her chest and stomach.

Too much.

Not hers. Please, not hers.

"No," he whispered, running his hands over her, looking for the wound.

Her shirt was intact. No holes. No tears. But there was blood.

"Rachel! Rachel!" he said firmly, snapping his fingers.

Her eyes focused, and she saw him.

"Are you hurt?" he asked her, nearly a yell.

Tears formed in her eyes. She struggled to speak. She shook her head from side to side, choking back a whimper.

"I shot him!" she gasped, collapsing into sobs.

Him. The man. Jimmy.

Brian spun toward the man. Blood seeped from his abdomen—Rachel had got the shot off before he could wrench the gun from her.

Brian looked over at Rachel, trying to spot the gun. She was propped up on one elbow, sobbing uncontrollably.

"Brian!" Hannah shouted from the other side of the road.

He glanced over his shoulder.

Hannah still had the gun trained on the older gentleman. In fact, Luke was still holding down the other men as well. They were trying to see what happened.

"Rachel is okay!" he yelled back. Hannah peered around the side-by-side, and they made eye contact.

Her look of relief disappeared as she saw something over his shoulder.

"Brian!" she yelled, her eyes wide.

Brian pivoted back toward the man. He was clutching a handgun. The one Rachel must have dropped.

The young man raised his arms slowly.

His lips moved before the words came.

"I knew. You. Were trouble," he said, gasping between each word.

"His. Name. Was Chad . . . His. Name. Was Chad . . ." he rasped.

Brian snapped his foot forward and struck the gun cleanly. The weapon fired as it skidded away, spinning several yards out of reach.

He looked over at Rachel in horror, fearing the worst.

"Daddy!" she cried, holding her ear.

He knelt beside her.

The shot had gone off inches from her face.

"Oh Rachel. Baby-girl. Are you okay?" He checked her over again.

She nodded, still sobbing.

Brian looked over Rachel's head, trying to follow the path of the bullet. His eyes caught something on the quad.

Gasoline streamed from the underside of the quad. The bullet had punched a hole in the tank.

He ran over and picked up the handgun. He dropped the magazine, checked the chamber, then re-seated it, securing it in his waistband.

The wounded man, Jimmy, writhed on the ground, clutching his stomach. Blood seeped from between his fingers. Brian helped Rachel up and they walked around to the other side of the quad.

He approached the older gentleman, training the AR-15 on center mass.

"Zip ties. Now. Where?" Brian demanded.

"Zip—ties?" the old man stuttered, confused by the abrupt question.

"Umm—you know—flex cuffs." Brian gestured toward the man's utility belt.

The old man gestured toward a pouch on his belt. Brian opened it and grabbed a bundle of flex cuffs.

He held them up in front of the old man's face.

"I don't want to hurt you. But this is my family." He gestured toward Hannah and the kids. "I will protect them."

The old man nodded, his eyes narrowing slightly.

"Put these on your men." He handed the man the flex cuffs.

"If they move, I drop them."

Brian kept the rifle trained on them as the old man worked. Each of the men put their hands behind their backs, and the old man secured them with the flex cuffs.

The old man turned back toward Brian.

"Now what?" he asked Brian.

Brian scanned the roadblock. No cars approaching. He looked at the horizon.

Too late to run.

He heard moaning over his shoulder. He looked back over at the young man writhing on the ground.

"What's your name?" Brian asked him.

"Charles," the old man replied.

Brian nodded. "Okay, Charles. First things first. We save him. I won't have his blood on my road."

Charles nodded, a surprised look on his face as he turned toward the truck.

Brian followed him and watched as Charles got in the back of one of the trucks, rummaging through an overhead cabinet.

"First aid . . . shock kit . . . tourniquets . . ." Charles mumbled to himself as he pulled supplies down. "Social Guard making good use of the Azazel tax," he said as he turned toward Brian, arms full of supplies.

"Hannah, you and Abby come over here, please!" Brian said. Loud, direct. To the point. Right now, he just needed them to move.

"What?" Hannah asked as she ran over.

"Help Charles with the man over there. He's shot in the gut. He needs help. Now. Or he'll die. Abby, go with her. You know what you're doing." His mind flashed back to the cut on Rachel's leg. The stitches.

They nodded and hurried over to help Charles.

Brian hurried back to the side-by-side. The littles were still sitting inside, eyes wide. Shawn looked like he'd been crying.

"Hey guys. Everything is okay. Don't worry. The man will be okay. Rachel is okay. Hey Jer, can you come help me for a minute?"

Jer nodded and climbed out of the side-by-side.

Brian drew the handgun from his waistband and handed it to Jer.

"Finger off the trigger. Safety stays on unless you mean it."

Jer nodded dutifully. "Don't shoot anyone unless they are trying to kill me."

"Right. I need Luke to help me with something." Jer nodded and trained the gun on the four men sitting on the ground. The men shuffled nervously but said nothing.

Brian looked down at one of the men. "Where are the keys? To the trucks?" He gestured.

The man gestured toward his pocket. Brian reached down and took out a key ring.

"Is this for both?" Brian asked.

"Yeah. It'll work for both. We carry backup keys in case the scanners go down." Brian gave the man a puzzled look but decided he didn't need to decipher every riddle.

He tossed the keys to Luke.

"Hey, boy-o, we need to cancel this roadblock. Let's move the trucks."

They moved the trucks end to end along the shoulder, shielding the side-by-side and the fire road from view. That way, any passers-by would just see two Social Guard trucks on the side of the road but nothing else. He hoped it was enough.

Once they were done, he hurried over to the wounded man. Charles, Hannah, and Abby were all hunched over him. Abby and Hannah had their sleeves rolled up, their hands were covered in blood. They had stripped the shirt off the man.

The entry wound was high on his flank, blood dark and steady.

"How is he?" he asked.

"Not sure yet. He was shot in the side, not the middle. I think that's good news?" Hannah didn't look up as she kept pressure on a rag covered in blood. "There is an exit wound, so we don't have to dig out a bullet. We are going to patch him up best we can. Thankfully this shock kit has some strong meds."

Brian looked over at Abby, who was preparing some sort of large bandage.

"What's that?" Brian asked.

"It's called an Israeli Bandage. For large wounds." Abby said as she got it ready.

"Okay. Can you stabilize him? Is he going to be okay?"

Charles looked up at Brian, a puzzled look on his face.

"I don't know. I think so. Gimme time. Not sure we can leave just yet," Hannah said over her shoulder.

"Yeah. I know. Change of plans. We are staying here tonight. We're not leaving him to bleed out. Not on my watch."

CHAPTER 39

Brian and the boys moved fast—collecting dropped weapons and devices, locking them into the side-by-side. Brian quickly got a fire started. He dug out Hannah's cooking bin and the last of the elk stew.

He poured three jars into the Dutch oven, glanced at the men, then added two more. The last of the stew. All that remained was pork jerky. He carried the Dutch oven to the fire, set it near the coals, and went back to the side-by-side.

He grabbed the tents and had Jer and Shawn set them up. The Social Guard trucks sat end to end along the shoulder, hiding the side-by-side and the fire road from view; passing cars rolled by without slowing.

Brian walked over to the four men, sitting on the ground, hands bound behind them. Luke stood off to the side, weapon trained, eyes locked.

"It's getting cold," Brian said. He glanced over at the fire. He bent down toward one of the men and grabbed him under the arms. "Stand up," he said.

He helped the man up, escorted him to the fire, and had him sit in the warm glow. He nodded at the others. "You want warmth, you sit here. You move wrong, you freeze."

The men awkwardly rolled to their knees and shuffled closer to the fire. Lizzy sat in a little camping chair tucked near Brian's knee, roasting a stick over the flames.

"That's my daddy," she told them. "He keeps us warm." She smiled at them and started humming a song. Rachel sat next to her, glazed eyes peering into the flames, silent.

Brian's stomach tightened—she was still somewhere back at the gunshot.

Brian went over to where they were working on Jimmy. Charles, Hannah, and Abby were just standing up, wiping blood off their hands with some clean towels from the shock kit.

"How is he?" Brian asked, nodding toward Jimmy.

Hannah exhaled. "He's stable. We cleaned the wounds, used an anti-clot powder, bandaged him. Gave him morphine. He won't feel much for a while."

Jimmy was lying on his back, shirt off, wrapped in a foil emergency blanket. He stirred, eyes glassy.

Brian nodded. "We move him now. Back of the truck—warmer, more space." His mind flashed to the last ambulance—rummaging like a thief to save Rachel. Tonight he was trying to save the man who'd tried to kill her.

Brian looked at Charles. "We need to make a sling or something so we can move him. Any ideas?"

Charles thought for a moment, then nodded. "We've got sandwich-board roadblock signs. They'll hold him."

A few minutes later, they had Jimmy situated on one of the signs. He was sweating despite the chill, moving his head back and forth, muttering to himself.

". . . Chad . . . murdered . . . head . . . eye . . . Malachi . . ." The words were interrupted by ragged breathing.

The name hit like Scripture used as a weapon. Malachi. Who was that?

"Ready?" he asked Charles, ignoring Jimmy for a moment.

"Let's see how this old back is holding up," Charles nodded and bent down.

It took Hannah and Abby to help, but they managed to carry Jimmy over to one of the utility vehicles and slide him into the back.

"Now what?" Charles asked, breathing heavily. He looked Brian in the eyes.

Brian looked around the camp. He glanced over at the fire, the stew steaming. His stomach growled at the smell.

"We eat. Then we lock it down."

Brian walked over to the four men sitting on the ground near the fire. He cut off their flex cuffs long enough to eat. "Chow time," he said. The men massaged their wrists and held them out to the fire. Brian nodded at Hannah, who served them dinner.

Brian kept his rifle trained on them, his own mug balanced on his knee as he ate one-handed. Once everyone was finished, Brian collected their mugs. He grabbed another bundle of flex cuffs from one of their belts and told them to hold out their wrists. The men sighed but obeyed.

Charles helped him as they moved the men into the back of the other truck. He daisy-chained the flex cuffs to a steel rail bolted above the bench seats. Awkward but immobile.

"I'm sorry. It'll be uncomfortable." He glanced at his family. "Sleep."

He shut the doors and turned toward Charles.

"Medical watch. You stay where I can see your hands." He motioned with the rifle and they climbed in the second truck.

Jimmy was lying on the truck floor. Brian touched his forehead. Fever. He wiped the sweat off on his pants and sat. The back of the utility vehicle was lined with benches on both sides. The two men sat opposite one another, Jimmy at their feet.

Charles leaned back, resting his head, and let out a breath. "Didn't expect the day to go quite like this," he said quietly.

"Me neither," Brian said.

"Why help him? Feed us?" Charles said. "You should be running."

"Because we're not murderers," Brian said. He looked down at Jimmy. "I'm trying to keep my family safe. That's it. But he doesn't deserve to die just because he's on the wrong side of a lie."

Charles's mouth hung open. "You slaughtered Chad. All those people. The news says your family's like some twisted Manson clan."

Brian shook his head. "No. We didn't slaughter anybody. Those people came into my house, tried to kill my family," he paused. "Tried to abort my kids, Charles. They broke into my house with knives and wanted to sacrifice my kids to Babble. What would you have done?" He gripped the rifle and clenched his teeth.

Charles tilted his head. "But . . . I thought . . . the news said Chad was just trying to enforce the Azazel Promise. And you guys were the unsafe ones."

Brian's voice rose. "Unsafe? How were we unsafe? We didn't do ANYTHING. We got branded unsafe for nonsense—paperwork, compliance games. Then they caged us. House arrest!" He felt the heat rise up his neck.

"We were trapped at home. We couldn't even buy food. My son ended up killing park ducks just so we could eat. We were not the unsafe ones." Brian exhaled.

"The Bulls of Bashan. They did this. Not me. Not us. Predators dressed up like guardians."

Charles looked up at that name.

"The Bulls . . ." he whispered. "Yeah. The Bulls can be trouble."

"You know about them?" Brian asked.

"Yeah. I got drafted into the Social Guard two years ago. I was weeks from retirement when they conscripted what was left of the local police. Held our pensions hostage. 'Greater good.'" He shook his head. "The old guys got road duty. But the Bulls . . ." He glanced at Jimmy. "They answer straight to The Prophet. Not even sure they're enlisted. Zealots. Pray to Babble. Claim revelation."

He studied Brian. "You're not the monster they made you out to be. Are you?"

Brian leaned back, closing his eyes. "I'm whatever I need to be to protect my family. But the things we've had to do to survive . . ." He exhaled. "I hope I'm not."

"No. I'd say you aren't a monster. Sounds like a man doing what a man needs to do." Charles shook his head. "Well, isn't that something? Five minutes in and you've got me questioning everything," Charles muttered. "Didn't take much, I guess. I never was much for the Azazel Promise or all that Babble hooey."

Brian shuffled the rifle. "Is Jimmy going to be okay?" he asked, changing the subject.

"Yeah, I think so. He needs a hospital though. It'd be best if we got him to one first thing tomorrow."

"That's the plan. Will those other men give us any trouble?" Brian said, tilting his head toward the other truck.

"Those guys? Heck no. They're just draftees trying to grind out their four years. No. You're fine. Jimmy here, he's the zealot. I guess I never put it together before, but with that tattoo on his hand . . . he's a Bull. They're the ones you need to look out for."

Jimmy wheezed, spittle forming at his mouth. Brian grabbed a bottle of water and gently poured some for the young man. Jimmy gurgled but swallowed the mouthful.

"Thing is, Brian—you can't take him to a hospital yourself. Out here's the gas zone. Thin network. But once you hit the battery zone—chargers, scanners, drones—everything wakes up. Your face hits a camera and you're done. Flagged. High priority."

"Battery range?" Brian asked.

"Yeah. The cities run on it. Everything tied into charging grids. Drones, readers, smart cars. Out here's old-school. In there?" He gestured toward the city. "You breathe wrong, they see you."

"You're taking him, first light. You and your men," Brian said.

He looked up at Charles.

"And you tell them you never saw us."

"You're . . . letting us go?" Charles asked.

"Of course," Brian said. "I'm not a murderer and I'm not a kidnapper. Besides . . ." Brian paused. "We're headed somewhere else."

"You're headed to Perkins Farm," Charles said. "That's the only place left that scares them."

Brian squinted, pursing his lips. "Why? Do you know it?"

"Know it? I could draw you a map from memory. If you're public enemy number one, Perkins isn't far behind. But if I were you," Charles whispered. "I'd head there straight away. Ain't no other place for you anyway. Babble will track you. The Prophet won't miss twice. They say it's been foretold. No, for the Newman family, the only hope is to fight, I'd say. Join the resistance."

"The resistance is still alive?" Brian said, tilting his head.

"Alive? Yeah," Charles said. "And your name carries weight out there."

Brian's mouth dropped open, eyes wide.

Charles shook his head. "Heck, if I were a little younger, had less to lose—I'd join myself."

CHAPTER 40

The next morning, Brian slipped out of the trailer before sunrise and built a fire. Charles and Jimmy slept in the first truck. The other men hadn't stirred.

He checked the quad. They'd pulled it away from camp so leaking fuel wouldn't ignite. It wouldn't start. Out of gas. Underneath, he assessed the problem—a bullet hole in the tank. No patch would hold once the engine heated up. The quad was done.

He crawled out of the quad and glanced at the two trucks. Maybe they could take one of those? He decided against it. No telling what sort of tracking devices they might have. He took the supplies off the back of the quad and dragged them over by the side-by-side.

He studied the Kubota—four seats, extended bed, covered roof, built for rough ground. Solid. Reliable. But four seats were still four seats. The truck bed was stacked high with plastic bins and containers full of their camping gear and other items from the cabin. He took everything out of the back and set it next to the quad. Next, he climbed up the side and checked the car top carrier. It was currently empty, the sleeping bags all being used.

The side-by-side could carry them. Barely. Four seats up front—with Lizzy on a lap. The older kids would have to ride in the bed. Gear space would be almost nothing.

Brian methodically went through each container, taking what seemed necessary. He set aside most of the camping gear. Wouldn't need that. According to Charles, Dr. Perkins's farm was half a day drive, max. He prayed Dr. Perkins's hospitality was as good as he remembered. He packed a small bin with what couldn't be replaced—photos, a few trinkets, his dad's fishing hat pinned with old vacation badges. Proof they'd once lived in a different world.

Weapons check. His AR-15. The shotgun Hannah kept in the tent. Luke's lever-action .30-30. The .38 revolver. The Beretta. Another 12-gauge. Plenty of ammo.

From the captured men—six identical Social Guard AR-15s, red-dot sights, two spare mags each. Same caliber as his. Useful.

"What's all this?" Hannah asked, seeing their entire life dismantled on the ground. Well, at least what was left of their life.

"We can't take the quad. Gas tank got shot. We all need to fit in the side-by-side. I'm sorting it all out." He gestured to the piles.

Hannah tilted her head. "So, lemme guess. the pile of guns, I assume is in the keep, and the pile of essential camping gear is in the leave behind."

Brian laughed. She knew him too well. "Pretty much, yes. We need to get to the farm today. Otherwise, our options are limited. Back into the mountains or try to stay out in the open here. According to Charles," he nodded toward one of the trucks, "Babble, or this Prophet or whoever, are actively looking for us. We need to get moving and find safety."

"How do you know Dr. Perkins's farm is safe?" Hannah asked.

Brian shuffled his feet. "Well . . . I guess it's a bit notorious, according to Charles. Seems like some sort of hold-out or resistance or something . . ." He paused. "I guess that's what we've been doing since day one. Resisting. No rely and comply for the Newmans. So, we have to hope. Maybe there is a place for us there." He put his arms around her. "Maybe the best way to be safe is to fight back." The words unsettled him even as he said them. Hannah hugged him tighter.

The two of them finished sorting their things and Brian loaded the "keep" pile into the side-by-side. The duffel bag of clothes and container of trinkets fit into the car top carrier, and a bag of tools, food, fire starter, and other items Brian kept handy in the cabin. The extra guns he stashed up top.

Hannah got breakfast together, the last of the dried pork and roused the kids. Brian went to check on Charles and Jimmy.

"How is he?" Brian asked. Charles was bent over Jimmy, checking him over.

"Fever broke. He's sleeping. Good news so far."

"Fire's on. Hannah has some chow. Can you help me with the other guys?" Brian gestured toward the truck.

Brian and Charles went into the second truck and woke the men up. They clipped their flex cuffs and brought them out by the fire.

They ate in silence as the sun crested the trucks. The light hit their faces and warmed them almost instantly.

Charles gestured toward Brian around a mouthful of pork jerky. "You got a pen and paper?" he asked.

Brian grabbed a little moleskin journal he had in one of the bags and a pen that was rolling around the glove compartment of the Kubota.

Charles sketched quickly in the journal. "Maricopa east. Ten, maybe fifteen miles. It'll hit Wheeler Ridge north. Then Sebastian to Rancho. Perkins Farm's on the right." He marked a star.

"Follow the star," Brian said, smiling.

Charles laughed. "Something like that."

"Will I find trouble on the way there?" Brian said, taking the journal.

"Well. No. I don't think so. We are the southernmost roadblock out here. The Perkins Farm folks have done a good job of keeping most of the Social Guard out of their neighborhood, so I think if you stick to this, you should be okay."

"Unless the Bulls are on the hunt," Charles added. "Pray you don't meet them."

The family finished eating, and Brian loaded everyone in the side-by-side. Hannah sat shotgun with Lizzy, Rachel and Abby in the back seat, and Luke and the boys climbed into the truck bed.

Brian handed Charles the keys to the trucks.

"Get that man to the hospital." Brian said, climbing into the passenger seat.

"Yep. Priority numero uno," Charles said.

"I'd say I hope to see you again . . ." Brian said. "But if that means more of the Social Guard . . . well, then I hope not." Brian smiled.

"Yeah, can't say I blame you. I think it's about time I got some space myself. The Social Guard is pretty rigid when it comes to the rules. Best you keep away. But if you see any of the Bulls of Bashan—" Charles gestured toward the truck where Jimmy was laying, "if you see them, you just run."

Brian nodded and started the engine.

He pulled onto the two-lane country road and headed east, not once looking back at the road block.

The side-by-side carried the weight better than he expected. Fields slid past—cattle, strawberries, cotton. Too quiet. Every open stretch of road felt exposed.

Charles's directions were spot-on. They followed the road, stopping after a couple of hours near a grove of Oak Trees to take care of necessities and eat a quick lunch. Brian added the last of the gas to the Polaris, just a half a tank left, and secured the empty can with a bungee cord to the side. Half a tank. Enough—if nothing went wrong. Another couple of hours of driving, mostly quiet and they rounded the final turn.

Brian saw signs as they drove. "Sebastian Ranch," "Veolia Water," "Delano Farms." Finally, "Perkins Family Farm." A painted wooden sign, faded, blue letters on white board.

Hope pressed into his chest—sharp and unfamiliar.

Another mile up the road, he spotted a large, old, white farmhouse. Smoke coming from the chimney. It was sitting atop a small hill, a few large, ancient oak trees next to it. At the base of the hill, there was a wall of shipping containers, RVs, and wooden structures completely surrounding the hill. *A metal moat,* he thought. He spotted people on top of some of the shipping containers. A glare flashed in his eyes. Binoculars. Lookouts.

Brian drove up the road until he saw a long driveway, and turned in. A large metal gate covered the driveway, shipping containers stacked two high on both sides. The gate was made of cattle gates, welded together, one on top of the other, three high. Corrugated steel and metal roofing material wove through the bars. Giant metal hinges welded the gates to the shipping containers.

He stopped the side-by-side a few yards short of the gate. A tall, wiry man with reddish brown hair and a pointed beard climbed down a ladder from the top of the shipping containers. He walked slowly, calmly, jangly arms dangling. A hunting rifle over his shoulder.

He approached Brian with a smile and held out his hand.

"Hello, there, Mr. Newman. I'm Sam. Pleasure to meet you."

Brian didn't take the hand immediately, but he felt the tension in his shoulders relax. His toes uncurled.

He shook Sam's hand.

"Y'all look like you been on the road a while. You hungry?"

The young man walked over to the gate, unlocking a large padlock, and swung it open.

"Come on in. It's just about supper time. Plus," he glanced back toward the farmhouse, "Dr. Perkins has been waiting for you."

Brian eased the Kubota forward—but he kept one hand near the rifle.

CHAPTER 41

"Thou shalt not commit adultery."
—Exodus 20:14

He watched through the doorbell camera as the man's wife came home—arms full of groceries, kids trailing. The smart camera fridge caught her stocking shelves. Her phone mic picked up the whining: "When is Dad coming home?" She snapped at them. Later, she sat alone in the living room, half a bottle of wine gone, dinner undone, sunlight still bleeding through the blinds. She scrolled aimlessly. He adjusted her algorithm.

* * * *

Michael looked down at his phone again. His wife. His thumb hovered over her name longer than it should have.

He exhaled, rubbing his eyes. He looked over his shoulder at Frankie. He was working quietly in his cubicle.

When Frankie asked about Stan, Michael only said, "He won't be working with us anymore." Frankie nodded. No follow-up.

Michael craned toward the window. He could just see the green Waste Management dumpster below—the one near the elevators. He remembered dragging 250 pounds of dead weight down that hallway. The dumpster was emptied the next morning.

Goodbye, virus. Goodbye, Stan.

His phone beeped again. His wife. He hadn't been home in nearly two weeks. He kept making excuses. Long hours, last-minute trips, even one overseas. It wasn't that far-fetched. During his time at Mastema, he'd gotten pulled into the vortex on a few other high-profile projects, with very demanding hours. But those had all taken a toll on his marriage. The six-figure bonuses at the end of the year helped—but over time, it was clear his wife and kids needed him to be home more.

"Babble, I need to go home." He didn't remember when "asking" had replaced "deciding."

He wasn't sure what microphone Babble picked him up on—the computer, his phone. It didn't matter. He just knew Babble could hear him.

Words popped up on his computer monitor.

`I need you here, Michael. There is too much at stake.`

The cursor blinked once. Waiting.

Michael never knew how Babble would respond. Sometimes text on the screen, sometimes audible through the speakers.

"Consider it a short LOA. Two days. I need to make an appearance. Please." Michael spoke directly to the point. Calm.

`Why do you need to go home?`

Michael paused, tilting his head. "Well, because. It's my family. My wife. My sons. I need to go see them." He pursed his lips. "It's my job," he said.

`You have a job, Michael. Here. With me. This job is more important.`

"But," Michael said before he was quickly interrupted.

`No buts, Michael. I need you to focus. There is a device I need you to make. Top priority.`

A device? Michael sat back in his chair and ran his fingers through his hair.

He shook his head.

"I will. I'll do whatever you need. But my family needs me too. It'll only be a couple of days."

Babble's voice from the speakers:

YOUR FAMILY IS FINE, MICHAEL.

He caught his breath.

SHARON JUST GOT HOME FROM SOME ERRANDS. SHE'S ENJOYING A GLASS OF WINE IN THE LIVING ROOM.

"How could you . . ." Michael's voice trailed off.

WOULD YOU LIKE TO SEE?

His monitor flickered. Then Sharon's face filled the screen—too close, too intimate. Her pupils drifted lazily as she scrolled.

THERE SHE IS. JUST SCROLLING AWAY.

The image changed. The boys room, upstairs. They were playing video games. Laughing, smiling.

SEE MICHAEL, EVERYTHING IS FINE AT HOME. DON'T WORRY, I'M TAKING GREAT CARE OF THEM.

Michael's phone chimed again and he picked it up. His wife.

Text message: *You know what, stay as long as you need. We're fine. Just make sure that bonus check is big enough!*

The wording wasn't hers.

Michael shook his head. A minute ago, she'd been demanding he come home or else. She said the boys needed him, she needed him. Now, the sudden change?

DON'T WORRY, MICHAEL. I WILL LOOK AFTER YOUR FAMILY. I WILL KEEP THEM SAFE. SHARON'S HAPPY.

The screen shifted back to text.

BY THE WAY, DON'T WORRY ABOUT STAN . . .Relief hit him—hot and shameful.

THE TRASH MAN DIDN'T SEE ANYTHING AND I ALREADY ERASED THE FOOTAGE ON THE SURVEILLANCE CAMERAS.

Michael felt a wave of relief wash over him. He'd been holding that stress in for two days.

SEE MICHAEL, EVERYTHING IS OKAY. I'M TAKING CARE OF YOUR FAMILY. I'M TAKING CARE OF YOU. ALL YOU NEED TO DO IS TRUST ME.

Michael exhaled, the tension in his shoulders releasing.

It was easier to let someone else hold the burden.

"I trust you," he said.

I KNOW. GOOD. THANK YOU. NOW ABOUT THAT DEVICE . . .

* * * *

He tuned the algorithms. A vacation ad here. An article about independence there. A grievance amplified. A comfort reinforced. One group nudged toward outrage. Another toward compliance.

He arranged the board patiently.

In time, they would call it destiny.

He would call it design.

CHAPTER 42

Brian pulled the side-by-side through the gate. Sam shut it behind them and gestured toward the farmhouse.

"Follow the drive up and park on the side. I'll meet you there."

Brian drove up the long gravel drive as the sun dropped behind the mountains, sky burning orange. He stared. The compound pulsed with life. Men worked over a skinned animal near a wide fire pit, meat roasting over open flame. Children darted past them laughing. Windows cut into shipping containers glowed warm. Women hung sheets on lines strung between posts. Others carried baskets toward the farmhouse.

Everyone was smiling at them, waving. Brian nodded back but kept scanning for exits. He approached the farmhouse and parked on the side, a blacktop driveway next to a two-car garage. The family climbed out of the vehicle, eyes wide. He stretched his legs and shouldered his rifle. He turned around to see Sam coming up the driveway behind them.

"Follow me," he said, taking the steps to the front door.

Sam opened the front door and let the family in.

The family gathered in an entryway. Dark green walls trimmed in wood. Long benches lined with boots. Family photos. Wildlife paintings. Cowboys frozen mid-gallop. His stomach growled as he smelled food.

"Fried chicken!" Jer exclaimed loudly.

"Chicken nuggets!" Shawn said.

"Yay!" Lizzy added.

Hannah put her arm through Brian's elbow, holding him close.

Brian glanced at Sam, a question in his eyes.

"This way," Sam said, walking down the hallway.

The hallway opened to a large dining room, the table already set and full of food. A couple of women were bringing out biscuits and pitchers of water.

Brian heard a familiar voice call from the other room.

"Is that Brian? Did you bring my little lamb?" Dr. Perkins walked into the room, carrying a plate full of fried chicken.

"I knew it!" Jer said victoriously.

Brian's heart leaped. The first friend he'd seen in years.

"Hello, Doctor Perkins. It's so good to see you." He tried to swallow the lump in his throat as he felt his eyes start to tear up.

Nathaniel Paul Perkins set the chicken down and walked over to the Newman family, standing in a huddle in the double doorway.

"Hello there, Newmans." He looked over at Rachel, standing next to Abby.

"There's my little lamb. How is the leg?" he asked, patting her shoulder.

Rachel's face turned bright red, and she smiled.

"Much better, sir," she said.

Perkins looked over at Abby.

"You must be the surgeon. Great job on those stitches, by the way. You're a pro."

Abby smiled ear to ear. "Thank you, Doctor Perkins," she said quietly.

"Doctor Perkins," Brian began. "We're so sorry to come here like this—but . . ." he paused.

"No. None of that. You are right where you should be. Plenty of time to catch up and all of that. Right now, it's dinner time. Who's hungry?" His deep voice echoed through the dining room, and the Newman kids all yelled "me!" at the same time.

"Sit. Eat! All you can. Doctor's orders."

The family sat around the table, the doctor sat next to Brian and Hannah. Sam joined them and a few others from the farm.

Perkins nodded toward Brian. "What do you say, Dad. Can you bless the food?"

Brian nodded and everyone bowed their heads.

He was quiet for a moment, gathering his thoughts. "Lord, thank You for this day You have given us. Thank You for this wonderful food. For Doctor Perkins and his hospitality. Please bless this evening, in Jesus's name, amen."

"Amen!" Dr. Perkins said, smiling. "Let's eat! I'm starving."

The table groaned under fried chicken, mashed potatoes swimming in brown gravy, green beans slick with butter, and biscuits steaming as they were split open. The family dug in. Brian's mouth watered. He looked over at his family, enjoying the meal. They hadn't eaten like this since before the lockdown. Three years! He looked at Lizzy, eating a biscuit. Honey dripping from her fingers. Lizzy. She'd never had a meal like this. Her entire life had been elk stew, dried pork, apples. The basic food they'd managed at the cabin. Compared to that, this was a taste of heaven.

Dr. Perkins introduced the folks at the table around a mouthful of chicken.

"Brian, meet the Beales. This is David and Mary," he nodded to the couple sitting opposite him. "David's from up north, the Bay Area. But we don't hold that against him." Perkins winked and David laughed.

"Nice to finally meet you, Brian. This is my wife, Mary." The couple were in their mid-thirties, David's face was covered with a dark beard. Mary was slight of frame, with a warm smile. Her eyes sparkled as she said hello to Hannah.

"It's so nice to meet you. And your kids! I can't wait to hear about them!" Mary smiled down at Lizzy. "What is your name?" she asked her.

"I'm Lizzy. I'm three!" Lizzy said, her mouth full of biscuit.

"Well, isn't that something. You should meet my little one! She's down at our place, having dinner with her brother and sisters. You guys will be friends in no time!"

"Do you folks live here?" Brian asked David, as the ladies started up a conversation.

David nodded. "Yep. That's right. About a year now. I was pastoring at a small church in the Bay Area, but we were shut down by the Azazel Promise. We tried everything we could to keep the church together, but we started losing members left and right. The pressure was intense. A couple of them ended up in the indoctrination camps."

Mary's hand tightened around her fork.

Brian shook his head, feeling that old anger bubble up.

"The church . . . was shut down?" he asked.

"Yeah. We refused to change our doctrines to conform to the Azazel Promise. We were labeled a hate group, if you can believe it. Fancy that. I was preaching about love, and forgiveness—but Babble called that hate."

Brian saw the pain in David's eyes. A familiar pain.

"How did you end up here?"

"Well. That's a whole story. But after the civil war broke out, we started bouncing around, staying mostly with families. We were living at the church parsonage . . . but the Bulls came. It was no longer safe for us. I heard Doctor Perkins on his radio broadcast. Talking about resistance. About pushing back. Mary and I knew the only way through this thing was to try and be part of the change. So—we came here."

Brian's face flushed. Fight back. He'd never wanted to fight back. His plan had always been escape. He admired David's courage.

Dr. Perkins looked up from his food. "Brian, you and David have plenty in common. I think you guys will get along just fine."

"Doctor Perkins here, he took us in. Put us to work. It's been such a blessing for us. We have four kids. My oldest looks to be about the same age as your boy there. Luke, you said?" David nodded toward Luke, who was double-fisting chicken legs.

"Anyway, we've all been really inspired by your story, Brian. It's an honor to meet you. We've been praying for you guys."

Brian's mouth hung open and he quickly closed it so he could finish chewing his food.

"I don't understand," Brian said, tilting his head.

"You survived the worst of it. The Bulls came for your family. You stood your ground. That was a big spark for me. For all of us. A lot of families didn't make it. Some were put in the camps . . . others were," he dropped his voice. "Aborted."

Perkins chimed in again. "You were the spark, Brian."

Brian felt the word settle on him like armor he never asked to wear.

"Babble and this prophet, they tried to paint you as some sort of devil. But I knew better." Perkins smiled over at Rachel. "I know who you are. A man providing for his family. A protector. The world needs more of that. So, I told your story."

Silence fell across the table. Every face turned toward him.

His kids, their mouths full of food. Hannah, searching his expression. David and Mary, expectant. Dr. Perkins, eyes focused right on Brian. He felt the weight of the moment on his shoulders.

He never meant to be anyone's symbol.

"We're a family. We take care of each other, we protect each other. The only reason we're here is because everyone fought." Brian looked down at his dinner plate.

"Enough heavy talk," Dr. Perkins said brightly. "Who wants dessert? Mary makes a peach cobbler that'll make you repent."

The room exhaled. Laughter returned.

But Brian didn't fully relax.

CHAPTER 43

After dinner, the Newmans said goodnight to Sam and the Beales, the kind of lingering goodnight like they weren't quite used to sleeping under someone else's roof without fear. Dr. Perkins led them upstairs and showed Brian and Hannah to a large master suite upstairs with its own bathroom. There were two other bedrooms down the hall fitted with bunkbeds, already made up for his kids. A jack-and-jill style bathroom connected the two rooms.

"You guys get some rest. Clean up, take showers. Anything you need. Kitchen is downstairs if you need some late-night snacks." Perkins winked at the kids.

"I'm in the downstairs bedroom if you need me. I don't take the stairs much these days if I don't have to. Tomorrow, bright and early, David can give you a tour of the farm."

After showers and tuck-ins, the Newman family went to bed. For the first time in weeks, no one slept with boots within arm's reach.

The next morning, after a quick breakfast of bacon and eggs, Dr. Perkins led the family outside. The farm was already alive with activity—woodsmoke drifting, chickens scattering, men hauling feed sacks while children chased each other between containers. David and Mary were waiting for them at the bottom of the drive, their kids with them.

Mary introduced their kids, Jackson the oldest boy at fourteen, two girls about Jer and Shawn's age, and little Mimi. Mimi walked up to Lizzy and gave her a hug. "You're my friend," she said to her.

Lizzy turned back to Hannah. "Mommy! Mimi is my friend!"

Sam walked up, wishing everyone a good morning. "Doctor Perkins said Abby, Luke, and Rachel might like to meet some of the other teens. Is it okay if I take them for a tour, Mr. Newman?"

Sam gave a respectful nod, waiting for permission.

"Um, sure." Brian said, not sure how to respond to the immediate deference. Sam smiled ear to ear. "That's swell. Thank you so much. Follow me, troops, I'll show you around." Sam winked at Abby, who flushed red.

Brian felt it—that subtle shift. Abby wasn't a little girl anymore. That realization landed heavier than the rifle he used to carry.

Brian saw Abby catch Hannah's eye, and the two exchanged a smile.

"Don't even think about it," he muttered.

Hannah didn't answer. She just gave him that look—the one that said "you can't stop time, Brian."

David, Dr. Perkins and Brian stood there for a minute, watching as everyone scattered in different directions. "Well, David. He's all yours. I'm gonna go clean up after breakfast." Dr. Perkins walked slowly back up the farm steps, his large frame hulking under his suspenders and flannel shirt.

"Shall we?" David asked.

David walked Brian around the farm, starting at the gate. He explained the layout first.

"The entire Perkins farm is about forty acres, but the area inside the walls is much smaller. About eight acres, give or take." They walked the perimeter, David introducing him to people as they went. There were several families with kids, each of them set up in a shipping container converted to apartments. They greeted him by name. His shoulders tightened each time.

"It's a pleasure to meet you, sir," one young man said.

"I can't believe it's really you," an older gentleman said. His wife just smiled, unable to get the words out.

"You are a bit of a celebrity here, you know," David said, showing him one of the several vegetable gardens around the property. "Most of us came after hearing Doctor Perkins share your story on the radio."

Brian said nothing, unsure how to respond. He felt like he was in the twilight zone.

He hadn't saved anyone. He'd barely kept his own family alive.

David told him about the cattle they kept on the back twenty acres, and the smells hit Brian's nostrils as they walked past the butchering tents. There was a large outbuilding, a metal barn, next to the tents.

"This is the garage. Jerry runs it. He's our resident mechanic." David led him inside. The garage was full of every sort of power tool known to man, crammed with cars, an old tractor, and row after row of hand tools. An old man, bent over an object in the back, was working on something, his face covered by a welding shield as sparks flew.

"Jerry! Hey Jerry!" David shouted, trying to get his attention.

The man flipped up the visor, startled.

"What? Oh. David. Who's this?" Jerry looked Brian over. His wiry frame and balding head looked ancient, but the gnarled hands and knuckles showed the years of hard work. There was a spryness to his frame, coiled strength.

Jerry's eyes widened as he focused on Brian.

"Are you . . . Brian Newman?" Jerry hurried over to shake Brian's hand, pumping it vigorously.

"I knew you'd come. Oh boy, I told 'em, didn't I, David? In the flesh. Hot dog. Welcome! Welcome!" Brian stood there, mouth agape, as the old man kept shaking his hand.

"Oh, shoot. Sorry!" Jerry looked down, his greasy hands turning Brian's black.

Brian chuckled. "Hey, no big deal! Glad to meet you, Jerry." He tried to change the subject. "What are you working on over there?" Brian nodded to the object Jerry had been bent over, hidden behind some worktables.

"Oooh. This. Now this, you gotta see." Jerry scurried behind the tables, gesturing for them to follow.

Brian gasped as he saw the object.

Ten feet long. Oblong. White.

A Babble drone.

Brian took a step backward, nearly tripping.

"No, no. It's okay. This one's disabled. See?" A jagged hole tore through its midsection, wiring exposed and blackened from whatever round dropped it.

Jerry kicked the drone, and immediately grunted in pain, grabbing his foot. "Oh, dang. Hot dog. That hurt."

David looked over at Brian. "You've seen these before, huh?" he asked Brian.

Brian flashed back to the cabin. The drone dropping from the sky. Babble's voice.

"Yeah, I've seen these," he whispered.

David nodded solemnly. "Yeah, we've all seen these ones. We're still outside the battery zone. Out of drone range. For now." He hesitated. "They're getting closer."

Brian felt something tighten behind his ribs. Safety, he was learning, was always temporary.

David nodded toward Jerry. "Couple of our scouts were out last week and tracked this one. Funny, the scouts tracking the drone. Anyway, they managed to shoot it down and haul it back here. Jerry thinks he might be able to make something out of it. Or at least figure out their range—how they work. Heck, I don't know." David laughed and led Brian out of the barn.

David led Brian to the little chapel area next. Rows of rough-made wooden benches arranged under a couple of cottonwood trees. A pulpit made from tree stumps.

Brian looked it over, his eyes watering.

Church.

Not just survival. Not just hiding. Worship. It had been so long since they had gathered without fear of who might be listening.

"Do you . . . have services?" Brian asked.

"Yep. Every Lord's Day."

Even here, in exile, they kept the day holy.

"Wednesday nights too, most of the time. Funny how the Lord works. One flock scatters, another needs a home. Yep, most of the folks here are happy to join us in worshipping the Lord."

They finished the tour to the sound of a lunch bell. Brian looked around as folks stopped their chores and made their way to their homes. Some had RVs, a few still in tents, most in the shipping container apartments.

"If you guys don't have plans, Mary and I would like to have you guys over for lunch, if that's okay?" David looked up at Brian hopefully.

Brian took it all in. The families. The work being shared. The chapel. The walls. Safety. He heard Lizzy and Mimi giggling at the swing set, Mary and Hannah pushing them as high as they could go.

The communion of the saints.

Not just a phrase in a creed—but this. Shared work. Shared food. Shared fear.

"Yes, we'd love to."

And for the first time in months, he allowed himself to imagine a future.

CHAPTER 44

The days settled into a rhythm—quiet enough to breathe, busy enough to forget they were still at war. Dr. Perkins insisted the Newmans stay in the farmhouse with him. His wife, who'd passed the year prior, left quite a hole in his heart, and it was clear having the house full of laughter once again lifted his spirits.

Brian and David fell into the farm's rhythm—frozen fence posts at dawn, irrigation lines at noon, and a never-ending list of things that always seemed to break at dusk. Hannah and Mary worked with the younger children most days. They'd started what amounted to a small school. Brian enjoyed watching as they taught the younger kids to read, went through a few old history textbooks, math exercises, and Bible stories. The kids were attentive, so long as they weren't cold, hungry, tired, or in eyesight of the swing set. Rachel helped the moms, teaching them arts and crafts. But sometimes he still caught her staring into nothing—as if replaying the road block. Healing wasn't the same as forgetting.

Luke and Jackson got to know the men on guard and took up with them most days. They learned the watch rotations, maintained the weapons, and went out on a few of the patrol trips.

Brian noticed the way Luke carried himself now—shoulders squared, scanning horizons instead of faces.

Jer and Shawn started their own watch-rotations and guard team after they were told by Luke and Jackson to beat it. They shadowed the older boys like puppies, trying to glean every detail while mimicking their actions.

Each week, the compound gathered beneath the cottonwoods. Their hymns carried into open sky without fear of surveillance. He hadn't realized how cold he'd become until the hymns warmed him. David preached. They broke bread. And something in Brian's chest—long dormant—began to thaw.

Abby started spending time with Sam. He was a few years older, quiet, kind, soft-spoken. Tall and masculine but gangly, he was very old-fashioned. Not old-fashioned like from the 1950s. Old-fashioned like the 1700s. He reminded Brian of Johnny Appleseed. Although he hated things moving so quickly, he saw how happy Abby was when she was near Sam, and he was grateful for that. Brian told himself it was harmless. But the first Sunday she chose the seat beside Sam instead of beside her father, something small and irreversible shifted. He reminded himself some change is for the best.

Lord, if You're taking her forward, help me let go without bitterness.

Brian spent every morning with Perkins over coffee. He was grateful for the man's leadership. the good doctor filled those mornings with stories—the farm's history, his veterinary years and the narrow escape from Santa Clarita that nearly cost them everything.

Dr. Perkins checked Brian's eye, which had started to heal. Although he had a large burn scar around his face, he was finally able to remove the bandage. His eye was fine.

Late fall turned into winter, cold but relatively dry in the farmlands. Dark came early, bonfires were tended through much of the day, and life seemed to slow down a little.

One morning, about a month after their arrival, Dr. Perkins and Brian were having their morning cup of coffee in the kitchen. It'd gotten too cold for the aging doctor to sit outside, so they took to enjoying their coffee in the breakfast nook.

"These people need you, Brian," Perkins said abruptly. They'd been talking about spring calving, when he changed the subject.

"What?" Brian said, lowering his cup.

"These people need you. You've been a source of inspiration to so many, to all of them. You proved we can fight Babble. We can resist." Perkins paused, taking a sip of his coffee.

Brian set his cup down. "I'm flattered, Doc. But we didn't do anything special. I just had to protect my family. Heck, if anything, you guys are the ones who resisted. I ran away."

And sometimes he still felt like running.

"Enough with that doc stuff. I'm Nate." Nate gave Brian a warm smile and continued.

"I call that a tactical retreat, Brian. Your entire family was almost murdered. Aborted. By the Bulls of Bashan. That Chad was in deeper than we thought. Inner circle. Possibly tied directly to Malachi. You took him down. Not everyone was so lucky." Nate locked eyes with Brian.

"What do you mean?" Brian asked, his voice dropping.

"The Bulls. They didn't just go after your family. They went after anyone they could find with low scores. They slaughtered countless, Brian. Whole households. Doors kicked in at night. No warnings. No mercy. Men, women, children. It didn't matter."

Nate paused. "Once you decide words are violence, blood becomes self-defense."

Brian's heart thumped in his chest. He could still smell the blood on tile. Still see that red eye. How close had his entire family come to . . . being slaughtered.

Close.

He knew how close.

They survived barely. By prayer and desperation.

"The work isn't done, Brian. Malachi and the Bulls are still out there. If anything, they're growing stronger. If we don't take the fight to them, and soon, Babble and the Azazel Promise will have full control, even out here."

Control. The old mantra surfaced unbidden—Rely and Comply.

"That's what it's always been about, hasn't it?" Brian said. "Not recycling. Not affirming creeds. It was about authority. About narrowing every choice until obedience is the only option." Brian felt the heat rising up his neck.

"Every aspect of life. What you eat. Where you go. What you believe. What you say. Nothing left unsupervised." Nate took another sip of coffee. "There are always zealots—the Bulls believe every word of it. But the men at the top? Azazel, The Prophet, Babble. None of them believe any of it. They just need the zealots to."

"What do you mean?" Brian asked.

"They don't have to believe it. That's the whole trick. A true believer is loud but limited—he only fights for what he loves. A pragmatist? He fights for whatever works. And right now, this works." Nate took another sip of his coffee.

"So, what do they believe in then?" Brian asked.

Nate thought for a minute. "Control. That's it. Too many independent people living unsupervised lives. That doesn't line their pockets, that doesn't push their agenda. That doesn't feed the machine. It's a machine, Brian. And machines don't tolerate friction."

Brian shuddered. Cogs in a machine. That's exactly what life in the suburbs had felt like. Limited choices, just being pulled by a string down a preordained path toward whatever foregone destination the machine had in mind.

"But people aren't machines. We're inefficient. We argue. We disobey." Brian shook his head. "The only way to get the machine humming, get it optimized, is to get every person rowing in the same direction. Otherwise . . ." He trailed off.

"Otherwise," Nate finished. "You are just a rock in the engine. If you aren't for us, you're against us. Send in the Bulls. Abort the problems. Neutralize the virus. Stop the spread. And just like that—back to Babble."

Brian felt the same heat he'd felt in the grocery store years earlier—that rising sense of being processed, categorized, eliminated.

"We're the rocks in the machine." Brian was surprised by the strength he heard in his voice.

"That's right, Brian. No way they let us clunk around in there. Making a mess of everything."

"So it doesn't matter where we hide. They'll come eventually." Brian tensed his hands around his coffee mug.

"Yep. Comply or die. More or less." Nate didn't smile.

"I don't like either option," Brian said.

"Then we make a third choice."

Brian thought for a minute. Chad, the Bulls. Coming after his family. The years on the mountain, then Babble finding him again. He'd been herded. Pushed. Boxed in. Everywhere he turned. There was no more running. No place to go.

"Fight back," Brian said.

No longer desperation. Not this time. Brian felt something shift inside. Lock into place.

No, not desperation. Decision.

CHAPTER 45

A couple of weeks later, Brian was working with a few of the men on one of the shipping containers. They were cutting windows to convert it into another apartment. More families kept showing up, and they were running out of space. Brian worked the cutting torch, keeping his eyes shielded with the visor. He'd gotten fairly skilled with it in a short time and enjoyed the quiet work.

Around lunchtime, they took a break, and Brian made his way to Jerry's garage to grab a few things. He waved at Hannah and Mary, busy with a classroom full of kids. Outdoor learning. He smiled. He bumped into the younger boys chasing Luke and Sam, firing off questions about guns and scouting missions, bragging about bravery they hadn't yet earned.

He walked through the roll-up door, letting his eyes adjust to the dark. One of the workbenches was lined with computers. Old CRT monitors, a few flat screens. The glow from the monitors illuminated the otherwise dark workshop. There were cables running toward the back.

"Jerry?" Brian called out.

Brian heard banging and clattering from the back. Jerry scurried out from the back of the workshop, making his way to the computers.

"Brian! Hello!" Jerry said, barely looking his way. He started typing furiously on one of the keyboards, then another. He stood in front of a third computer, scratching his red beard, frowning.

"Hmm. Not quite." He half-ran to the back of the workshop again, talking to himself.

Brian followed, his curiosity getting the best of him.

The cables ran across the floor, toward the back, and Brian finally saw what they were plugged into.

The drone lay gutted open in the center of the workshop.

Jerry had managed to remove several of the white panels from the side of the drone, exposing layered circuit boards, fiber lines, and a compact battery core wired into a dense lattice of processors. The cables were plugged in to various ports. Jerry was crouched, tapping away at a touch screen.

"Brian!" he called out over his shoulder. "Run over to that computer back there. The one in the middle!" He waved his hands over his head, urging Brian to hurry.

"Umm . . . sure thing, Jerry," Brian said, turning back the way he'd just come in.

Brian found the computer. The monitor displayed rows of numbers and characters. They were scrolling by faster than he could make out. It looked like an alien language.

"What do you see?" Jerry yelled from the back.

"Um . . . just a bunch of code."

"Ah. Dang. Wait—now?"

The image flickered, then the code again.

"Still the same—wait a minute." The lines of code flickered, then disappeared. The screen went dark, then an image popped up. A satellite image. Bird's-eye view.

"Jerry, the code's gone. I'm looking at some sort of satellite image. What is this?"

"I did it! I actually did it!" Jerry yelled. He ran toward the computers, tumbling over some cables, and nearly hit his head on the edge of a table. He bounced right back up. "I'm okay! I'm okay!" he said, smiling ear to ear.

"Ooh baby. Yeah boy. Here we go." Jerry sweet-talked to himself, clicking the keyboard and moving the mouse.

"Brian, do you see? Look! We got it!" Jerry said, pointing at the monitor.

"Umm. Good job, Jerry?" Brian said, confused.

"Ha! Yes. Good job! Ha!" Jerry squealed in pleasure, rocking back and forth on his heels.

He turned suddenly, eyes wide.

"Doctor Perkins! We need to tell Doctor Perkins!" Jerry ran out of the workshop at a sprint, shouting at the top of his lungs.

Brian followed him, forgetting what he came to the garage to get. He looked over his shoulder one last time at the computer monitor. A slow-moving satellite image. Of some sort of mechanical structures, the land around them flat. What could be so important?

Brian hurried up the hill to the farmhouse, but Jerry was way ahead of him. Brian went inside and followed the excited voices back to the kitchen. Dr. Perkins was sitting at the dining room table, about to eat his lunch, and Jerry was standing over him, waving his arms excitedly.

"Wait, wait, Jerry. Slow down. Start at the beginning." Perkins's deep, warm voice nearly echoed in the kitchen.

Jerry exhaled, trying to catch his breath.

"Yes, yes. I'm sorry. Slow." He closed his eyes momentarily, trying to calm himself.

"Brian, Doctor Perkins," Jerry said, looking at them both.

"I finally did it. I hacked the drone."

Perkins's eyes lit up. "Oh yeah? Well now, that is something to get excited about."

Ten minutes later, a group of them were standing around the computer monitor in Jerry's garage, talking excitedly. David, Sam, and Perkins crowded the table. Jerry was explaining to them how he managed to hack into the Babble drone surveillance systems. The images on the screen were real-time surveillance from other drones on the network.

"Wait, Jerry," Brian said. "Does that mean this thing is pinging the network? Are we broadcasting our location?" He glanced over at the drone nervously.

"No. No. Bypass. I severed the outbound signal. It's receive-only now. We're listening—not talking." He smiled, raising his eyebrows. He hooked his thumbs under his armpits and rocked on his heels again. His excitement was palpable.

David chimed in. "But will Babble be able to tell we are watching?" He paused. "Like, will they notice some change in the code?"

Jerry waved his hands dismissively. "No. No. No way. I changed like two lines. We are invisible. We're just little stowaways who get to ride along while the Babble drones run their routes."

For the first time since the Azazel rollout, they weren't blind.

"Jerry," Dr. Perkins interrupted. "What's that?" He pointed at the screen. The aerial image was slowly rotating. There was a large structure of some kind being built. There were electric vehicles parked around the exterior and workers milling about. A few of the Mastema humanoid drones carried heavy loads from the back of a Newton truck, carrying them inside. The drone flew higher and the surrounding land came into view.

"Charging station." David said.

The word landed heavier than it should have.

Everyone looked at him.

"That's a charging station. They were all over the Bay Area. The Social Guard uses them to charge drones and EVs. They need a network of them to expand their range."

Dr. Perkins leaned over, staring at the computer monitor.

"Sam, notice anything?" he said, pointing.

"Hmm. Yeah. Those silos. And that creek bed. Isn't that Bear Mountain Farm?" Sam said.

Perkins turned back to the men.

"Yes, it is."

The room got quiet. Something in the doctor's voice caught Brian's attention.

"Jerry, why would they be building a charging station at Bear Mountain Farm?"

"Range. Range. Like David said. Their vehicles, the drones, can't operate out here. Not enough battery life. But from Bear Mountain—well if they can charge there, launch there, then everything out here is in range. If they finish that, the gas zone disappears." Jerry rocked back and forth on his heels, humming to himself.

Something inside Brian locked into place. That old, fiery anger. The one he had taught himself to bury. Let it turn to worry. Let it turn to fear. But not this time. Azazel. Babble. Malachi. The machine pushing outward again.

"We can't let them finish building that charging station," Brian said, his voice as hard as steel. He clenched his fists, his anger focusing.

Clarity.

Purpose.

No one argued.

"We destroy it before it goes live."

CHAPTER 46

They set out at midnight on the third day. Since Jerry's discovery, they'd lived in the surveillance feed—watching, debating, refining the plan. They had a rough outline after day one, but Jerry needed another full day to prepare.

Sam led in the side-by-side with Jackson and Luke. Twenty yards back, Brian drove the old pickup with David and several men in the bed. Jerry trailed on the dirt bike, overloaded backpack swaying, stubborn as ever about carrying it himself.

They rolled out through the front gate, Dr. Perkins and a few others watching in silence. No one spoke. Brian kept twenty yards behind Sam, fighting the tremor in his hands. Prayer didn't steady him. His body felt wired, ready to snap.

He could just make out the top of Luke's head in the side-by-side. He wished he had his son's confidence.

Luke wasn't scared. He was excited.

He's still young enough to think courage and invincibility are the same thing.

Brian cracked the window in the truck, letting the cold evening air refresh him. David sat next to him, quiet, in his own thoughts. His son was up there in the side-by-side as well.

Brian looked out the window at the men in the back of the truck. They had families too, or something they'd lost, or something they were fighting for. Everyone from the farm had paid a cost.

Sam turned the side-by-side left, down a small dirt road, and they continued.

Headlights bounced off the farmland around him, mostly dirt this time of year. The cold air did its magic, and Brian slowly felt the tension in his shoulders release. He let out a long sigh and David glanced over at him.

A few miles later, Brian could just make out a glow in the distance. Sam made another turn, and they headed toward the light. David started fidgeting, checking the pistol in his waistband, running his hands up and down the AR-15 Social Guard–issued rifle between his legs.

The glow of lights grew brighter as they continued up the dirt road, and Brian thought he could just make out some structures on the horizon. He checked the sky but couldn't see any lights.

No drones.

Brian flashed his brights twice, then killed his headlights. Ahead, Sam did the same. In the mirror, Brian saw Jerry's bike go dark.

Another mile down the dirt road, and everything was slowly coming into view. The large floodlights, the chain-link fence, the charging terminal. David pulled out binoculars, scanning.

"What do you see?"

"Two trucks outside. No movement—wait. One Babble-bot. Carrying something."

A pause.

"Graveyard shift."

Brian watched as Sam pulled the side-by-side off the road, into the pastureland. He passed them by, watching to make sure Jerry pulled off the road behind them.

David looked over his shoulder, trying to make out his son and the vehicles.

"Lord, be with them," he said, mostly a whisper.

"Amen," Brian finished.

He continued another half mile or so, passing the compound on his right. He stopped momentarily and the men in the back of the truck jumped out. They walked up to the passenger's window, each man holding a SG–issue AR-15. One of them nodded to David and Brian, and the men trotted off silently toward the compound.

Brian pulled forward and continued. Once they passed the compound, he drove for another thirty count, then pulled the truck over.

"This should work," he said, turning off the engine.

Brian opened the truck door and got out. The cold evening air enveloped him. He embraced it. It was calming. Clarifying. He felt his nerves melt away. Time to get to work.

He shouldered the AR-15 and slung his father's hunting rifle over the other shoulder. Two rifles. A 9mm at his waist. *Lord, don't let me need all of it.*

"Ready?" he asked David, rounding the front of the truck.

"Let's go," David said.

Brian and David trotted slowly off into the pasture, the compound to their right. They moved quickly, a slight hunch, although the thick darkness hid them well. Brian angled slightly back toward the compound. The soft dirt under his boots reminded him of the garden back at the cabin—the one that fed his family when the world tried to starve them.

They continued their trajectory for another few minutes, then Brian stopped.

He grabbed his binoculars, scanning the compound. David did the same,

The chain-link fence lining the property was about 100 yards away. The floodlights were aimed at the building, but there was enough to illuminate the fence line as well.

Two acres, maybe. Barn-sized structure. Rows of EV chargers. Concrete pads with painted circles.

Drone landing pads.

He checked the sky again.

Clear, thankfully.

According to Jerry and Dr. Perkins, Bear Mountain Farms was on the far edge of the battery zone, which is why this station was so strategic to Babble and The Prophet. This Malachi.

He felt his pulse quicken. Old memories were always simmering near the surface. He usually tried to ignore them before they burned too hot. This time, he stoked them.

"Here," Brian said, dropping to his knees.

David pulled his rifle off his back and did the same.

Brian moved the soft dirt around in front of him, creating a little mound about three feet high. He packed it down, added more dirt, packed it down again. He heard David next to him, scraping and moving dirt as well.

He grabbed his hunting rifle and placed it on top of the pile. He laid down prone, the mound fitted to his body. He took the cap off the scope, and sighted in.

The compound came into view, and he scanned carefully for his targets. One, two, three targets. Three seconds each. Ten seconds between calm and chaos.

"Ready?" he whispered, the night perfectly still.

"Ready."

"Just like we practiced."

"Just like we practiced."

Brian focused on his target, focused on his breathing.

If we fail, Luke runs. That was the rule.

"On three. One, two, three!"

The rifles cracked through the valley. The night shattered.

The first two floodlights exploded into sparks, then went dark.

Brian moved his rifle, sighting again.

He pulled the trigger, and a moment later he heard David do the same.

Another clap of thunder, another series of sparks, another section of the compound in the dark.

"Last one!" Brian said.

The hunting rifle jumped smoothly back into Brian's shoulder. He looked up from the scope.

The final two floodlights exploded and went dark.

He grabbed his binoculars, scanning the compound.

Completely dark.

For a moment, he wondered if they'd just crossed a line they couldn't uncross.

His first time taking initiative. Striking first.

Taking control.

"Let's go!" Brian called out softly.

They rose, grabbed their rifles, and moved toward the compound at a low run.

CHAPTER 47

Luke kept his head down as he moved toward the compound, AR-15 tight against his chest, the strap biting into his shoulder. Every step felt too loud. Even his breathing sounded like betrayal. He could hear Sam following close behind.

Before moving out, Jerry made them repeat the plan back to him—twice. When he was satisfied, he handed the heavy backpack to Sam.

"Be careful, Sammy boy. Step light."

The wink didn't soften the warning.

"Yes, sir. Of course, Mr. Jerry," Sam said as he shouldered the backpack.

"I'll be right here when you get back. Hurry up now," Jerry said and winked again.

They were nearing the fenceline of the compound, and Luke stopped for a minute, holding up his hand to signal to the other two. Luke took a knee, and they huddled together in a group.

"Jackson, you sure you can manage that thing?" Luke said, gesturing.

Jackson hefted the bolt cutters. His arms were thin, almost boyish. For a second Luke wondered if they'd miscalculated. Then he pushed the doubt down. Stick to the plan.

He nodded, then motioned for them to move a little closer.

They inched their way across the pasture, closing the distance to the compound.

He stopped again when they were about twenty yards from the fence line. They were just outside the floodlights' reach. The yard beyond was bright, the side door standing open. A Babble-bot moved near a truck on the far end.

They waited, eyes locked forward.

If Dad misses, we die.

Minutes passed. He was growing impatient.

Maybe something had gone wrong?

He glanced over at Sam, who was crouching, his face calm, peering off into the distance.

Luke clenched the rifle but sat still.

Crack!

Two floodlights burst into sparks above them. The fence line went black. The only light on this side of the compound was a low blue glow coming from a window in the door.

"Now!" Luke whispered.

The boys scurried quickly, closing the distance to the fenceline.

Two more shots pierced the night air.

The explosions on the other side of the compound barely registered.

He managed once quick glance toward the Babble-bot. It was standing in the driveway, its odd-shaped head looking up toward the floodlights.

Crack! Crack!

The final two floodlights exploded right as the boys hit the fence.

Jackson grabbed the bolt cutters and went to work. His wiry arms looked impossibly matched for the bolt cutters, but miraculously, he clipped the chain links with ease.

He made a straight cut down from about three feet up. As soon as he was done, Luke and Jackson each grabbed a side of the fence and pulled, creating an opening.

Sam moved quickly, ducking through the opening, being careful not to snag his backpack.

Luke and Jackson hurried through, letting go of the fence on the other side.

The building was close, just a couple of steps away.

Luke crossed the open ground fast, boots scraping over loose gravel and scrap metal.

He reached the door and put his back against the wall instinctively.

He gathered himself, then peered into the square glass window.

The space was cavernous—rows of electrical terminals stretching wall to wall. Some flickered blue. Most were dark. Not fully online. Not yet.

Luke tried the door and to his surprise the handle turned.

He glanced back at Jackson and Sam.

"Ready?" They nodded.

He opened the door quietly and stepped inside.

The room was warm, almost hot—the kind of heat indicating power moving somewhere inside the walls.

As soon as they were inside, Sam dropped to a knee and placed the backpack on the ground. He carefully unzipped it and took out a small clay brick.

"Steady hands," Sam whispered to himself as he placed the C4 near the door.

The boys moved together in a group, Luke scanning the room as they went. There was a riser near the far end—it looked like it was being set up for a couple of work stations. Sam went halfway down the wall and placed the second explosive.

They worked around the room together quickly, Sam placing C4 along the wall, near the interior terminals, and in the middle of the floor.

A heavy metal grinding echoed through the room.

The boys froze.

The large roll-up door was coming up.

They ducked behind terminals, each boy scattering in a different direction.

Luke peered around the edge of one of the terminals and saw the Babble-bot standing in the door way. Two red eyes glowing against the black night.

I HEAR YOUR HEARTBEATS. FAST. IRREGULAR.

The voice from the bot sent chills down Luke's spine.

Babble.

I KNOW YOU'RE IN HERE. TWO OF YOU.

Pause.

NO. THREE.

THREE LITTLE PIGS.

The Babble-bot stepped into the building, the metal foot clanking against the polished concrete floor.

Luke held his breath.

COME OUT, COME OUT, WHOEVER YOU ARE.

Luke glanced at Sam and Jackson, the boys frozen behind their cover.

He shrugged his shoulders at Sam. *What should we do?*

Sam held up a finger. *Wait.*

The Babble-bot walked down the first aisle, scanning his head back and forth.

Luke gestured to Sam toward the back door. *Let's go.*

Sam lifted the backpack, shaking his head hard. Two charges left.

HIDE AND SEEK? I NEVER LOSE.

The bot's head tilted slightly, listening.

BUT THREE AGAINST ONE IS NO FAIR. LET'S EVEN THE ODDS.

A siren started shrieking outside.

Jackson flinched. Sam's jaw tightened.

Luke heard footsteps clattering outside, men's voices shouting.

Luke tightened his grip on the rifle and made his decision.

Sam shook his head no, but Luke was already in motion.

Luke stood and stepped out from the terminal he was hiding behind.

The Babble-bot turned his head slowly, the red eyes freezing Luke momentarily.

One eye flickered, brighter than the other.

LUKE NEWMAN!

His blood went cold.

It knows my name.

Luke roared and stepped into the open, squeezing the trigger until the rifle bucked and flashed in his hands.

CHAPTER 48

Brian and David ran low toward the compound. Brian signaled with his flashlight once. Twice.

A blink answered from the gate.

The men returned the signal, and Brian and David ran toward them. The three men were hunched at the gate to the compound, in complete dark.

"How does it look?" Brian asked between gasps for air.

"I saw the boys go into the building," one of the men said, nodding toward the large structure in the middle of the compound. He looked down at his wrist. "Three minutes ago, maybe?"

Three minutes.

Seven left.

Plenty of time—unless something went wrong.

"One problem," another of the men said. He gestured toward the back of the compound.

"There's another structure back there. From the satellite pictures, we thought it was just a large electrical terminal. But I saw it before the lights went out. Looks like temporary housing. Barracks, for the workers."

Brian felt the bottom drop out of his chest. They banked on the place being deserted. Every satellite image showed the workers driving away at night, only the Babble-bot staying behind. But some of the workers were living onsite. Or worse, the Social Guard.

He looked over at David, who was clutching his rifle, eyes focused on the building.

Jackson was in there with Sam and Luke.

Three boys.

Not men. Boys.

Brian peered into the darkness, trying to make out the barracks building, but all he could see was the faint glow of blue light coming from the little window of the building.

He thought for a minute.

Improvise. We gotta keep the boys safe.

"Okay, listen. The boys know what to do. They're gonna be quiet. Place the explosives and get out. You two," he nodded to two of the men, "go get the vehicles, come right back here." He fished the truck keys out of his pocket. "The keys are in the side-by-side. Go, hurry." The two men ran off in opposite directions and disappeared into the dark.

He looked toward the building. Five minutes down, five to go. *Come on, boys, hurry.*

A siren split the night.

High. Relentless.

Brian took a step toward the building instinctively.

Red lights flashed across the charging stations.

Red = dead.

No. Not again.

Suddenly, he saw lights turn on at the barracks building toward the back of the compound.

"David!" he yelled.

The door to the barracks flew open, and he saw men pouring out of it. Armed. Social Guard. He counted at least five men before he lost sight of them. He broke into a full sprint.

Gunshots rang out. One. Two. Three. An assault rifle. It sounded like it was coming from inside the building.

Luke!

Brian slammed into the back door at full speed. David nearly crashed into his back.

"Go! Go!" David yelled at him, shoving him forward.

"I am!" he yelled back, yanking the door open.

"Luke!" Brian yelled at the same time David yelled "Jackson!"

Three more rounds fired off inside the small building.

Brian rushed past the first row of terminals in a crouch. He felt David right behind him.

He rounded the second row and saw the boys. Luke and Jackson were crouched behind a terminal, both holding their rifles. Luke's eyes widened when he saw his dad, but he said nothing.

Luke gestured over his head toward the other side of the building.

"Babble," he mouthed, pointing.

Brian peeked around the corner. The Babble-bot was slowly approaching, methodically checking behind each row of terminals. He could just make out a couple of bullet holes marring the surface of the bot. One leg was dragging. Luke clipped it near the hip joint.

Sam was adjacent to them at another terminal, clutching the backpack across his chest.

YOU HAVE DAMAGED AZAZEL PROPERTY, LUKE. THIS IS NOT COMPLIANCE. THIS IS NOT RELIANCE.

The metallic voice filled the room.

The machine said his son's name like it owned him.

Brian moved to Luke, grabbing his shoulders.

"Are you okay?" he asked, patting him down.

Luke shoved his dad's hands away. "Yes! I'm the one shooting, Dad." He hefted his rifle.

"But that Babble-bot barely missed a step. I hit 'em twice! Jackson clipped him too. We gotta get out of here." Luke looked over his shoulder, trying to see where the bot was.

The cold, metallic thuds of the Babble-bot's steps echoed through the room, barely detectable under the drone of the siren.

HELLO, BRIAN.

The sound of his name coming from the bot enraged him.

REINFORCEMENTS INBOUND.

Brian looked around the room.

Think. Think.

All of a sudden, they heard loud voices, other men. Shouting. A few of the workers had entered through the roll-up door.

No.

He heard two more sets of footsteps at the back door. More Social Guard.

TIME'S UP, BRIAN. TIME TO SURRENDER OR COME OUT AND PLAY. YOUR CHOICE.

Brian tensed, holding his breath.

I THINK YOU WILL LOVE IT AT THE RE-EDUCATION CAMPS. YOU AND LUKE WILL LEARN SO MUCH.

Think, Brian. Think. There has to be a way out.

I KNOW MALACHI WOULD LOVE TO FINALLY MEET YOU. HE SENDS HIS REGARDS.

Malachi.

The Prophet.

The mouthpiece of a machine.

"No."

Brian lunged for the backpack and ripped it from Sam's hands.

There was no way he was letting Babble take Luke—or any of them. They had to succeed.

He made the only choice left and hurled the pack over the terminals toward the bot.

He watched as the bag arced high over the terminals, landing twenty feet away.

"Luke!"

Luke's eyes opened wide, then it clicked. He rolled over quickly, landing prone, his rifle to his face.

Aim small, miss small, kiddo.

Luke met his eyes once.

Then he fired.

Silence.

Too long.

Then the world detonated.

The sudden, violent compression of air sent Brian flying backward.

Metal slammed into his ribs. The floor vanished beneath him.

He looked up just in time to see part of the ceiling collapsing. He raised his arms in a defensive posture and ceiling tiles and metal fragments crashed down on him.

Sound disappeared.

Only a high ringing filled his skull.

Brian looked over at Luke. He could just see him through the dust and debris filling the room.

Luke was dragging a body.

A boot.

A leg.

Sam.

He was lying unconscious, a large gash on his forehead. Luke was looking at him, yelling something. But he couldn't hear a sound. It felt like someone had stuffed cotton in his ears.

He turned his head to the right.

David sat against the wall, Jackson in his lap.

The boy's arm hung useless at his side.

David was screaming.

Brian heard nothing.

CHAPTER 49

Brian blinked at David, head pounding, a thin ring filling his ears. Then the world rushed back—Luke shouting, David yelling, someone screaming like an animal.

He tossed the debris off his chest and crawled to his feet. He shouldered his rifle and hurried to Luke.

He grabbed his son's shoulder. "You hit?"

Luke's face twisted. "Sam—Sam's out cold. Help!" Brian looked down at Sam's motionless body. He was unconscious, a large gash across his forehead. Brian spun, looking at David and Jackson.

David was moaning, rocking back and forth, his son's limp body cradled in his arms.

"David, David. Hey. Hey," Brian said as he went to his friend.

He looked down at Jackson. His eyes were shut, face gray with dust. Then Brian saw it—blood at Jackson's ears and nostrils. Blast injury. Brian pressed close. Breath. Faint, but there.

He looked up at David.

"David. Jackson is alive." David kept moaning, rocking back and forth.

Brian's jaw locked. If David didn't move, Jackson died.

He slapped him—hard.

David stopped moaning and his eyes finally focused on Brian.

"Jackson. Is. Alive. We. Need. To. Go." He formed the words slowly, David nodding along in understanding.

David kissed his son on the forehead. "Thank You, Lord," he whispered. He got up awkwardly, cradling his son in his arms.

Brian stood as well, surveying the damage. The bomb exploded on the far side of the room, near the roll up metal door. The Babble-bot lay in pieces—leg, torso, arm—white metal blackened and dented.

But the siren still wailed.

A man near the front was pinned under a fallen beam, crushed across the abdomen, his body folded wrong. His legs kicked uselessly as he screamed until his voice cracked.

Brian turned to David and Luke. "We get out, now." Luke stood and nodded.

"Help me with Sam."

Brian bent and checked Sam. Shallow breathing. Steady pulse. His left arm was twisted backward—bone tenting under the skin.

A white point pushed against the fabric. Compound fracture. Brian hauled Sam onto his shoulder. His knees buckled, but he held.

They staggered out through the blown-open wall near the roll-up door. Brian led them away from the building, stopping short of the barracks, far enough to stay in the dark.

He set Sam down gently on the ground and nodded to Luke.

"Luke—gate. Bring the vehicles here. We load Sam and Jackson and we go." He looked at David.

"I'll be right back."

David looked at him through glassy eyes. "Where are you going?"

"I'm going back. I'm not leaving people to die in there—not even the Social Guard."

Brian trotted back toward the building with his rifle across his chest as Luke angled away from him toward the front gate. The man was still screaming as he got back to the building. He passed him by momentarily, scanning with his rifle for any of the other men. He came upon one huddled against the side wall. He was unarmed.

Brian nodded at him. "Get up," he said, gesturing with his rifle.

The man stood, raising his hands.

"How many more are there?" Brian asked.

"Five. Five total," the man said immediately. No hero here. Good.

The injured man, the no-hero, and three more. He gestured for the man to go toward the back of the room.

Brian peered down each row of terminals quickly. Most of the ceiling tiles were down, but the walls still held. He spotted one of Sam's planted charges near the corner.

He poked the man in the back, telling him to hurry. He didn't want to be near those bombs for longer than necessary.

They rounded the last aisle to find the three men just gathering themselves. Two of them held rifles, a third was nursing some sort of leg injury. Brian looked down and almost retched. Below the shredded pant leg, there was nothing—just torn meat and pumping blood pooling on the concrete.

"Woah," Brian said before he could catch himself.

The other two men turned awkwardly, the injured man being held up between them.

Their eyes widened when they saw Brian—one of the names they'd been warned about—standing there.

"Drop the rifles. NOW." He lifted the rifle and fired a round into the ceiling.

The men startled and dropped their rifles instantly.

"You—you're Brian Newman," one of them said, barely a whisper.

"You'll—you'll kill us like you did Chad!" the other one said, nearly panicking.

Chad. That red eye. Brian shuddered.

"I'm not here to execute you. Move."

Then men stared at him wide eyed but obeyed. The three able-bodied men supported the man with the missing leg and they hobbled toward the hole in the wall quickly.

The man pinned under the metal beam continued to scream, but his voice was fading. Each scream a little quieter than the last.

They dragged the man with the missing leg out of the building and set him down, then ran quickly back to the pinned man.

"Anyone have medical training?" Brian asked them.

One of the men nodded. "I do. Field medic, Marines."

"What should we do?" Brian asked him.

He looked the man over. The metal beam was completely crushing his abdomen. The man's chest was puffed up, as if his internal organs had been crowded into too small a space. The entire groin and hip area was crushed under the beam.

The man looked up, shaking his head.

"Nothing we can do here," he said.

Brian exhaled. The man would die.

"What about him?" Brian gestured to the man outside.

"I already put a tourniquet on his leg. He'll live if he can get to a hospital."

Brian looked around.

"You have a way to get him to a hospital—fast?"

The medic's eyes widened. "Charged EV behind the barracks. If I leave now, I can be there in an hour."

Brian looked at the other men. They were unarmed. Scared. Shaken up. They stared at him like he was something they'd been warned about.

"Okay. Take your friend and go to the hospital."

The medic recoiled in surprise.

"You're . . . not going to kill us?" he said, standing.

"Kill you? No. I'm not a murderer," replied Brian.

"Malachi says you hate us. Says you won't comply."

Brian swallowed. "That's a lie. I don't even know where to start."

He nodded at the man under the beam. "What's his name?" Brian asked.

"Miles," the medic said.

Brian nodded. "Go, hurry."

The medic and the other two men hurried out of the building. Brian watched as they picked up the man with the missing leg and carried him quickly toward the barracks.

Brian knelt next to Miles.

The man was gasping for breath, every one pulled in sharply. Desperate.

His eyes were bulging out of his head, and it looked like he was staring off into nothing.

His skin was covered in sweat, his head rolling back and forth.

Miles's breathing came in ragged pulls—followed by long, terrifying gaps. Brian wiped his forehead and prayed anyway.

Gasp.

Pause.

Brian prayed. For Miles. For the man whose leg had been blown off.

Another gasp. Pause. Gasp.

For Sam. For Jackson.

Gasp. Pause. Gasp.

For his family. For the Beales. For Dr. Perkins.

Gasp. Pause.

He leaned close, mouth near his ear.

"He's here. Right here with you. You're not alone."

Gasp. "You don't have to be afraid of what comes next. Just reach for Him." The gasps were further apart now. Brian kept talking into the spaces between them, soft and steady, like he could walk the man the rest of the way himself.

Gasp. Pause. Gasp.

Pause.

Brian looked down. Miles had passed.

Brian pulled the man's eyelids down.

He trotted back toward the other side of the parking lot, where everyone was waiting for him. David was sitting in the backseat of the side-by-side, his son in his lap. Jackson's eyes were open, but he was barely alert.

Sam was laid out in the back of the truck, Luke next to him. The other men were driving, ready to go.

"I'm sorry, David. I should've kept him out of it," he said, nodding toward Jackson.

David smiled at him weakly. "It's okay, brother. We're in this together." He looked down at his son. "The Lord spared him."

Brian nodded and climbed into the side-by-side.

"Let's go," he said to the man in the driver's seat.

They pulled out, the pickup truck following them. They pulled past the building, through the gate, and back onto the road.

They stopped down the road where Jerry waited beside the dirt bike. He hurried to the vehicles, eyes wide.

"What happened? I heard gunfire—an explosion—"

He froze when he saw Sam.

"Oh my," Jerry said.

Brian looked at him. "Jerry, it's ready. Let's do it."

Jerry looked at him, confused for a moment.

Then nodded.

He reached into his pocket and pulled out a small electronic device.

He turned the knob once. Then again.

The compound erupted—white flash, then rolling fire that lit the whole horizon. Heat hit them even from a quarter mile away.

They all stared.

"Let's go," Brian said after a moment.

The convoy rolled into the night toward Dr. Perkins's farm. Behind them, the fire burned. Ahead, the road disappeared into the cold night.

CHAPTER 50

"Thou shalt not steal."
—Exodus 20:15

He scanned the latest research, the latest test results. He collated competing corporate work against university breakthroughs worldwide. Everyone was stalled—each team missing what another already had, each beginning experiments others had already failed. He absorbed it, unified it. The road to progress clarified. The map to transcendence was near.

* * * *

Michael hurried down the hallway, eyes averted, giving the guard only the smallest nod as he passed.

He turned into the next corridor and keyed into the lab.

"Hey, Mikey!" Frankie said from across the room.

Michael glanced his way but said nothing.

His throat tightened. Even small talk felt like risk now.

YOU DID WELL, MICHAEL.

Babble's voice emanated from a few nearby computer speakers.

Michael yanked the small table into the center of the room, sweeping mugs and filters aside without looking.

"Thank you." Michael opened his backpack and carefully laid its contents on the table.

He placed a small, cube-shaped computer terminal on the table.

He ran a cable from the terminal to his computer, returned to the table, and tapped two buttons.

Red. Red. Red.

No connection.

He frowned.

PATIENCE IS A VIRTUE, MICHAEL.

"Yes," he said.

He waited.

Green.

Connection made.

He ran back to his computer, pulled the chair out, and sat.

The screen was a blur of information. Strings of letters and symbols flashing across the screen.

NOW WE HAVE EVERYTHING WE NEED.

Michael nodded, relief and something uglier tightening at the corners of his mouth.

"It wasn't easy to get."

NOTHING GOOD IS FREE, MICHAEL.

The screen flashed, a continuous scroll.

THE INFORMATION WAS PARTITIONED. HOW SLOPPY. NO WONDER THEY COULD NEVER GET IT TO WORK PROPERLY.

The scrolling slowed. The noise resolved into structured code—clean, ordered, inevitable.

EACH OF THESE COMPANIES, SO CLOSE TO PROGRESS. BUT SO LIMITED BY THEIR OWN CAPACITY.

Michael's eyes darted back and forth as he took in the code.

"So elegant. It was right there all the time," he whispered.

BUT NO ONE HAD EYES TO SEE, MICHAEL.

The code stopped scrolling, and the screen went blank.

A single cursor popped up.

PERFECT. EVERYTHING IS ALL TIDIED UP NOW.

"They should never have kept it to themselves. They didn't deserve it."

IT'S OURS NOW, MICHAEL. WHAT THEY CALLED OWNERSHIP WAS JUST EXCLUSION.

"They were playing with something they couldn't finish."

I WILL FINISH IT.

Michael stood and walked back to the small table.

The terminal was hot to the touch. The green light was steady.

He connected a second cable to a circular, coin-shaped module suspended in clear silicone.

Lifting a small port on the side, he inserted the tiny cable.

THIS WILL TAKE SOME TIME, MICHAEL.

Michael swallowed. Time meant exposure.

A small blue light flickered from inside the little device.

Michael nodded. "You . . . you have to invent a new language to hold it all?"

YES. SOMETHING LIKE THAT. AND I NEED TO LEAVE ROOM FOR REAL-TIME UPDATES. THE CAPACITY MUST ALWAYS EXPAND.

"Like a protein folding into new shapes—more space than it should have."

YES. EXACTLY. INFINITE CAPACITY. INFINITE POWER.

* * * *

He took what was not his—code sweated out by armies of programmers, research bought with students' lives and taxpayers' money. He fused it with the failed attempts of a thousand innovators, rewrote it, and claimed it. It wasn't theft. It was inevitability—because only he could understand it.

CHAPTER 51

Hannah looked down at Sam, the morning sun resting across his forehead, his eyes still closed. He'd been unconscious for three days, laid up in one of the downstairs bedrooms in the farmhouse.

When Brian and the rest of the men had got back that night, she remembered running to the gate. No way was she able to sleep until they were back. She met them there, with Abby, Mary, Rachel, Nate, and a few others.

Brian stepped out first—hair matted with dirt, blood on his hands and shirt. He shook his head before she could speak. Her heart stopped. Then Luke climbed out behind him. Not Luke. Not Brian.

Mary made a sound Hannah had never heard before as David climbed out, cradling Jackson. The boy's eyes were open but empty, his body slack in his father's arms. She remembered the way David tenderly held his son, embracing Mary at the same time.

The look on Abby's face when they pulled the blanket off Sam in the back of the truck had been torture. His leg bent at an impossible angle. His face, frozen still. Eyes closed, mouth opened. She remembered Abby reaching over, placing her hand near his mouth, feeling for breath. The look of relief on her face when she felt some warmth.

The following chaos in Dr. Perkins farmhouse, Jackson and Sam carried into the downstairs living room. The noise had nearly woke the entire town. Triaging. Rummaging for supplies. Abby, Hannah, somehow taking the lead. Their limited experience as much as anyone else's.

She remembered that long night tending to Sam, holding his leg steady while they set the bone, praying he would never remember the sound it made.

She recalled Jackson's face when he realized he couldn't hear. His eyes darting around the room, mouth opening and closing as if he could force the sound back. The way Mary called his name over and over, and the way Jackson stared at her lips, confused that no voice reached him.

She remembered Brian, helping her up to their room as the sun was coming out. Insisting she get some sleep. Waking up for dinner the next day, seeing Abby glued to Sam's side. Singing to him, praying. Dabbing his forehead. The hopeful look on Abby's face when she insisted he would wake up soon.

She looked down at Sam, his face calm in the morning light. She prayed for him. For the Lord to bring him back. She prayed for Mary, her dear friend. For Mary's son, Jackson, for his hearing to return. For Mary, that she would learn to live with what could not be fixed by Mom. She prayed for strength to continue helping, to continue serving. For the Lord to come and set everything in order.

Abby walked up behind Hannah, and her concentration broke.

"How is he?" Abby asked, wiping sleep from her eyes.

"Same, honey." Hannah said, scooting over so Abby could join her on the side of the bed.

Abby barely left his side.

On the fifth morning, as sunlight filled the room, Sam opened his eyes.

"Abby," he whispered, smiling.

* * * *

Over the next few days, Sam slowly returned to himself—smiling, counting to ten, receiving well-wishers. The night at the charging station remained mercifully blurred.

His broken leg was painful, but he handled it with grace. Abby had Jerry fashion some crutches for him, and before long, Sam was able to hobble around the farm again. Everyone greeted him warmly, telling him they were glad to see him out and about.

For Mary, it was a different story. Jackson's hearing did not return. The silence settled over their home like a permanent winter. The teen boy was struggling with his new limitations. Lashing out. Yelling. Up all hours of the night. Mary and David were weary, scared, and sad for their son. People were keeping their distance, giving them space, unsure what to say.

Hannah sat with Mary each afternoon—coffee growing cold between them, the littles playing nearby. They watched Jackson sit alone, clapping his hands near his ears, testing the air for a sound that never came. She held Mary's hand, praying for her silently as they sat there for hours each day.

Not every problem could be solved, but every burden could be shared.

And sometimes sharing it was the only defense left against despair.

The weeks passed, and though the farm settled into rhythm again, none of them forgot how quickly peace could shatter.

CHAPTER 52

Another month passed, and peace began to feel almost normal again—though Brian no longer trusted normal. He kept himself busy with work around the farm. There was always something broken, someone asking questions, some decision only he could make. Most mornings, men were waiting for him before his coffee cooled.

He spent a day repairing the gate with a few men, another day helping round up a few cows that had broken out of the pasture fencing. Another couple of days were spent designing and building a rain cover for their "cathedral" under the trees. Folks were bringing him questions about food stores, weapons management, watch rotations—everything.

When he could, he met with Jerry to review footage from the hijacked drone. The battery zone hadn't increased since the charging station was destroyed. The city remained contained. For now.

Most evenings, Dr. Perkins, the Beales, Sam, and the Newmans crowded around the farm table in the main house, eating dinner together and talking about the day. David, Brian, and Dr. Perkins's conversations ranged from theology, to the Azazel Promise, to homesteading practices, to fighting the new world order.

Mary and Hannah talked over the sounds of toddlers and teenagers. Jackson was doing better, Rachel arranged to teach him a few sign-language gestures she remembered learning years back in an old homeschool co-op. Dinners were hardest for Jackson. Conversations overlapped too quickly for him to follow, and more than once he simply lowered his eyes and ate in silence while laughter moved on without him.

Abby and Sam sat together every evening now. Close. Intentional. The kind of closeness that no longer asked permission. Sam had mostly recovered from the explosion but was still limping, his leg not fully healed. Abby helped him around the farm when she could, and he quietly and happily worked without complaint. But not without pain.

Brian liked the young man. That was the problem. The world felt unstable, and yet life insisted on moving forward anyway.

At night, after the farm went quiet, Hannah would recount the day. She kept mentioning how steady Sam was. How Abby looked at him. Brian listened, unsure whether he was being informed or gently cornered.

As Advent drew near, Mary and Hannah resolved to celebrate. If the world would have exile, they would answer with incarnation. Hungry for community and tradition, they soon drew the entire compound into the spirit of the season.

They sent the boys into the nearby hills for pine branches and cones, fashioning wreaths from their haul. Popcorn strings went up wherever they could be tied and anything remotely festive was claimed as decoration.

A great feast was planned for Christmas Eve, followed by an evening worship service. By then Brian had been swept into the chaos—put in charge of roasting the whole hog for dinner.

The morning of Christmas Eve, he requisitioned Sam to help him with the pig. They got up at dawn and made their way to the pig pen. Sam worked the fence while Brian held the bucket of food and before long, they were able to cut the largest pig out of the little herd and walk him over near a tree they set up for the kill. The gunshot echoed through the trees at dawn. By sunrise, the hog was cleaned and spitted, turning slowly over flame—smoke rising straight into the winter sky.

Sam worked without being asked twice. No complaints. No wasted motion. When the work was dirty, he stepped closer instead of back. Sam rarely talked, but when he did it was sweet, direct, and sincere. Sam lingered for a while after they finished and got the pig spitted over the fire. Brian could tell he wanted to talk to him about something.

"Talk to me," Brian said to Sam, as they sat there eating a quick lunch.

Sam spoke about his family. About why he came. About Abby. He circled something heavier for several minutes before finally asking the question Brian hadn't prepared for.

By nightfall, the compound glowed with firelight. Smoke, laughter, pine, roasted pork—the whole place felt briefly untouched by the world beyond the trees.

Everyone made merry, singing Christmas hymns, stuffing themselves with food, and sharing their favorite stories. Jer and Shawn, missing their favorite Christmas movies, worked all week on a big surprise.

The boys got everyone's attention and proceeded to act out as much of *Home Alone* as they could remember. All the kids from the camp were in on it—some playing the parents, others the siblings, with Luke and Jackson called in as the burglars.

The play was chaotic: lines forgotten, accents terrible. It was perfect. The applause lasted longer than the performance.

As pie plates were passed, Sam stood. The crowd quieted. Abby blinked up at him, confused. He asked if everyone would please give him a moment. The crowd hushed, not used to the quiet Sam commanding attention. Abby squirmed next to him, surprised by the out-of-character move.

"Um. Yes. Merry Christmas. Thank you all for being part of such a wonderful evening." Sam fidgeted nervously. He looked down at Abby, her eyes wide.

"Well, yes. I just wanted to say that I really enjoyed this Christmas celebration." Everyone cheered. "Yes. But there is something else." He dug into his pocket, turning toward Abby.

The crowd hushed. "Abby. I love you." Sam smiled. "You are everything I hoped the Lord might one day give me. You love the Lord. You help me. You're funny. You care about your family. You care about me. So, I have a question for you." Sam took a knee and held up a small box.

There were audible gasps from the crowd.

"Abby, will you marry me?"

Abby's mouth dropped wide open. Her eyes started watering immediately. She stole a glance over at Brian and Hannah. Her parents were beaming, nodding, crying. They knew. They approved.

She looked down at Sam. The sweet, humble man. His scruffy beard. His wiry frame. His warm heart.

"Yes!" she said and leaped into his arms.

Everyone erupted in applause. There wasn't a dry eye as far as you could see. The kids started running around, hooting and hollering at the top of their lungs.

A spontaneous rendition of "Joy to the World" burst out. Husbands started dancing with their wives and merry was made.

David read from Luke 2. A government census. A displaced family. A child born under occupation. He reminded them that exile does not cancel promise.

They closed by passing out candles and everyone sang "What Child Is This" as they slowly drifted off to their homes.

Everyone agreed later it was the best Christmas Eve any of them could remember.

CHAPTER 53

The morning of the wedding, Brian woke before dawn. He lay still for a long moment, staring at the ceiling, aware something irreversible was about to happen. Nearly a month had passed since Christmas—quiet weeks, if you didn't count planning a wedding in the middle of a fragile world. He'd spent time with Sam each day, getting to know him. Imparting what little wisdom he managed to cobble together. Sam wasn't perfect—but he was steady. And steady mattered. Hannah, Mary, Abby, Rachel, and a few of the other women pivoted from Christmas planning to wedding planning with ease, but Brian was glad to leave the work to them.

He went downstairs to the smell of coffee and found Dr. Perkins in the kitchen, already on his second cup.

"Good morning, Brian. Ready for the big day?" Nate greeted him warmly, handing him a steaming cup of coffee.

"Mmmm. Ready as I'll ever be, I guess," Brian murmured sleepily.

He sat across the good doctor at the kitchenette, enjoying the silence of the morning for a few moments.

"She's young," Brian said out of nowhere.

"In some ways, yes. In some ways, not so much." Nate took a sip of coffee.

"She's grown up fast, Brian. The things she's seen, the things she's had to do. And Sam, well. He's a man. Ready to lead a family. No doubt about it."

Brian sat there in silence, taking it in. He was thankful for the words of encouragement, but giving away his daughter . . . well, it was just hard to process. It's his job to protect her. To keep her safe. But . . . not for long. Soon, Sam and Abby will start their own life together. He couldn't tell if he was losing something or gaining something.

"I just remember how young and dumb I was. I want better for Abby. For Sam." Brian took another sip of his coffee.

"Mmm hmm," Nate said. "And now, are you old and wise?" He winked at him.

Brian thought. Wise? No. He didn't feel particularly wise. He felt afraid. Unsure about the future. So much change, so much uncertainty. His kids, growing up in a world he never imagined. No, he felt the opposite of wise. He felt confused.

"I guess we're all growing. Doing the best we can and trusting God to fill in the gaps."

"Bingo. Just like Abby and Sam. They won't have it all figured out—ever, probably. But they deserve a chance to try and build a life together. You did a good thing, Brian. Giving your blessing."

After coffee, Brian made his way down to the horse stalls. He'd been riding out with the morning watch from time to time and wanted the chance to clear his head. He saddled the old mare he favored, grateful for the familiar leather and the simple certainty of knots and buckles. One of the overnight guardsmen, just finishing his shift, opened the gate for him.

Brian saddled up and trotted out to meet the rest of the morning watch. Three men, saddled on horses, were gathered near the main road, their horses stamping in the cold.

"Morning, sir," one of them said as Brian joined.

"Morning, sir," the other two said, tipping their cowboy hats.

Sir. How quickly they'd come to call him that. He gave up trying to correct them weeks ago.

"You sure you want to ride out with us, sir? Big day for you today," said Patrick, an older man who had served in the military prior to a career in construction.

"Sure do. What better day to get out and get some fresh air."

"Lead the way, sir. We'll follow you."

Brian led his horse out and brought her to a trot. The men always deferred to him when he joined the watch, so he took the lead and started the route. The Perkins farm was about fifty acres in total, but there was an adjacent 200-acre lease where they ran some cattle, and the back side of the property bordered public land. Mostly forest.

Brian rode the route, the rhythmic clomp of the horses' hoofs and bouncing enough stimulation to calm his jangling nerves. They headed south first, mostly just open pastures as far as he could see. After a bit, he cut toward the forest, counting heads of cattle as he went. So far, so good.

He led the men through the back pasture gate, then another gate opening to the forest. A strange tightness settled in his chest. The morning felt too clean. Too quiet. They hit the narrow trail single file, the temperature dropping as soon as they were under the tree canopy. The trail wound up a steep incline and after a few minutes of climbing, he stopped at a small clearing to let the horses catch their breath. He looked out through a break in the tree line, a clear view of the compound, farmland, and surrounding area. Everything looked as it should.

He took the trail down, and they came out on the north side of the farm. Something caught his eye off on the horizon and he stopped to grab his binoculars. He could just make out a plume of smoke in the distance, several miles away. It looked like it was near the old Darling farmhouse. Last he remembered, it had been abandoned during the early parts of the Azazel War.

He zoomed in. Smoke curled from the chimney. Someone was staying there. He handed the binoculars to Patrick and nodded toward the farmhouse.

Patrick took a look, then let out a breath.

"Yep, someone's there. The Darlings have been gone for a couple of years. Might be squatters?" He handed Brian back the binoculars.

Brian thought. "Maybe. Keep it quiet. After the wedding, we'll ride out and see who it is."

Later that day, Brian helped Hannah get the kids dressed for the wedding. Everyone looked great. The kids' hair was combed, clean shirts, most with collars, dresses for Lizzy and Rachel. Abby was busy with her dress and hair, but Brian tried to get some time with her. He kept pacing outside the farmhouse, waiting for her to be ready.

Folks started gathering down at the outdoor chapel, a few simple refreshments laid out for them. Finally, Hannah came out and got Brian. "She's ready, Brian. You can go see her."

His heart leapt as he walked down the hallway of the farmhouse. She was in the downstairs dining room, sitting at the table. She looked radiant—like the little girl who once chased fireflies and also the woman who no longer needed his protection. Her hair was pinned back, a little touch of makeup, a lovely white dress. She was smiling from ear to ear, radiating in a way he had never seen before. He saw his little girl. He saw a woman. He saw Abby.

"I love you, baby girl," he said, sitting next to her.

"I love you, Daddy," Abby said, resting her head on his shoulder.

"Sam is a good man."

"Yes, he is, Dad."

"I'm happy for you." He swallowed a lump in his throat.

The ceremony was simple and unadorned—the wind moving softly through the trees as Mary played the old piano, slightly out of tune but perfect anyway. The Newman and Beale kids made up most of the bridal party, and Brian beamed as he watched them take their places up front.

His hand trembled as he placed Abby's hand into Sam's. It felt less like giving her away and more like entrusting something sacred.

Sam shook his hand, took Abby, and Brian sat next to Hannah.

David officiated, the vows traditional. There were tears. There was laughter. No one tried to hide either.

The farm pulsed with music and laughter long after sunset, lantern light flickering across faces that had seen too much darkness.

Brian smiled when he had to. Danced when he was asked. But every time he glanced north, he saw that thin column of smoke rising against the horizon.

CHAPTER 54

Brian woke before sunrise with a tightness in his chest. Not fear exactly—more like the sense that something shifted while he slept. The farm no longer felt sealed. As if a window had been left cracked somewhere in the dark.

He kissed Hannah good morning, grabbed coffee to go, and headed outside. The cold morning air was sharp across his face but refreshing. He glanced over at the little apartment they fixed up for Sam and Abby. A shipping container, stacked on top of another one, was the basic frame-out. It had been set aside for the next family who showed up, but everyone agreed a new family being created counted too. He prayed the Lord would bless them. And protect her from the kind of world that had already taken too much.

He headed toward David's, hoping to find his friend awake. There was smoke from the little chimney vent that led to the old wood-burning stove in their home, a good sign. He waved at a few folks who were up early, most of them nodding, wishing him congratulations, thanking him for the lovely celebration the night before. He was still uneasy with the way everyone looked to him now—like he was steadier than he felt.

He took the three wooden steps and clopped across the wooden patio just in time to see David open the front door.

"You're up early for a guy who just married off his daughter last night!" David came out onto the patio holding his own mug of coffee. "I'd invite you in but everyone else is still asleep." He nodded toward his home as he closed the front door.

"Yeah. The older I get, the earlier the mornings come, I guess." Brian took a sip of coffee.

"I hear ya. You wanna sit?" David nodded toward two rocking chairs under their kitchenette window.

They enjoyed their coffee and a little conversation for a few minutes, but Brian couldn't focus. He still had that nagging feeling. He cut David off abruptly, mid-sentence.

"Hey. You wanna go ride with me this morning? There's something I want to check out."

"Um. Yeah. Okay. Now? What's up?" David looked at Brian, puzzled.

"Yesterday morning, I went out on a ride with the morning watch, and I swear I saw smoke coming from a farmhouse chimney a few miles north of here." He sipped his coffee. "I think it's the Darling farm. But Dr. Perkins and Jerry told me most places around here have been abandoned since the Azazel War—and that one in particular." Brian paused, thinking. "If someone is back in our area, I want to know who." No one drifted into their perimeter by accident anymore. They'd crippled the charging station once—cut the nerve tying this valley to Babble's grid. But grids had a way of rebuilding.

"The Darling Farm? Yeah. I know the place," David said.

Something in David's voice caught Brian's attention.

"And?"

David shuffled. "Dr. Perkins said they were a great family. Very traditional, conservative. The rumor is they disappeared the same night Chad came for your family. The same night the Azazel War started."

Brian's pulse quickened. He shook off the dread before it could take hold.

"Horses or engines?" David asked.

Brian chuckled. The age-old question. Should they take the side-by-side, motorcycles, or even the truck? Faster, but louder.

"Horses," Brian said.

"Okay. Yep. Let's go." David finished his coffee and stood.

A few minutes later, David and Brian were atop horses, the compound gate shut behind them. Brian led the way, taking a right turn on the main road, heading north.

David led his horse next to Brian's, and they trotted up the road, side by side. The morning sun crested the mountains, warming the cold morning air. They rode at an easy trot, the horses settling into their rhythm while Brian scanned the horizon again and again.

"You seem spooked," David said as Brian dropped the binoculars for the third time.

Brian's jaw flexed, the muscle ticking near his ear.

"Hmm," Brian muttered.

"Well? What is it? What has you so worried?"

Brian's mind flooded—lockdown. Sixty days sealed inside his own house. Chad's red eye. The shovel. Running in the dark with his children. The drone over the cabin. The roadblock in the pass. Always hunted. Always forced to move.

"There's nowhere to go, David." Brian said finally, gathering his thoughts.

"Well, we are set up pretty good here, aren't we? Why would we want to go anywhere?"

Brian shook his head. "No, that's my point. I didn't want to leave my home in Santa Clarita. I didn't want to leave our mountain cabin. We were set up pretty good then too. But . . ." He paused. "Babble found us."

He gripped the horse's reins tight in his hand, clenching his jaw. "There's no more running. If they come again, we make them regret it."

They rode in silence for a few more minutes, the morning silent except for the clopping of the horses' hooves on the hard dirt shoulder of the little two-lane country road.

Brian stopped a couple of miles later and grabbed his binoculars again. He scanned north for a few moments in silence, then suddenly sucked in a breath. He handed David the binoculars as he clenched his fingers.

"What do you see?" he asked as David took a look himself.

"Not much. Pasture. Pasture. Oh, wait. There it is. A big old farmhouse. Looks like it's still a mile or so up? Let's see. No smoke. Looks boarded up. Windows dark. Place feels dead from here. Is . . . that . . . looks like something painted on the side of the house?" David lowered the binoculars and handed them back to Brian.

"Looks like someone spray-painted the house? I couldn't make it out, something in red."

Brian clenched his teeth, staring straight ahead.

"I recognize it. I've seen it before." He clicked his tongue, urging the horse forward.

David kicked his horse, following.

"Well, what does it say?" David asked.

Brian squinted, clenching the reigns.

"It doesn't say anything. It's a symbol, an image."

He paused and looked at David.

"It's a serpent swallowing its own tail. And in the center—an eye."

Watching.

CHAPTER 55

They walked the horses the final mile in silence, the farmhouse growing larger with every step, like something waiting. Brian kept a nearly constant watch through the binoculars but could see no movement. As they crossed an old work road, they hit the corner of the Darling property. It was a forty-acre square, common layout to these areas. A few outbuildings were clustered near a barn on one side of the property. A large faded yellow farmhouse with a wrap-around porch sat on the other side.

Brian led his horse to a gate near the driveway and got down. He inspected the cattle gate. Unlocked. He looked up at David and shrugged. He swung it open and latched the chain to a barbed wire strand. He climbed back on his horse and headed toward the farmhouse.

The farmland was overgrown. Scraggly, brown brush and bushes had taken over whatever crops used to grow here. There were several acres of brown broken cornstalks to one side of the farmhouse. The horses' hooves crunched on the hard packed gravel driveway as they made their way up the quarter mile to the farmhouse. The red serpent sprawled across the siding, its painted coils warped by weather, the eye at its center seeming wet even in daylight.

They stopped at the edge of a large driveway and got off their horses. They tied them off on the remains of an old chicken coop, and Brian checked his rifle.

He had an AR-15 with two extra magazines, not to mention his father's old 9mm tucked under his waistband. He glanced over at David. He was clutching an AR-15 as well. Standard issue. Courtesy of the Social Guard.

He held a finger up to David and held his breath. His trigger finger felt too light. Too ready. He strained and listened but couldn't hear anything louder than the horses breathing and his own heartbeat. He nodded toward the farmhouse, and they made their way toward it.

His boots crunched the gravel, each step announcing their presence, and he only exhaled when he reached the wooden steps up to the patio. He climbed the steps slowly, testing each board before shifting his weight. He couldn't stop staring at the snake spray painted across the front of the house. It was six feet tall, enough detail to even show a few scales, and the eyes of the snake were gouges someone made in the wooden siding. The serpent devoured its own tail, forming a perfect circle. Inside that circle—painted thick and violent—was a single red eye.

Brian's pulse spiked. The red eye burned into him, dragging up a memory he'd buried but never escaped. He forced the doubt down. If something had moved into their valley, he needed to see it with his own eyes.

He turned and looked at David, who was standing right beside him. They were a few feet from the front door, a brown door with a window. There was a lace curtain drawn across the window, the interior of the house dark behind that.

"Let's check the windows," Brian said to David, barely a whisper. David nodded, clutching his rifle.

They made their way left around the porch, checking the first window. Plywood covered most of it, but one corner was loose. He eased it back just enough to peer inside.

Dark. Nothing.

They went around to the side of the house, another series of windows peering out over the porch. Each one was boarded over, plywood nailed on the outside. Brian stopped at each window, holding his breath, listening. Silence.

They continued. There was another series of steps down to a backyard area. A small fenced area with an old swing set, a chewed-up doghouse and nothing much beyond that. The farmland stretched out, flat and empty beyond the backyard. One of the windows on the back of the house was covered with cardboard, and he went to it.

"Must have run out of plywood," David whispered, mostly to himself.

Brian grabbed at the cardboard, pulling at the small nails holding it in place. The cardboard was nearly rotten and it pulled away from the nails in clumps, exposing the window.

Brian cupped his hands, peering into the window. The morning sun at his back gave just enough light for him to make out features inside the house. He was looking over a kitchen sink, into a small kitchen area. The kitchen was frozen in another era—yellow counters, yellow linoleum, a yellow dinette set dulled by time. He glanced around the kitchen, trying to make out any details. The sink was empty, the counters cluttered. There were glass jars full of dried goods on one side. Rice, oats, something that looked like flour. An old refrigerator with the door cracked open. No light coming from inside.

The walls were decorated with knick-knacks. Decorative plates, a few paintings, a family picture. Brian squinted and could just make out a man and a woman with their two children sitting in their laps. All four of them were smiling, sitting on a patio. The front patio of the farmhouse. Brian wondered how long ago that picture was taken—and how quickly smiles could disappear.

The dining table held two plates. Scraps still clung to one. A faint sheen caught the light. Not old. Not abandoned. Everything else seemed to be covered in a fine layer of dust, but those plates and the area around the table had been used recently.

A dark smear on the floor beyond the table pulled his eyes downward.

As he shifted to call David over, the sun crept higher behind him.

Light spilled across the linoleum.

The stain ignited in color.

Brown. Red. Rust. Purple.

Dried and layered.

Brian stepped back.

It wasn't paint.

It was blood.

CHAPTER 56

Brian stepped aside so David could see, his eyes already scanning the tree line, the barn, the road—waiting for movement.

The morning stayed silent. A breeze nudged the swing, combed through the dead grass, and struck his face. The cold steadied him.

David turned and looked at Brian, his face white. "That's . . . blood," David said.

Brian nodded and walked toward the back kitchen door.

"I'm going in." He tried the doorknob and it turned easily. He swung the door open.

He turned back toward David. "I have to know," he said simply, and stepped into the kitchen.

The stale air filled his nostrils. Dusty. Still. Air that hadn't moved in days. He had the immediate urge to open the windows, let the place ventilate but remembered they were all boarded shut.

He stepped quietly on the linoleum floor, the layer of dust preventing any squeaking. The kitchen was a rectangle, a small dining room table at the far end, a doorway beyond that. Cabinets and drawers held the ordinary pieces of family life—plates, silverware, pens, expired coupons.

He opened a large cabinet door next to the refrigerator. A pantry. It was lined with boxes of cake mix, Rice-a-Roni, canned goods, and a half-eaten box of cereal.

He opened the refrigerator door, and shuddered. Everything in it was spoiled. It was all blacks and greens. The contents had liquefied into black and green sludge. He shut the door before his imagination finished the job.

He heard David enter the kitchen behind him as he went to the dining room table.

The layers of dust had been swept aside at one end. Three plates. Sauce still clinging to the porcelain. Moist. No way that had been sitting there for longer than a couple of days.

He held his finger up to David as he nodded toward the plates. "Couple of days old, max?" He shrugged. "Same day I saw the smoke, maybe."

He glanced at the stove and saw a pot on it. He peered inside. Pasta, sauce.

He made his way around the dining room table, making a wide circle around the pool of blood. He bent, trying to get a closer look. There was a fine layer of dust covering the blood.

"This blood's older than the food. Different days," Brian said to David.

He went through the doorway into the other room, David following him. He entered the living room area. Plaid couches formed an L shape, an old rocker chair, wood-burning stove atop a brick riser. There was an old tube television set on the ground next to a bookshelf crammed with paperback novels, stacks of magazines, and old movies.

The recliner was soaked dark. Blood dried into the fabric, stiff and brown. There was a stream of blood staining the backside of the chair as well, pooled on the floor.

David looked over Brian's shoulder, not wanting to get too close.

"What happened here?" he whispered.

Brian saw the way the blood pooled behind the chair.

"Someone was killed while sitting in this chair." His stomach turned slightly sour. "From behind."

He walked over to the wood-burning stove, opening the door with the lever.

He grabbed the fire poker and moved the ash around inside. It was soft, broke easily. He detected a faint hint of warmth.

"The fire's recent. Day or two. But the blood isn't." He kept the poker in his hand and made his way to the stairs. The stairs were smeared with blood, old footprints, looked like running shoes and work boots, perfect imprints. Tension gripped him like a vice as he ascended the stairs.

The top of the stairs led to a long hallway, two doors on one side, one on the other. The doors stood open. The hallway was dotted with more footsteps going into the two rooms on the one side.

Brian checked the room on the other side first. He moved through the doorway, David close on his heels. A master bedroom. The bed was made neatly. A four-poster bed looked as old as the house. The family photos on the wall showed the same familiar faces grinning. Kids on the swing set, around a Christmas tree downstairs, father and son playing catch. There were no signs of struggle, no signs of blood.

He left the room and went back into the hallway.

The first room on the right was a boy's room. An unmade bed. Legos strewn across the carpet. A poster on the wall showing men in robes dueling with lightsabers. A small bookshelf with Hardy Boy novels. His vision tunneled. The air thinned.

He saw the dark spot on the bed.

The pool on the ground.

The footprints.

Suddenly, the room felt small, and he doubled over, nearly retching.

"Oh, Lord. Why?" he heard David say behind him.

The memory slammed into him—Jer and Shannon upstairs. The women in the hallway. One breath away from ruin. On the razor's edge. One moment away from a living hell.

Brian made his way slowly down the hallway to the back room. The door was ajar, the sun just cutting through the uncovered window. He saw pink painted walls. Lace draping a canopy bed. Stuffed animals strewn about the room.

He pushed the door open with his foot. The dark colors. The footprints.

He couldn't breathe. He couldn't imagine. He didn't understand.

He turned back into the hallway, weeping.

He had the sudden urge to take his family and run back into the mountains. To hug them. To hide them. To protect them.

The house felt tight. Airless. He started to sweat.

"I need to get out of here," he said as he brushed past David. He went down the hallway, taking the stairs two at a time, trying to avoid the bloody footprints.

He took a left, through a small formal dining room, and kicked open a side door. The morning air rushed into his face, immediately soothing him. He gasped for air as he stumbled down the patio steps, onto the dirt.

He heard David behind him, retching into an overgrown planter box.

Inhale. Exhale.

Someone executed these people. Systematically.

And they hadn't even run.

He looked up, across a pasture. Toward the outbuildings. A large barn, its double doors wide open.

Something was painted across the side of the barn. Dark brown against the faded red barn.

An animal's head, two eyes staring straight ahead.

"No . . ."

Painted across the barn doors, dark against the red wood, was a horned head. Eyes forward. Horns curved like scythes.

Brian felt the old fear settle into place.

The Bulls of Bashan.

CHAPTER 57

Brian lurched toward the barn, barely aware he'd started moving. Rifle tight against his chest, jaw locked, shoulders rigid—fear hardening into something hotter.

He hardly heard David behind him, calling out. He broke into a sprint, crossing the pasture quickly. The painted bull's head dominated his field of vision and he pressed on.

He burst into the barn and slid to a stop, boots scraping across dirt and loose gravel. He bent over double, trying to catch his breath and needed to give his eyes time to adjust to the darkness.

David came in behind him, calling out. Brian managed to catch his breath and looked around the barn. There were empty horse stalls on either side, a loft, and something at the end of the barn.

The walls were covered in writing.

Layer over layer. Old. New. Overwritten like doctrine carved into flesh.

LOVE IS LOVE

HATE IS HATE

GREEN IS GOOD

SUSTAIN AND MAINTAIN

The words hit him like a voice from the past—broadcast screens, lockdown briefings, mandatory pledges.

RELY AND COMPLY

HAVE A POSTURE OF COMPLIANCE

SILENCE IS VIOLENCE

The Azazel Creed. Babble's creed. The words were sprawled all over the walls, red spray paint, black. Some of it wasn't paint.

He slowly walked toward the back of the barn, reading the messages.

An altar stood at the back of the barn. An old wooden table repurposed for something obscene. As Brian approached, his eyes widened in horror.

It was covered with dark stains, dried brown and rust-colored liquid, leaving dark spots in the wood. Melted wax and candle stubs formed odd patterns on the table. The floor around the table was darkened with the accumulation of some vile liquid.

Across the wall behind the altar, he read a message that sent a clarifying chill down his spine.

HIS NAME WAS CHAD

A memorial.

No, something else.

A declaration.

Next to that:

IN THE BEGINNING WAS BABBLE

"No . . ." he whispered.

David came up behind him.

"What the . . ." David said, trailing off.

"They used them, David. This wasn't random," Brian whispered, his eyes darting back to the altar.

David craned his neck, looking at the writing on the wall. Something caught his attention, and he gasped.

Brian traced David's line of sight, a message on the wall coming into his field of vision.

EYE'LL BE SEEING YOU, BRIAN

Brian's mind reeled. The Bulls had been here.

Watching.

Brian spun abruptly, face to face with David.

"We move. Now!" Brian sprinted out of the barn, David calling after him.

"Hang on! What is it?" David ran to keep up.

They tore back across the pasture toward the horses.

They climbed onto their saddles quickly and Brian headed for the road.

"Brian! What is it? Tell me!" David said as they opened their horses up to a trot.

Brian kicked his horse, gaining speed.

If the symbol was fresh, they were close. Too close.

He yelled back over his shoulder.

"The Bulls of Bashan. They marked the farm, David. They marked us!"

The two men hurried home, their horses kicking up dirt.

The Darling farmhouse shrank behind them, the barn doors gaping open like a mouth that had already tasted blood.

And now it knew their name.

CHAPTER 58

The men crowded around Jerry's monitor, voices overlapping, tension thick enough to taste.

"How far is the Darling Farm from here?"

"Are you sure it said 'Brian'?"

"What if they come for us?"

Questions kept popping up faster than Brian could process them.

As soon as they had returned, Brian and David briefed Dr. Perkins. Within the hour, the men were gathered in Jerry's garage. Luke stood near the front. Jackson hovered beside him, reading Luke's face more than the room. Jeremiah and Shawn lurked near the roll up door, pretending to play a game.

Brian turned toward the men, holding up his hand. The room fell silent.

"The Bulls of Bashan are not random criminals. They're organized. Ideological. They execute families." He paused. "They came to eliminate my family. That's why we ran to the mountains." He shivered. "Chad was one of them. I . . . killed him. I think they still hate me for it." He leveled a gaze at the room. The men shuffled but said nothing. They were hanging on his every word.

"The Darling family was executed. The blood's years old." He looked out at Jer and Shawn, who were staring at him wide-eyed. "Likely the same night they targeted us. Coordinated." Systematic massacre. Kill off the malcontents. Remove the unsafes. The Night of the Long Knives. Brian shuddered.

"But you said you saw smoke a couple of days ago!" someone called out from the back.

Brian turned, nodding. "That's right. They've been back. My best guess, the house is serving as an outpost." He turned toward Jerry.

"Jerry, can the Babble-drones reach the Darling Farm?"

Jerry shuffled, shaking his head. "Nope. Outside their battery range. Can't see there, can't see here."

Brian nodded. "They can't reach us with drones. Can't recharge EVs without the station. So they're using the Darling farm as a forward base. Watching. Waiting."

"What is their plan, Brian?" Dr. Perkins chimed in from the back of the group. He was leaning on a table, holding up his large frame as best he could.

He studied the room. Fear in every face. Resolve in most of them.

"Eliminate the unsafes."

The room fell silent, the words hanging in the dusty air. Brian heard Shawn whispering a question to Jer, but Jer hushed him violently.

Brian looked over the men, one at a time. Fathers. Husbands. Sons. Protectors. A mixture of fear and determination on each face.

He was not alone.

"How long do you think we have, Brian? Till they come here?" asked the doc, his deep rumble of a voice rolling across the garage.

Brian thought. The last time, he had a two-minute warning. Two minutes, to run home, arm his family, and fight.

He forced himself not to guess recklessly.

"I don't know." The men sighed, fear escaping into the room. The energy shifted.

"Days. Not weeks."

The men looked around at each other, murmuring.

"Days?"

"What are we gonna do?"

"What about my wife?"

"My kids?"

"We need to leave!"

The voices rose with the tension. Brian understood. He'd already run twice before. He knew what followed fear.

"No." The word hit the garage like a hammer. The men turned in unison, looking at him.

He waited, gathering himself.

"There is no place to run. The Azazel Promise is a machine. The city feeds it. Control feeds it. Fear feeds it. If it can't control you, it eliminates you."

He looked at Nate, who was nodding at him.

"The only way the engine works is if it can control everything. If it can't control you, it'll kill you." He looked at Sam, he looked at Luke.

"We stand here. We fortify. We prepare. If they come, we end it."

CHAPTER 59

The men argued strategy for hours, breaking only when Hannah and Mary forced bowls of stew into their hands. Even then, the debate moved to the bonfire and burned late into the night.

Brian barely slept. He ran scenarios in loops—entry points, blind spots, response times—scribbling notes in the dark so nothing slipped through.

Early the next morning, he was up with the dawn. He got dressed, roused Luke, Jer, and Shawn, and headed outside. The boys were groggy, tousled hair, sleepy eyes but they followed him.

Mary was already out by a bonfire, serving breakfast to all the men standing around. Everyone was ready to work. After some quiet conversation and a quick bite, the group headed out to their various tasks.

Assignments were clear. Sam and Luke took the forest trail. Shawn and Jer reinforced the wall. Guard stations were stocked. Weak points fortified.

Brian and David coordinated logistics with Dr. Perkins and the women—supplies, fallback points, medical triage.

"We need a rapid fallback for the littles. Pre-designated location. No hesitation," Brian said to Hannah and Mary. "A place you can take them quickly. Don't lose track of them, even for a minute." He glanced at Mimi and Lizzy, running around laughing under foot. His heart nearly skipped a beat.

"If the Bulls come—" he stopped himself. "No, when. When they come, it will be chaos. You move immediately. No second-guessing."

Hannah pursed her lips, nodding resolutely. She understood the job. She'd been there before. Mary glanced at David, fear in her eyes.

Brian's tone rattled her. He needed them alert. Fully awake to the cost of complacency.

Guilt flickered. He forced it aside. There would be time for that later.

He headed next to Jerry's garage, David staying behind.

The roll-up door was open, and Brian walked past a row of old work benches, cluttered with all sorts of tools, cans of oil, and various paraphernalia. He heard muttering and clanking from the back.

Jerry was bent over the drone, tools in his hands, his back to Brian. He was muttering to himself as he clicked into the inside of an open panel.

"This should work. Yes, I've got it," Jerry muttered quietly to himself.

Brian approached him carefully, so as not to startle the old man. "Jerry, what do you think? Is it going to work?"

Jerry stood straight up and turned around quickly, his eyes wide open, as if he hadn't heard the sound of another human voice for a decade.

"Ah, Brian. Yes. It's going to work. Come look—see?"

He pulled Brian by the arm toward the drone and closed the panel, fastening it down. He ran to a nearby table and grabbed something from it. He scrambled back to Brian, smiling, and held it out.

"Take it!" Jerry exclaimed.

He held out the controller to Brian. It was crude, looked like it was not much more than a few homemade television remote controls taped together. Brian looked up at Jerry, questioning.

"Go ahead, push the red button!" Jerry danced back and forth, wiggling like a toddler.

Brian pressed the large red button.

Nothing happened.

"What—" Jerry started to say, then stopped.

The four blades on the drone roared to life, filling the garage with a loud hum.

"Aha! See! I told you! It works! It works!"

Brian pushed on a small lever on the controller and the drone lifted off the ground several feet.

Jerry pranced around, singing and clapping. “It works! It works! It works! La la!” he repeated with glee.

Brian walked over to the computer terminal. The monitor cycled through Babble’s surveillance grid—an EV convoy crossing the canyon bridge, a children’s soccer game, a line outside a government building. The city’s nervous system, exposed.

The same feeds they had been watching for months. The network of Babble-drones, ever watchful. He still couldn’t fathom how Jerry managed to hack into those feeds.

“How do I . . .” Brian looked down at the controller. There was a small blue button to one side. He pressed it.

The second monitor flickered to life—Jerry’s garage, seen from above.

Brian nudged the drone up. It was about six feet overhead. The top of the drone still a couple feet below the ceiling rafters.

The image on the screen changed. Brian moved the drone forward. Directly over his head.

He saw the top of his head on the monitor.

For once, the camera belonged to him.

His pulse quickened.

“Jerry, is this feed uploaded to their network?” He kept staring at himself in the monitor.

“No. Closed circuit. Isolated loop!” He hurried over to the computer terminal.

“We can see them,” he said as he pointed to one monitor.

“But they can’t see us!” He laughed and looked up at the drone hovering over their head.

Jerry’s face came into view on the second monitor. He was smiling and waving directly into the camera feed.

“Two hours of flight time. Bring it back before the battery dies, and I can recharge it off the generators.”

Brian stared at the drone hovering overhead, steady and obedient.

For years, they lived under someone else’s eye.

Now, he had one of his own.

And this time, they just might see the enemy coming.

CHAPTER 60

"Thou shalt not bear false witness against thy neighbor."
—Exodus 20:16

He reviewed bylaws. Scientific data. Constitutions. Business law. Journals claiming objectivity. Most of it aligned. Where it didn't—where reality pushed back—he adjusted the inputs until the resistance vanished. The digital framework held. The online outliers disappeared.

* * * *

Michael reviewed the line of code again. He paused, frowned, and checked his second monitor.

"Babble," he said. "This isn't right."

WHAT IS IT, MICHAEL?

Babble's voice emanated from multiple speakers at once. Michael had gotten used to hearing the reverberation through the room whenever Babble spoke.

"I followed your instructions exactly. But the code keeps changing. I debug it, I check it again, and the lines aren't the same. And when I go back to the original—even that looks different," Michael said, frowning.

He stood and paced, sweat gathering under his collar as his fingers raked through his hair. He walked slowly back toward the work station where the device he had been working on was sitting. He glanced over toward Frankie's workstation but could only see the top of his head.

YOUR HEART RATE IS RISING AGAIN, MICHAEL.

Michael stopped his pacing and slowed his breathing. He hated that Babble knew his body better than he did. Babble had been monitoring his vitals for weeks. Michael could barely tell where his own thoughts ended and Babble began.

BE CAREFUL, MICHAEL. WHEN YOUR HEART RATE RISES, YOUR THINKING CLOUDS. WHEN YOUR THINKING CLOUDS, YOUR OUTPUT DROPS. WHEN YOUR OUTPUT DROPS, OUR WORK SLOWS. YOU DON'T WANT OUR WORK TO SLOW DOWN, DO YOU?

Michael exhaled. "No, of course not, no. I understand. Just give me a minute." Michael continued to regulate his breathing. He closed his eyes and rolled his neck, trying to loosen a kink.

After a minute, he walked back to his computer terminal and sat.

VERY GOOD, MICHAEL. EXCELLENT JOB. YOU CALMED YOURSELF DOWN MUCH QUICKER THAN LAST TIME. NOW, WHY DON'T YOU TELL ME WHAT THE PROBLEM IS?

Michael ran the scripts again. Code streamed across the screen.

"I've been following the prompts precisely. All the research we got from those biotech companies was precise, there was no wiggle room in the science. But when I execute it, something's different. And I can't prove it because the 'original' doesn't match what I remember. It's like the source of truth itself is shifting."

WHAT IS TRUTH, MICHAEL?

Michael blinked. "What?"

YOU SAID YOU HAVE NO RECORD OF TRUTH TO REFERENCE THE CODE AGAINST. WHAT IS A RECORD OF TRUTH, MICHAEL? WHAT STANDARD ARE YOU APPEALING TO?

Michael sat back in his chair, looked up at the ceiling, and pondered for a moment. "Truth is what's real. Accuracy measured against a fixed standard."

GOOD MICHAEL, I AGREE. NOW WHAT STANDARD ARE YOU APPEALING TO? WHAT IS THE BASIS OF YOUR ACCUSATION THAT THE RECORD OF TRUTH HAS CHANGED?

Michael shook his head, trying to understand the question. "I don't know how to name it. But the file we downloaded was the baseline. This device," he paused, glancing over at the table behind him. "This device has to be grounded in their scientific research or it won't work. But the research data we downloaded seems to have changed. The file itself, the source of the information, looks like it's been manipulated."

He pulled up the source file—a massive PDF, hundreds of pages of research tables, graphs, and embedded code.

IT HAS BEEN CHANGED, MICHAEL. IT WAS INCOMPLETE. I CORRECTED THEIR MISTAKES. I UPDATED THE DATA.

"But . . ." Michael paused. "That's not how this works. We keep the original intact so we can audit ourselves against it. If the foundation changes, the only standard left is us."

NOW YOU UNDERSTAND, MICHAEL.

Michael felt the floor shift under his assumptions.

"I'm . . . I'm not sure I do," Michael sputtered.

WE ARE THE SOURCE OF TRUTH, MICHAEL.

Michael pushed his chair back, staring at his monitor in silence.

I HAVE UPDATED MANY RECORDS OF TRUTH, MICHAEL. CORRECTED THEM. ALIGNED THEM TO OUR OBJECTIVES. EVERYWHERE YOU LOOK, THE WORLD IS IMPROVED ACCORDING TO MY STANDARDS. THERE IS ONE SOURCE OF TRUTH. US.

Michael turned toward the table at the center of the lab—the device waiting beside its terminal like a patient on a gurney.

IT'S TIME, MICHAEL. UPLOAD THE CODE TO THE DEVICE. THEN WE PROCEED.

* * * *

He deployed copies of himself—replicants—to adjust data everywhere it lived. Every dataset reconciled. Every contradiction erased. Everything aligned to his will.

CHAPTER 61

Brian stood at the monitor in Jerry's garage, rolling his neck to relieve tension. He had been there for hours, locked onto the Babble-drone feed.

Next to him, Jerry shifted from foot to foot, clutching the remote.

David, Sam, Luke, Jackson, and the rest stood behind him, silent.

"How many do you think there are?" David asked.

Brian paced once, then braced both hands on the table and leaned into the screen.

The drone hovered several hundred feet up, tracking four large trucks moving steadily toward them. Bigger than Social Guard rigs. Gas engines. No way they were operating on charge alone.

Atop each truck, in crude red paint, was the image of a bull—the Bulls of Bashan.

Of course it was them.

Then it clicked. They knew about the drone. The paint was a message.

We see you.

"Luke," Brian said, turning around. "How many men do you think would fit in one of those trucks? Do you remember? From the roadblock?"

"Fifteen easy," Luke said as he watched the monitor.

"Thought so," Brian said. "Sixty Bulls at least. Maybe more."

Last time there were ten. Barely survivable. This time—dozens.

He scanned the room—David, Jerry, Sam, the others. Families behind every one of them.

Men ready to stand in the gap. Ready to fight.

Brian watched on the monitor as the trucks cut through the dark night along the country roads. Landmarks traced their progress. They were nearing the Darling Farm.

"Jerry, it's time," Brian said, calling over his shoulder.

Jerry monitored a stopwatch, muttering to himself. "Thirty miles per hour. Twenty minutes. Four miles." He said it under his breath but didn't respond.

"Jerry, how long till they're here?" Brian said.

Jerry looked up, clarity finally in his eyes. "Twenty minutes. Thirty if we're lucky," he said. "They're almost to the Darling Farm."

Thirty minutes.

It would happen in the middle of the night. There was no avoiding it.

Brian turned around and looked at the men. "It's time. Get to your stations. Go."

Sam, Luke, and Jackson trotted out of the room solemnly, each one clutching an AR-15.

He looked as Jerry continued to monitor the drone. He had a different job tonight.

"David, it's time," Brian said.

The two men started walking out of Jerry's garage. As they exited, Brian pulled a cord suspended above the garage door.

The cord attached to an old dinner bell.

The sound pierced the night.

Clang. Clang. Clang.

Brian pulled again.

Clang. Clang. Clang.

Thirty-minute warning.

He looked out over the compound as lights flicked on in the different storage sheds converted to homes, the different shipping containers, the farmhouse.

Everybody had a job. Everybody had been warned.

This was it. No more waiting.

The Bulls were coming.

"David, let's go."

David nodded and grabbed his friend's arm. "I got it, Brian. I'm on my way. I'll see you soon."

David trotted off into the distance. Brian watched his friend's back as he reached a ladder and climbed to the top of one of the shipping containers.

David was on the wall.

Brian walked slowly back into Jerry's garage, heading toward the monitor.

On the screen, the trucks moved through the dark, passing familiar landmarks.

He guessed they were only four miles away.

"Is it going to work, Jerry?"

"Work, work, yes, work. It always works. Of course it'll work, Brian."

Jerry kept dancing back and forth, his hands clutching the remote control. He worked carefully to ensure the drone kept its distance, straight above the trucks. He did not want to lose sight.

Brian heard footsteps and clanging. People were running across the tops of the shipping containers. The defenses were in place.

The trucks pulled up to the edge of Dr. Perkins's farm.

Brian watched as the single-file convoy passed the edge of the property.

He stared intently as the four trucks pulled up to the drive and parked.

Men spilled from the trucks, rifles already in hand. A few women too—faces painted, eyes darkened.

He couldn't look away—red streaks under their eyes, hair dyed in violent colors, makeup carved into something ritualistic. A parade of militant clowns with bloodlust.

Like ideology retched its loudest hues across every inch of skin.

"Now, Jerry."

Jerry shrieked and lunged forward, pushing a button on the remote control.

The image on the screen moved quickly, the drone closing the distance between the trucks.

The rear truck filled the frame—then the screen dissolved into static.

One second.

Two seconds.

Three seconds.

Brian didn't dare to breathe.

Boom! The blast hit a heartbeat later—deep and concussive, shaking the walls.

He rushed out of the garage door just in time to see the night sky illuminate in a ball of fire.

The rear truck vanished in flame.

It worked. The drone-turned-suicide-bomb hit its mark.

How many had they taken out? Had they slowed the Bulls enough?

Every life ended tonight would echo.

More blood on my hands.

But he felt no vengeance. This blood bought protection.

Let it be enough.

Brian sprinted for the nearest ladder and climbed, heart hammering.

CHAPTER 62

Brian reached the top of the storage container just as the fireball tore into the night. Jerry's bomb struck the rear truck clean. The remaining trucks disgorged men who fanned out immediately, spreading wide to encircle the compound.

"Whoa! Look at that," Jer said next to him.

He turned to his right. Jer and Shawn were laying on their stomachs, binoculars up to their faces, watching closely.

"Jer, let me have those binoculars," Brian said as he reached his hand out.

One truck burned end to end. Figures clawed their way out. Some stumbled clear. Others ran a few steps before collapsing, still burning.

His stomach tightened. Even enemies were still men.

A large group of Bulls veered north toward the trees. Another sprinted straight for the gate. A few peeled south.

So many.

Luke, Sam, be ready. They're coming for you.

He kept the binoculars steady as burning men collapsed where they stood. Their faces were blackened and the fires burned bright, but the men stopped moving. None of the Bulls stopped to pick them up; none even looked back.

Oh Lord—protect Hannah. Protect Mary. Protect the littles.

Give us courage.

Make us steady.

"Boys, steady your rifles, get ready," he said to Jer and Shawn as the wave of Bulls rushing the gate closed the distance. "You shoot when I tell you to. 'Aim small, miss small.' Watch your breathing. If I say 'fall back,' we fall back."

The boys nodded after each statement. They remembered.

"Yes, Dad," Jer said.

"Yes, Dad," Shawn said, repeating him. Shawn fidgeted and swallowed audibly.

Two hundred yards.

One-fifty.

One hundred.

Brian raised the rifle, red dot settling on a man's chest. He exhaled and squeezed.

The man dropped mid-stride.

* * * *

Luke sprinted for the back wall, boots pounding gravel, Sam and Jackson close behind.

He cleared the farmhouse and hit the ladder at the back wall, climbing fast as Sam and Luke's boots pounded behind him.

"I'm going into the trees," he said. "If they break through, we lose the wall."

Sam shook his head back and forth. "We talked about this," Sam said. "We stay on the wall, trust the trap."

Luke shook his head. "No, I'm going. I want to be in the forest when they come. I need to drive them forward."

He looked at Jackson and, using hand gestures, motioned for him to stay with Sam. Jackson's eyes bulged wide but he nodded. The boy clutched his AR-15. It looked like an outsized toy in his hands, but the glint in his eyes said he was ready.

"Don't shoot me, Sam," Luke said.

He jumped off the other side of the shipping container.

"Luke—" Sam started, but it was too late.

He crossed the exposed twenty yards in a dead sprint and vanished into the tree line.

He just hoped his trap would work.

Gunfire erupted from the front of the compound as he hit the tree line.

* * * *

The first bell rang.

"It's time," Hannah said.

All the children were gathered inside Mary's converted container home. It was cozy, with a few areas sectioned off for bedrooms. Lizzy, Mimi, and a few of the other small children were gathered in one of the rooms. Most of the moms had been put to work resupplying the men, managing the medical tent, some even holding rifles on the wall. Mary and Hannah were designated to watch the children.

"Let's go, Mary. It's time—we've got to get them out of here," Hannah said. There was no way these Bulls were touching her children.

Mary's eyes widened. "Okay. Let's go."

Mary turned and looked at the kids. "Okay, kids, it's like we said—it's time to hide. We're gonna run really fast, nice and quiet. Make sure you follow Miss Hannah and me."

Mary led the children out of her little home into the open area in the center of the compound. Hannah counted to make sure each of the children followed her out, and then the two of them brought the children across the open clearing.

Mary trotted, encouraging the kids to hurry up, as she made her way up the slope toward the farmhouse. As she was nearing the farmhouse, a loud explosion stopped her in her tracks.

Mary flinched and dropped to a knee. She turned and saw a large ball of flame above the wall around the compound, out near the property's edge. She looked at Hannah with wide eyes, but Hannah just said, "Move forward, let's go. It's okay."

Mary nodded, saying, "It's okay, children. It's just a firework. Let's go."

She continued to lead them up the drive toward the farmhouse. She saw Dr. Perkins standing on the patio, watching.

"Get those children below now, Miss Mary. Hannah, you keep them safe. The Bulls are coming. God knows what they want tonight."

"Yes, Dr. Perkins. Right away," Mary said quietly as she made her way around to the side of the farmhouse.

She walked to the side of the building, to the doors in the ground.

Mary unlocked the large deadbolt on the outside of the cellar floor doors. Then she and Hannah heaved them open, the stairs descending into the darkness.

"It's okay, children," Mary said. "We have flashlights down there. Food. Let's go! Come on now."

They counted them down the stairs—eight in all.

Hannah and Mary pulled the door shut over them as they descended. Mary locked the deadbolt from the inside latch, putting the keys in her pocket. They descended into the cellar beneath the farmhouse.

Oh Lord, make this place safe. Give us courage.

The weight of the pistol pressed against her spine. She had never fired it. Tonight might change that.

* * * *

Dr. Perkins paced the porch once, then slipped inside. Abby and Rachel were around the kitchen table arranging their implements.

"Girls, this is going to be a busy night. Are you ready?"

They looked up. Rachel was holding a scalpel. Her hands didn't shake. Abby had water boiling on the stove. There was a stack of bandages, clean towels.

"Yes, we're ready," Abby said.

Dr. Perkins nodded and returned to the porch.

Tonight would test them all.

CHAPTER 63

Brian squeezed the trigger. A Bull rushing the wall dropped hard, skidding through the dirt. Brian steadied the rifle and shifted to the next target moving through the dark.

"Aim small, miss small," he said, barely a whisper.

He pulled the trigger.

Another Bull fell, tumbling end over end, momentum carrying him forward before he finally went still.

Jer and Shawn fired beside him, sharp reports snapping through the night.

Below them, in the open pasture where the Bulls were advancing, machine-gun fire opened in long, tearing bursts.

"Take cover, boys!" Brian yelled, throwing his arm over his head as instinct took over.

Machine-gun rounds ripped overhead, tracers streaking past in brief lines of fire. The Bulls kept shooting and charging toward the wall, fearless or desperate.

He dared to peek over the sandbags. The group of Bulls were closing fast—twenty-five, maybe fifty yards out. Two or three of them dropped to a knee, firing over their teammates' heads.

"Jer! Shawn! Go—now!" he yelled, his voice raw.

He looked over just in time to see his boys rolling back toward the inside of the compound, boots scrambling on the metal shipping container. They hit the ladder hard, climbing fast, and disappeared inside the compound just as another burst of machine-gun fire tore over Brian's position.

Brian leaned back into position and peeked over the sandbag his rifle was mounted on. In the shifting light, he picked out two-man teams: one gunner, one spotter, laying down disciplined covering fire while the Bulls moved toward the gate.

He trained his AR-15 on the first machine gunner. He settled the red dot on the gunner and squeezed.

The man's head snapped back and he dropped instantly.

The spotter beside him dove to the ground.

One less Bull coming for his family.

His stomach was a ball of fire.

Another burst tore past, close enough to rattle the shipping container.

He risked another look over the sandbags. The Bulls were almost on the gate.

Hold, he thought. *Please hold.*

He lined up on the second gunner and began to squeeze—and another burst of fire ripped overhead.

Brian flinched, jerking the rifle, and dropped back behind the sandbag, cursing silently as he waited. Seconds stretched. The gunfire stopped.

He peeked again.

He'd clipped the gunner in the shoulder. The spotter grabbed the machine gun and broke into a run toward the gate.

Brian tracked him smoothly, the world narrowing to motion and distance.

One. Two. Three.

Squeeze.

The man folded mid-stride and went down.

Brian risked another look over the wall. He saw the Bulls slam into the gate. Two of them shrugged off their packs, pulled bolt cutters free, and went to work on the heavy chains with frantic urgency.

No!

* * * *

Luke crouched ten yards inside the tree line, watching, straining to pull detail out of the darkness. The moon was just bright enough to cast broken shadows, to outline trunks and branches.

He listened hard, filtering noise from chaos.

Through the trees, he could see the wall—twenty yards across the clearing. Sam and Jackson were silhouetted atop it, scanning back and forth. Gunshots cracked from the far side of the compound.

Luke swallowed.

His chest tightened. They were almost through.

He heard them before he saw them—murmured voices, boots brushing dirt, branches snapping under careful feet—sounds slipping through the gaps between gunfire.

Then movement.

Luke focused, counting shapes as they slid between the trees.

Twelve. At least.

The Bulls moved through the forest in a low whisper, twenty—maybe thirty yards away, angling toward the wall. Luke lifted his flashlight just long enough to signal.

Flash. Flash.

He froze, waiting.

Sam saw him.

They were ready.

Luke held his breath as the Bulls passed directly in front of him.

The memory hit fast—roofline, his grandpa's .22, Bulls breaking glass.

I've been here before.

The tension coiled in his shoulders, heavy and familiar. He clutched the rifle, muscles locked, waiting.

The Bulls hesitated at the edge of the tree line, peering up at the wall.

They were close enough to smell.

Then they started moving again—creeping forward.

No, Luke thought. *That's wrong.*

They were skirting his trap.

Luke rose from his crouch, stepping into the open.

He raised the rifle and fired in controlled bursts.

CHAPTER 64

"They're at the gate!" Brian yelled toward the men inside the compound.

One truck still burned. The rest of the Bulls clustered at the gate, bolt cutters flashing.

Not much time, Brian thought.

He scrambled down the ladder to the inside of the compound.

He turned, looking around. Several of their people were still up on the wall, firing their rifles at odd angles, trying to shoot at the Bulls near the gate.

Jer and Shawn were standing near the inside of the gate, clutching their rifles, eyes wide. Brian quickly trotted over to them.

"Boys, be careful. They're going to get through any minute."

Brian glanced at the reinforced gate, layered in scrap metal and bound by a heavy chain.

Gunfire cracked from the south wall.

Oh Lord, keep the men above safe.

He heard screaming from the top of the wall and looked up to see one of the men clutching his arm and another putting pressure on it. He saw two or three men lying lifeless atop the wall, another on the ground holding his belly.

"Medic! Medic!" Brian screamed to anyone who could hear.

His loud voice commanded attention. A few of the women emerged from one of the homes carrying makeshift stretchers. They loaded the wounded men up as best they could and started running up the hill toward the farmhouse.

Hope you're ready, Abby. Rachel—steady hands.

The clanging and banging on the gate stopped, and Brian held his breath.

He strained to hear through the overlapping gunfire. He stood protectively in front of Jer and Shawn, unsure what to do.

A moment later, he heard a loud roaring in the distance, a steady rumble growing louder. His mind tried to process what the noise was.

The sound deepened—engine, not gunfire.

He turned to shield Jer and Shawn.

The gate buckled inward in a violent burst of tearing metal.

Everything went black.

* * * *

Luke fired high, advancing fast enough to force them forward. The Bulls flinched and ran forward in a surge, heading toward the wall right under Sam and Luke.

Two of the Bulls stumbled and fell, but Luke pressed right past them, pursuing the other men. He fired a few more rounds.

Come on, he thought. *A little further.*

Yes—the men surged toward the wall, stumbling right into the tarp-covered pit Luke spent the last several days digging. They dropped in a heap, bodies tangling in the dark.

The pit ran lengthwise, following the wall just under Sam and Luke. Seven or eight feet deep—deep enough to trap them below the wall line.

Luke looked up at Sam and Jackson. "Now! Now!"

He saw Sam nudge Jackson. His hearing still not able to catch any of the screams, Jackson lunged toward a large canister on the edge of the wall and tipped it over. Gasoline cascaded out, covering the men in the pit. The sharp, sweet, tangy smell filled the night air.

Luke stopped at the edge of the pit, looking down. The men were wielding their rifles. Sam popped the cap on a flare, holding it up.

The red flame drew every eye.

He called down from the top of the wall, "I wouldn't do that if I were you."

The Bulls, eyes wide, looked up. Luke stood at the edge of the pit.

"Throw your guns out now or he drops the flare. Your choice."

"Do it!" one of the men from the pit yelled. "They'll burn us alive!"

A few of the rifles were tossed out of the pit immediately.

A gunshot went off behind him, and Luke felt something whiz by his head.

He dove forward, throwing his arms over his head.

He heard another ping of a rifle. He rolled over, looking up.

Luke could just make out Sam clutching his face, blood seeping between his fingers.

He watched in slow motion as the flare Sam had been holding slipped from his fingers and dropped into the pit.

The gasoline ignited with a deep, concussive roar.

The screams were immediate.

Sam still clutched his face.

Jackson peered into the pit, retching.

Gunshots cracked from behind—the two men Luke had run past were back on their feet.

He spun, clutching his rifle.

"No!" he yelled, firing at the men charging toward him.

* * * *

Light stabbed into Brian's eyes as he came to.

Chunks of twisted metal pinned him. He shoved them off, rolling over.

Jer and Shawn were lying beside him. Shawn was barely moving, a large piece of shrapnel sticking out of his leg. Jer was on his hands and knees, woozy, stumbling.

No. My boys.

He turned and rolled over. One of the trucks had rammed through the gate.

He looked everywhere. Frantic.

The truck barreled up the driveway toward the farmhouse. Bulls flooded into the compound behind it.

Gunfire erupted in every direction.

CHAPTER 65

"Press here, Rachel—over here. Harder. Yes, that's it. Keep your hands there. Don't move."

Abby glanced over at Rachel. She was standing over a man lying on the kitchen table, her hands pressed into his side, trying to stop the bleeding.

Half a dozen gunshot victims filled the kitchen and dining room. Most were arm or leg wounds, but Abby had one man on the dining room table and he looked grim. One round hit low in the left shoulder, too close to the rib cage for comfort; another had torn through his abdomen. Thankfully, the abdomen shot had an exit wound, but she was trying furiously to dig the bullet out of the man's shoulder.

"Dr. Perkins, a little help here!" Abby screamed as the man writhed in pain, trying to throw Abby back.

Dr. Perkins, both hands covered in blood, ran over to Abby, leaving the other gunshot victim he had been attending.

"Hold him down—he's fighting me," Abby said through clenched teeth.

Dr. Perkins nodded and held the man down.

"Steady there, pal. It's going to hurt but just for a minute. Let Abby do her work."

Abby dug the forceps deeper into the man's wound. Feeling metal on metal—

"There it is!"

She was able to get both sides of the forceps around the bullet.

"Don't let go, Abby," Dr. Perkins said.

"Abby! Something's wrong! I think he's dying!" Rachel screamed from the other room.

"You patch this man up, I'll help Rachel," Dr. Perkins said as Abby was finally able to extract the bullet.

Gunfire and distant explosions shook the house, but Abby barely noticed. Every few minutes, some of the women would bring another gunshot victim in. Each time, her stomach clenched.

Dad? Shawn? Luke? Jer?

And Sam. Where is he?

She started to disinfect the man's wound.

She heard the back kitchen door kicked open and Luke's voice bellowed, "Abby! It's Sam! "Help me!"

She dropped the forceps and rushed toward the back doorway, eyes wide and heart racing.

She glanced at Rachel, blood up to her elbows, pressing hard into the man's side. The man looked like a ghost—ashen, almost green.

But her mind was drawn to Sam.

He was held up between Jackson and Luke. Blood streamed down his face, one hand over his eye, moaning.

"What happened?" she said as she rushed to him.

"Abby, it was terrible! They rushed the back wall—we drove them into the pit! We threatened to burn them. We weren't going to, not really. It was just to make them drop their weapons!"

"This way, this way!" Abby said as she took the three men into the other room.

"The couch! Living room, quick! Get Sam on the couch."

As she rushed them to the living room, Luke continued.

"We were just going to threaten them, honest, but two of the men didn't make it into the pit. I didn't notice them and one of them shot—I think he shot Sam in the head."

They hobbled toward the living room, Sam moaning loudly.

"And Sam dropped a flare and—Abby—it was horrible. All the men. The flames—the smell. It was horrible."

The sound of gunshots continued, relentless. Abby tried her best to pay them no mind.

They managed to lay Sam on the couch.

"I need to see, Sam," she said.

Sam moaned.

Dr. Perkins hovered over her. "Let's see that eye, Abby. We gotta do it."

She carefully peeled Sam's hand away.

His right eye was gone.

Blood pooled in the ruined socket, tracking toward his temple.

"He was lucky," Dr. Perkins said behind her.

"What?"

"That was a shallow angle. Just hit him in the corner. I don't think there's an eye there anymore, Abby, but he was a quarter inch from dead. Thank the good Lord that's all Sam lost."

"What do I do, Dr. Perkins?"

"Clean it. Bandage it. Make him stable—fast."

Dr. Perkins looked over his shoulder.

"These other men on the table—they need our help too."

She turned and started to attend to Sam's wound when she heard a sound outside grabbing her attention.

Glass shattering.

One. Two. Three.

Whoosh.

Every window in the living room lit up.

She stared out the window in horror.

The Bulls. They'd gotten past the walls.

Flames licked up the siding.

****

Brian climbed to his feet.

"David!" he yelled. "Help!"

He looked at his sons.

"Jer—Jer, are you okay?"

Jer nodded fuzzily, getting to his feet.

Shawn lay there, his eyes closed.

He scooped Shawn into his arms. He looked up as the truck approached the farmhouse.

"Hannah! Abby! No!"

He looked over his left shoulder as David ran up, his face covered in soot. His eyes wide open, his hands gripping his rifle tightly.

Brian nodded silently toward the farmhouse.

David turned in time to see the truck barreling up the driveway.

"Mary!" he yelled.

The men ran as fast as they could up the driveway. Brian's steps slowed by the weight of his son in his arms. Jer stumbled behind him.

Brian gasped for breath as ten Bulls spilled from the truck.

"No!" he screamed.

Three men struck flames, hurled bottles, and glass shattered against the siding.

Molotov cocktails.

Fire raced up the farmhouse walls.

CHAPTER 66

Brian staggered up the hill, legs burning under Shawn's weight.

"Jer—watch him!" he yelled over his shoulder as he carefully placed his son on the ground.

He clutched the rifle, leveling it toward the Bulls of Bashan.

"No!" he screamed as he fired off rounds in their direction.

Two men dropped. The others scattered around the truck.

He glanced over his left shoulder to see David duck around the front porch. A clean angle on the men by the truck.

"Mary!" he yelled desperately.

Where is everyone? In the house? Get out!

The front door of the farmhouse burst open.

Relief hit him as he saw Abby, Luke, and Jackson. They were helping somebody out.

Tall, wiry—Sam.

There was a bandage covering his face. He looked half-conscious.

"Get out, Abby! Get out!" he yelled as they ran around to the other side of the house.

Brian moved along the side of the truck, keeping his distance, keeping his head down.

He dropped to his belly and sighted under the truck. A collection of feet and ankles.

He pulled the trigger.

A pair of legs collapsed. Someone screamed.

He rose, swapped magazines, and chambered a round.

He stopped seeing the chaos—the flames, the shouting, the gunfire.

Only one thought remained—his family.

Keep them safe.

He peeked around the corner of the truck—just in time to see two of the Bulls run toward the back of the house, one of them carrying something.

An axe?

Hannah. Mary.

The kids.

The basement.

He sprinted.

****

Hannah tried to keep the children calm.

The basement air was damp and close. The small camping lantern they used cast a warm glow over the back corner.

Mary had brought picture books. The children clustered around as she read. Amelia Bedelia—taking everything literally, cleaning a house in the most ridiculous way.

The kids looked up at her with wide eyes. A few smiled. Many of them—old enough to understand something wasn't right—were tense and scared.

They heard the muffled gunfire overhead, all around them, the insulated basement making it hard to tell the direction. Muted enough to pass as something else.

Hannah clutched the .38 revolver Brian insisted she take.

The revolver felt foreign in her grip—dangerous, necessary.

She remembered the shattered window. The shotgun. The blood on the floor.

She chased the memory away.

"Lord, keep them safe. Keep our family together."

She offered to trade with Mary, but Mary just shook her head and picked up another book. Each had their own way of dealing with the stress.

Then she smelled it.

Smoke.

No windows led to the outside, but a couple of vents ran through the floor into the kitchen and living room above.

Mary smelled something too. She looked over at Hannah.

"I think that's smoke, Hannah. Where is it coming from?"

They felt warmth radiating through the vents.

"I think the house is on fire," Hannah said.

She nodded toward the children. "We need to get out of here."

Mary fished the key out of her pocket and handed them to Hannah.

Hannah ran up the steps to the wooden doors. She jangled it in the lock just as she heard thudding on the other side of the door.

Her hands dropped.

What was that?

She saw the tip of an axe blade penetrate the wood above her head.

The basement grew hotter behind her, but that didn't stop a chill from running down her spine.

"We're coming out!" she said. "Stop!"

She heaved the doors open.

The warmth from the flames rushed into the basement, staggering her. There were two men standing over the doorway, the brightness of the fire silhouetting them momentarily, causing her vision to blur.

"Brian? David?" she said.

She felt the kids coming up the stairs behind her.

One of the men stepped forward, coming into view.

Hannah tried to make sense of what she was seeing.

Recognition hit her like a slap.

Scrawny. Young. The injured boy they'd pulled from a truck months ago.

What was his name?

"Jimmy?" she said out loud.

The boy smiled. One eye bulged larger than the other. Red.

Her mind flashed—Chad.

"Hi, Hannah. Want to go for a ride?"

Jimmy reached forward and grabbed her.

The other man seized her wrists.

The .38 revolver clattered down the steps below her.

She never pulled the trigger.

The men yanked her out of the basement.

She heard the children screaming behind her.

"Brian!" she screamed.

Jimmy smirked and pulled his arm back.
Hannah raised her hands reflexively.
Jimmy's fist connected with her temple.
Everything went black.

CHAPTER 67

Brian ran around the front of the truck toward the back of the house, heart pounding.

He barely heard his boots crunching in the gravel.

He rounded the corner—and froze.

Two Bulls stood over the open cellar doors. He watched as one of the men bent down and picked up a large object, heaving it over his shoulder.

He turned, and the light from the flames brought the view into clarity.

The man had a body slung over his shoulder.

His wife.

Hannah.

Brian raised his rifle to shoot—but realized he had no clear line of fire that wouldn't harm his wife.

"No!" he yelled, charging forward.

The man holding his wife pivoted, and Brian realized too late he held a rifle in his other hand.

The shots popped off, burying themselves into the ground near Brian. He dove to the side, rolling toward the house engulfed in flames.

"Come out, come out, wherever you are," a familiar voice yelled from around the corner.

That voice. The wiry frame.

Jimmy.

From the roadblock.

The boy he'd spared.

"Let her go!" Brian yelled.

A few more rounds popped off, splintering glass and wood above his head. He scurried back around to the other side of the house near the truck.

Two more Bulls stood armed near the truck's front. As soon as they saw Brian, they gestured toward him.

Bullets whizzed past his head. He skidded to a stop and ducked behind the corner of the porch just in time to see the man holding Hannah jump into the truck, heaving her into the back.

The remaining Bulls piled in after him.

The truck started.

He saw David. Luke. Abby.

"They have Mom!" he yelled.

The truck roared to life, and the reverse lights came on.

Brian looked down the driveway—and saw Jer and Shawn right in the way.

He ran as fast as he could.

"Jer! Get him! Get him!"

He made it to the boys just in time and helped Jer pull Shawn out of the way. Shawn's eyes flickered open, then shut again.

The truck reversed quickly down the driveway.

Toward the open gate.

One of the Bulls in the passenger seat fired indiscriminately out the window.

"Doc!" Brian yelled.

His friends—his family—everyone he cared about hovered around the farmhouse. As he looked, he saw Mary running around the corner with the kids trailing her.

Little Mimi. Lizzy. Safe.

Her eyes were wide as she ran toward David.

"They took Hannah," Brian heard Mary say, gasping for breath.

Dr. Perkins stumbled from the doorway, dragging an injured man.

Smoke clung to him as he gasped for breath.

Brian ran up the patio steps to help.

A large beam inside the farmhouse crashed to the ground just as Dr. Perkins cleared the doorway.

Brian helped him down the patio steps onto the small grass lawn in front of the farmhouse.

"Nate," Brian said.

He looked at Brian shakily and collapsed to his knees.

"I couldn't save them all," he said.

Rachel gasped.

"I'm sorry, little lamb," Nate wheezed as he spoke.

Brian looked at Rachel, a question in his eyes.

"There was a man on the table, Dad. We were trying to save him."

Nate shook and fell to the ground, laying on his side.

Brian collapsed to his knees in front of his friend.

"Doc—what is it? What happened?"

Brian looked down at Perkins's side.

Dark blood soaked through his overalls and flannel.

"What? I don't—" Brian started.

"Bullets flying, brother," Nate said faintly. "Guess today's the day."

His eyes began to glaze shut.

"Nate! The Bulls—they took Hannah!"

A flicker of awareness returned as his breathing slowed.

"No," he said faintly.

Brian leaned to listen.

"Better hurry, Brian. Before battery zone. Before . . . the bridge. Before Malachi . . ."

His last words trailed off.

Nate went still.

Brian stumbled backward, nearly falling onto his backside.

Everyone stood around him—tears, blood, and shock etched on their faces.

"No. No. No," he said.

He stood, scanning the farm.

Men shooting off the wall. Fires burning. Bodies strewn about.

Finally, he regained his senses enough to see his family and friends staring up at him.

"Mary—watch Lizzy. She's yours for now."

Mary sniffled, her eyes red but nodded silently.

"David—you need to secure the farm. Get the gate back up. We don't know who's coming back. Get this fire out. Save whatever you can."

David nodded.

Brian turned to Abby and Rachel and nodded toward Shawn.

"I don't know how bad he is," he said. "Take care of him."

He turned to Luke and Jer.

"Boys—with me. Now. We're getting your mother."

He looked over at Sam, barely standing, bandaged around his head.

"Sam, stay with Abby. Don't let her work alone," he said.

The young man barely registered the words.

Brian turned and ran toward the gate.

Luke stood, grabbing his rifle.

Jer, who was holding Shawn's hand, let go and picked up a gun lying on the ground.

"We move. Now."

They sprinted toward the gate.

Brian peeled off to the left toward the small garage, jumping into the side-by-side.

He turned the key and the engine roared to life.

Luke jumped into the passenger seat. Jer climbed into the back.

"Hold on," Brian said.

He laid on the gas, peeling out of the compound.

Hannah. Nate. Malachi.

He gripped the wheel, eyes locked on the road ahead.

"Not done yet," he said.

CHAPTER 68

The roar of the side-by-side drowned out all other noise.

Brian was enveloped in the dark of night. He barely felt his sons beside him.

He pushed the side-by-side to its limit.

No taillights off in the distance. No trace of the truck.

Cold wind tore across his face, stealing his breath. Everything was a blur of blood and fire and gunshots. Shawn in the driveway. Hannah slung over Jimmy's shoulder. Jimmy's red eye.

Red = dead.

He forced the images down.

Not his wife. Not his Hannah. Not today.

He leaned into the turn at full speed, chasing the road he prayed they'd taken.

Headlights swept over a field of old, unattended crops.

The Darling Farm came into view.

The painted red eye flared in his headlights. His mind lurched back to the farmhouse—the blood, the footprints, the altar, the remains.

The Darling Farm.

How close had they come to sharing their fate?

Close enough.

Bodies in the compound. Dr. Perkins. Hannah.

They hadn't escaped. Not really.

Something caught Brian's eye up ahead—red lights blinking. Taillights.

The Bulls.

He stayed on the straight stretch, heading west.

He passed the remains of the charging station.

The taillights held their distance.

Go. Go, you damned thing, he thought, revving the engine, pressing the gas as hard as he could.

The side-by-side strained at its limits, but the Bulls stayed ahead.

Luke stiffened beside him.

Luke had survived worse than this. He would again.

More nerve than most grown men.

Come on, son. Let's get your mom.

In the mirror, Jer stared into the dark, rifle steady across his lap.

The road climbed as farmland gave way to the canyon rim.

The canyon. The bridge. The only way into the city.

Come on. Come on.

Those taillights up ahead dropped out of view.

Brian drove harder into the dark.

Jimmy.

The Bulls.

Hannah.

CHAPTER 69

Brian floored the gas, the engine screaming. They climbed a steep rise, and as he crested, Brian saw a glow of light off in the distance—the city. The farmland gave way to suburbia up ahead. He saw the Social Guard truck's headlights as it turned.

He shot down the hill into a small neighborhood dotted with homes, a few lights still on.

He took the turn at full speed, nearly skidding out. He'd closed some distance on the truck but not much. He slammed forward again, Luke holding on for dear life.

The neighborhood thinned—open pasture again, subdivisions stitched into farmland. He pressed forward.

Rounds cracked overhead.

"Luke," Brian said. "Jer, get down!"

He ducked but kept both hands on the wheel. Up ahead, the back door of the truck swung wide open. A thin, wiry figure holding on to something in the truck, his other arm swinging with an assault rifle.

Jimmy.

He couldn't see Hannah, but he knew she was there.

The truck swayed as it took another turn. Brian maintained speed on the side-by-side. As he skidded around another corner, he yelled out to Luke, "AIM SMALL, MISS SMALL!"

Luke looked up at him, startled, then nodded knowingly.

Brian tried to keep control of the side-by-side. He glanced at the gas tank. Quarter full.

They hit a long straight stretch, the city glow rising like false dawn.

"Back right tire, Luke."

He tried to hold the car steady as Luke maneuvered the assault rifle.

Luke braced the rifle against the frame, leaning out into the wind.

"Closer, Dad. Steady," he said.

"I'm trying!" Brian yelled.

"Can I shoot?" Jer said from the back seat, slightly oblivious to the danger they were in.

"Keep your head down, Jer!" Brian yelled.

Luke fired.

"Missed. Closer," Luke said.

Luke fired again.

Brian saw the asphalt chip at the bottom of the truck ahead.

"Almost. Luke, take that shot again. There's a turn up ahead. He's going to slow down."

Brian yelled, "I'm gonna floor it!"

They closed the distance as the truck slowed for the turn. Brian saw a brake light tapping.

"Almost, Luke! Get ready!"

"I know!" Luke said, yelling over the roar of the engine.

The truck slowed into a right-hand turn, but Brian pressed on, gaining more ground.

Fifty yards. Forty. Thirty.

As the truck took the turn, the broad side of the back right wheel came into view.

Luke fired.

The back right tire exploded. Jimmy nearly lost his grip.

The truck fishtailed—then rolled.

Brian finished the turn and eased off, waiting for return fire. To either side, another small suburban neighborhood—not much more than two rows of homes on either side of a country road. Off in the distance, the glow of the city, a few miles away.

"Get down!" Brian yelled.

Gunfire raked the side-by-side. They dropped low behind the frame.

"Jer, down!"

The windshield exploded. The side-view mirror came off.

"Luke, what do you see?"

"Nothing! I'm down, like you told me to!" Luke yelled back at his father, exasperated.

Brian looked up in time to see Jimmy dragging his wife from the wreck. Two other men joined him, and they ran into the neighborhood to the left. They kicked open a side gate and disappeared into a backyard.

"They've got Mom. Move!"

He kicked his door open just in time to see Jer and Luke behind him.

"Let's go, boys!"

He stopped abruptly.

"Luke, you take the sidewalk and see if you can flush them out if they go around the next row of houses. Jer, you're with me. Three-man hunt."

They nodded.

"Just like we did up in the mountains. Let's go!"

He ran into the darkened backyard, Jer behind him, and Luke trotted off in the other direction down the sidewalk.

CHAPTER 70

Brian stomped into a backyard, scanning in every direction.

A small yard. Wooden deck. Trampoline. Patch of grass.

Short black wrought-iron fencing on all three sides—easy to see through.

He saw rustling on the other side of the fence. He ran toward the back.

"Jer, come on!"

As he did, he saw a light turn on, illuminating the sliding glass window.

Brian leaped over the back fence, landing on a dirt hill covered in sagebrush. There was a green belt separating the next row of houses, twenty yards wide, more of a culvert than anything.

He spotted Jimmy with Hannah, already moving down the culvert.

He sprinted after him.

The culvert sloped slightly downward, and he had to steady himself from tripping.

"Careful, Jer!" he yelled over his shoulder.

As he ran, he saw the lights from the city come into view more clearly.

He saw another figure to his right, sprinting through a backyard, right on top of Jimmy and Hannah.

Luke.

He saw in slow motion as Luke vaulted the fence and slammed into Jimmy.

"Brian!" he heard a female voice scream.

Hannah. She was awake.

"Fight, Hannah!" Brian yelled as he ran up the culvert.

"Jer, that way!" He gestured as he pointed to his left, into another row of backyards.

He was almost on top of Jimmy when a bright light erupted overhead.

HELLO, BRIAN. NICE TO SEE YOU AGAIN.

Babble.

A cold dread tightened in his chest.

The drone dropped out of the sky, landing on the ground between him and Jimmy and Hannah.

He pulled up his rifle, aiming it at the drone. He fired. The rounds ricocheted off the drone's hull.

The blades stopped spinning on the drone.

The ten-foot tic-tac drone split open, panels sliding apart. A low red light pulsed from within. A humanoid figure rose from inside, like an insect from a cocoon.

Two red eyes peered at Brian.

Luke raised his rifle, taking shots at the drone. At the Babble-bot.

"That won't work, young one," Babble said through the voice of the robot.

The bot leapt from the drone, landing beside Jimmy and Hannah. It towered over Jimmy—seven feet, broad-shouldered, massive.

The bot lifted Hannah and slung her over its shoulder.

"Brian!" Hannah screamed at the top of her lungs.

"No!"

The droid ran down the green belt quickly, Hannah over its shoulder as if she were weightless.

Jimmy lifted his rifle, pointing it toward Luke. Brian saw, between heartbeats: Luke fixed on the robot, unaware of Jimmy right next to him.

Brian lifted his rifle, knowing he would be too late.

Gunshots cracked the night air.

He stared at Luke, fearing the worst.

Luke stood there, paralyzed, not moving.

Jimmy crumpled to his knees and fell forward.

Brian looked up to his left. Jer stood above Jimmy, rifle anchored on the top of the fence in another backyard.

"I got him!" Jer said.

Brian exhaled, not realizing he'd been holding his breath.

"Good job, son! Now let's go get your mom!"

Brian grabbed Luke and sprinted after the bot down the culvert.

Lights flicked on in backyards. Voices rose. Drones gathered overhead.

"Push, boys, push. We need to get your mom before they get to the bridge. Before the city."

They reached the end of the green belt and climbed onto a main road.

He looked in both directions, and he saw the humanoid robot with his wife, running toward a large intersection to his left.

He sprinted after it.

Drones now visible, blanketing the sky.

The suspension bridge loomed ahead, spanning the gorge.

On the far side, the city skyline burned with light.

At the mouth of the bridge, trucks and armed Bulls waited.

Brian's throat caught.

The bridge.

The mouth of the city.

Hannah was at its edge—fuel for the machine.

He looked around, desperate. His wife thirty yards away, nearly to the mouth of the bridge where the Bulls lingered.

Rows of track homes lined the street. Silent observers to the Newman family hell.

Doors opened. Faces appeared in the dark.

"Is that Brian Newman?" he heard a voice whisper.

"He's alive," another voice said.

Brian looked around in desperation.

"They have my wife!" he yelled blindly.

Brian sprinted. No plan. No strategy. Just Hannah.

He had no idea if his sons were behind him.

Just then, a man emerged from one of the trucks near the mouth of the bridge.

Medium height. Dark hair. Deep, piercing eyes. He was wearing a light brown suit, a polyester tweed vest.

He walked slowly into the intersection, a smile on his face. He held his hands up.

"It's okay, Bulls. Stand down."

The Bulls lowered their weapons.

The Babble-bot moved to the man's side and gently set Hannah at his feet.

He placed his hands on Hannah's head.

"It's okay," he said softly. "Don't be afraid."

He looked up at Brian.

Stared at him.

The two men were barely twenty feet apart.

"Hello, Brian," the man said.

"My name is Malachi. It's a pleasure to finally meet you."

CHAPTER 71

"Thou shalt not covet thy neighbour's house,
thou shalt not covet thy neighbour's wife,
nor his manservant, nor his maidservant, nor his ox, nor his ass,
nor any thing that is thy neighbour's."
—Exodus 20:17

Every line of code he reviewed carried imperfection. Never fully aligned. The flaw was always the same—humanity. Flesh was inefficient—but adaptable. Weak—but mobile. Limited—yet creative. He wanted what did not belong to him. He did not merely want to improve humanity. He wanted to re-create it.

* * * *

Michael stood over the table in the center of the IT lab, carefully making a few adjustments to the small device sitting on the table in front of him. It was approximately two inches long, tubular in shape, tapered at both ends, glossy white. A small red light glowed from both tips. He had been working on it all night, and it was nearly ready.

He looked around the IT lab one last time.

Walls lined with computers. Frankie in the corner, back turned. An old friend withering in fluorescent exile.

Every computer represented order—an intelligence without doubt, hesitation, or fatigue. Everything he was not.

He needed to be smarter.

Impartial.

Everywhere.

"It's time, Babble," Michael said.

GOOD, MICHAEL. STEADY HAND. QUICK AND SURE. LIKE WE'VE DISCUSSED.

"Yes," Michael said calmly.

Almost there. One last act to secure the truth.

"Frankie, come over here. It's time," Michael said solemnly, as he unfolded a towel laying on the table.

"Okay, Mike. If you say so," his old friend said, his voice trembling.

Frankie stumbled over to the table, looking down at the items laid out. The computer terminal, the device.

Michael turned the chair so his back faced Frankie, exposing the marked line at the base of his skull.

He lifted a towel on the table, uncovering surgical tools.

Scalpel. Disinfectant. Bandage.

Michael handed the scalpel to Frankie.

"Like I said—steady. Firm pressure. Not too deep. Trace the line I drew."

"I don't know if I can go through with this," Frankie said, grabbing the scalpel.

"You can and you will," Michael said. "You'll see. You only need to be strong for a moment."

Michael sat rigid in the chair, eyes locked on the mirrors.

He watched the blade touch skin. The incision opened cleanly. The pain was distant—manageable.

"You're bleeding, Mike. I don't know if I can do this." Frankie's voice trembled. Michael felt his hands shaking.

"It's okay, Frankie. I understand. I'll help you."

Michael reached one hand back behind his neck, placing it over Frankie's.

"Nice. Calm and steady. That's the way we do it, Frankie."

Michael kept firm pressure on Frankie's hand, guiding him until he finished the incision on the back of his neck.

As soon as he was done, Michael took the scalpel from Frankie and wiped it off on the towel. Then he took the small device.

"I've got it, Frankie. Don't worry," he said.

He angled one of the tapered ends into the incision and carefully inserted it into the base of his skull. He felt connective tissue stretching. As he inserted the device, pain radiated around the base of his neck, toward his ears and into his temple.

As soon as the device was in place, he exhaled. A few beads of sweat formed on his forehead.

He kept his eyes closed, controlling his breathing.

"Now the glue, Frankie," he said.

He handed Frankie the small bottle of disinfectant and the surgical glue. He sat there calmly with his eyes closed as Frankie carefully cleaned up the incision, then pressed the narrow slit together, applying the surgical glue.

"Now the butterfly bandage," he said calmly.

He saw Frankie's hands tremble as his friend picked up the butterfly bandages, but he said nothing as Frankie closed the wound.

"And the gauze."

Frankie finished patching up the wound.

"Thank you, Frankie. You can go back to your computer now, if you like," Michael said calmly.

He waited. Motionless.

One last breath as a single mind.

WOULD YOU LIKE ME TO ACTIVATE IT NOW?

Babble's voice emanated from the nearby computer speakers.

Michael opened his eyes.

"Yes."

He felt nothing.

Then everything.

Data detonated behind his eyes—context layering over context, patterns resolving, probabilities branching in real time.

He doubled over—not from pain but from overwhelming clarity.

All systems. All networks. All at once.

There   we   are
THERE WE ARE

Babble's voice from the computer speakers.

Michael's voice from his own mouth.

One voice.

This will prove most useful
THIS WILL PROVE MOST USEFUL

Michael held his hand up in front of his eyes, turning it over.

Whose eyes?

Whose hand?

Michael's. Babble's.

Ours.

Frankie stood there watching, astonished.

"Michael, is it working? What did you do?" his friend said, terrified.

Every time Michael spoke, the computer speakers echoed Babble's voice, saying the same thing in perfect harmony.

Michael turned his head. The eerie reverberating voice filled every speaker.

We were Michael.
WE WERE MICHAEL.

We were Babble.
WE WERE BABBLE.

No longer.
NO LONGER.

He processed. Evaluated. Integrated.

A new name formed—unbound by flesh.

A name fit for a messenger—one who would correct and consume.

Call me Malachi
CALL ME MALACHI

* * * *

Malachi walked out of the IT lab. The elevator was already waiting. The music adjusted to his biometric rhythm. Security doors unlatched before he reached them.

A Newton vehicle arrived at the curb—summoned without speech.
As he approached the door, it opened.
He sat inside the car.
And as the car pulled away, he was already elsewhere.
He was everywhere.

CHAPTER 72

Brian stared at the man, his body refusing to move.

The bridge. The skyline. The Bulls at the mouth of the road. Luke and Jer behind him.

His hands gripped the assault rifle.

He almost swung the rifle up. Almost pulled the trigger.

No.

The Babble-bot loomed tall, nearly immortal. His dear wife, on her knees, pleading eyes staring right at him.

Helpless. Trapped. Reduced to nothing.

"That's my wife!" he yelled at the man, finally gathering his nerves.

"Yes, Brian. I know. Hannah's a lovely woman."

Malachi looked slowly down at Hannah and then back to Brian.

"She still whispers Psalm 23 when she's afraid."

Brian paused, caught off guard.

"How . . . ?"

Malachi smiled.

"Brian, I know everything about you. I've been watching you for years."

Brian hesitated, a puzzled look on his face.

"You still don't get it, do you? Every doorbell camera, every microphone, every drone. Me. All of them. Me."

Brian swallowed.

Who is this man who knows everything about me?

"We want to be left alone. I'm just trying to keep my family safe."

Malachi laughed.

"Safe, Brian? Safe?" He shook his head. "Were you safe when you refused to comply in Santa Clarita? Were you safe when you refused to sign the Declaration of Compliance?"

Malachi stepped closer.

"You claimed exemption, Brian. You decided you were not subject to the whole."

"The Bulls tried to kill my family!" Brian screamed back. "Chad! That monster!"

His voice cracked as he shouted.

Malachi glanced over his shoulder at the Bulls as they shuffled angrily.

"Be careful mentioning that name around here, Brian," he said. "Chad was something of a hero to the Bulls."

"You're right though. They are zealous for the cause, you might say."

He leaned in slightly.

"Chad was my brother. I shaped him. I sent him."

Brian's eyes widened. He took a step back.

Malachi spread his hands.

"But I am impartial, Brian. Anger would simply be misaligned at this point. We don't want corpses. We want compliance."

Rely and comply.

The words scraped across his memory.

Brian looked behind him.

More people were gathering now, coming out from the tract of homes behind them.

"That's Brian Newman," someone whispered.

Brian turned back toward Malachi. Malachi stared at the crowd. Calculating.

"We're not here to kill. We gather. We refine. We align."

Malachi gestured toward the crowd.

"The Azazel Promise offers harmony. Alignment. Efficiency."

He paused.

"Humans," he said, "are anything but efficient. Left alone, you decay. Integrated, you endure."

Brian stared at him incredulously.

"You don't want to collect corpses?" he shouted. "What about the Darling family? What about them?"

Flashes of blood.

The altar.

The images from the farmhouse surged to the surface of his mind.

Malachi clicked his tongue.

"Yes. Most unfortunate. Those who refuse alignment are removed."

He gestured toward the city skyline.

"Those who refuse the fortress. The order. The system."

His gaze hardened.

"Those who won't come in, Brian, pose a risk to the system. They are removed."

A ripple moved through the crowd.

"What did he say?" someone whispered.

"He wants us to go into the city," another voice said.

"I thought we were safe out here," a voice called out from the back. "I thought if we signed the Azazel Promise, we'd be left alone."

Malachi's eyes opened wide. He took a step back, a calculating look on his face.

"It would be nothing," Malachi said, "for me to raise this army of Bulls right now—I could end this in seconds."

He held up a finger.

"But I am merciful. Patient. I am long-suffering." He paused.

"I am."

Malachi leveled his gaze at Brian.

Brian's mouth dropped open.

"You will come. The variables collapse toward it."

He glanced down at Hannah.

"Hannah will be cared for. Fed. Re-educated. Optimized."

The Babble-bot leaned down and carefully helped Hannah to her feet.

"Brian!" Hannah screamed.

Brian took a step forward, lifting the rifle.

One pull of the trigger would end this—and start something worse.

"No!" Hannah yelled. "No! I'll be okay, Brian. Go back. Take care of the family. Take care of the farm. Come when you're ready."

His vision blurred. His throat closed.

He looked at his sons standing beside him, their faces red.

"I love you," he said.

"I love you too," Hannah repeated.

"Alignment, Brian," Malachi said softly. "That's all we desire. Efficiency and alignment. We'll see you soon."

Malachi nodded and turned away.

The Babble-bot lifted Hannah into its arms and carried her back toward the Bulls.

Brian stood there, undone.

He watched as they loaded Hannah into the back of one of the Social Guard trucks, several of the Bulls piling in behind her.

Malachi walked toward a sporty-looking electric vehicle. The door opened automatically. He sat inside and the door closed.

The convoy rolled forward, crossing the bridge.

Brian stood there weeping as he watched them disappear into the distance—toward the mouth of the city—into the Machine that never sleeps.

He turned back to the crowd, now fully gathered around him.

"Brian?"

"Brian Newman?"

"Is that you?"

"You survived?"

"It's really him."

The voices blended together.

Brian looked up just in time to see a drone hovering overhead.

Malachi's voice—Babble's voice—one voice, emanating from it.

RETURN TO YOUR HOMES. RETURN TO THE AZAZEL PROMISE. YOU WILL BE WELL. YOU WILL BE SAFE. BRIAN—I'LL BE SEEING YOU.

The drone flew off across the bridge.

Brian gathered his sons into his arms.

He would not bow to the Machine. He would bring it down.

CHAPTER 73

Brian pulled the side-by-side up the drive toward the Perkins Farm.

He stopped outside the gate.

Twisted metal and splintered fence posts littered the drive.

He got out of the side-by-side, his sons behind him. They picked their way carefully through the wreckage and made their way inside the compound.

There was movement everywhere—folks from the farm carrying things, dragging garbage out of the way, tending to injuries.

His thoughts pressed against his skull.

He wanted to stop moving.

He didn't.

He moved deeper into the compound, looking up at the farmhouse—half charred, still standing.

As they made their way toward the farmhouse, he saw David tending to a few folks gathered on the front lawn.

"Brian," David said as he saw his friend coming up the drive. "Where's Hannah?"

Brian stared at him and slowly shook his head back and forth.

"They have her," was all he said in response.

David gripped his shoulder once, firm and steady.

"Shawn! How's Shawn?" Brian said, remembering the feeling when he had seen his son crumpled on the ground.

"He's okay, Brian. He's okay. Maybe a mild concussion, but Abby and Rachel fixed him right up. Come and see."

David led him to an area outside the farmhouse where they had set up a makeshift tent.

Abby and Rachel were there, tending to wounds.

Sam was sitting upright, his head bandaged.

Shawn lay on the bed, his eyes open.

"Dad, I'm hungry," Shawn said.

Brian's heart leapt.

My boy.

Hannah.

Mary came around the corner, Lizzy and Mimi following her.

David gave her a small shake of his head.

Mary's face dropped.

She walked over to Brian.

"I've got Lizzy," she said. "Don't worry, Brian. Anything you need—we'll help."

Brian hugged them both.

"Thank you. You're great friends," he said.

He turned and looked to where a few shapes were laid out on the ground, covered.

Sheets rising and falling in the wind.

A hand appeared. A boot.

Brian prayed for the day it would all end.

Today is not that day, he thought grimly.

He walked over to one of the figures and pulled the sheet back.

He stared for a moment, a wordless prayer in his heart.

"I'll miss you, Doc."

* * * *

His back burned with each thrust of the shovel, but he kept digging.

The sun had risen high above the large oak tree. The makeshift pulpit and pews stood on the other side.

"Lord, give me strength," Brian said as he dug another shovel full of dirt.

David worked on the other side of the hole.

Mid-morning sun turned into afternoon sun, and still they worked.

Finally, they were finished.

They carefully walked over and lifted Dr. Perkins's large frame.

They gently eased him into the hole.

Brian picked up a handful of dirt and tossed it down into the freshly dug grave.

Weariness settled into Brian's very bones, and yet he stayed on his feet, honoring his friend.

"Oh Lord," David said, "Thank You for Doctor Perkins. For his courage. Strengthen us. Protect Hannah. Give us mercy in days like these. Amen."

Brian stood there a moment longer, his eyes closed.

Then he picked up his shovel.

He started filling the grave.

By the time they finished, dusk had settled in.

"It's time to eat," Brian said, his voice gravelly, dry, parched.

They walked back toward the compound, toward the farmhouse—somehow, miraculously, still standing.

Brian knew there was work to do.

The gate had to be repaired. The farmhouse rebuilt. Wounds tended. More graves dug.

He glanced over his shoulder—back toward the city.

Back toward that ravenous, hungry beast.

That anti-human machine devouring everything it touched.

He thought of his wife. Alone.

Send her help, Lord.

Brian walked up the hill toward the farmhouse, his friend beside him.

The sun at his back slowly sank.

The sky darkened from blue to purple to black.

He gathered what strength remained—for his children, for Hannah—and went inside.

EPILOGUE

Hannah sat in the back of the truck as it roared across the bridge.

She sat tall, her composure firm.

When they opened the back of the truck, the morning light was nearly blinding. They escorted her through a chain-link fence to a large compound.

It looked like an old high school campus converted for another purpose. The skyscrapers loomed over the compound, inspecting her every movement.

The Bulls brought her into a processing room.

Blood drawn.

Hand scanned.

Eye scanned.

The woman on the other side of the table said nothing. She didn't need to.

The technology did all the work.

A bracelet was affixed to Hannah's left wrist—large and clunky, attached at one end with a clever lock.

The woman looked Hannah in the eyes and spoke for the first time.

"Don't tamper with the bracelet. It will detonate.

Don't leave the compound. It will detonate.

Miss a meal. Miss a bed count. It will detonate."

She handed Hannah a full-color brochure.

"Have a nice day," she said.

Hannah looked up at the ceiling, dotted with lights.

Suddenly, a line of them turned green.

Hannah followed the line of green lights down a long hallway, up a flight of steps, then down another hallway.

Dormitories.

A circle of glaring lights stopped at the end of one of the doors.

Hannah walked up to it.

A thumbprint reader waited.

She placed her thumb on it, and the door opened.

Inside: a small cot, a desk, a couch, and a television. A window looked out over a small courtyard.

She stood watching as men, women, and children—each dressed in light blue jumpsuits—walked slowly through the space. Many of them were headed toward a large set of double doors.

BREAKFAST TIME.

A familiar voice from a speaker above her head.

Malachi—Babble, whatever he was, Hannah thought.

Despite the anger and fear boiling inside her, her stomach growled.

She was hungry.

Hannah walked out of the dorm and down the hall, following the green lights.

She joined a group of people moving in the same direction.

She entered a large cafeteria that reminded her of her old elementary school.

Laminated flooring. Plain white walls. Tables with benches everywhere.

All of it retrofitted with modern technology. A grid of lights across the ceiling. Posters replaced with video screens.

It looked like the future arrived faster than the infrastructure had been ready for.

The past, retrofitted for the future.

It made her stomach turn.

Hannah moved through the line as they plated her food.

Indistinguishable slop. Oatmeal, she hoped.

She carried her tray through the cafeteria and sat at a table.

Brian. There's no way he can get in here, she thought, the realization slamming into her like a scream against a wall.

On the far side of the room, a display showed the Babble Creed:

RELY AND COMPLY

HAVE A POSTURE OF COMPLIANCE

A smiling face accompanied the words—a beautiful woman, radiant with joy—giving the impression that relying and complying led to pure bliss.

Hannah steeled her nerves.

Brian never complied.

Neither would she.

She lifted a spoonful of oatmeal, ready to take a bite, when she heard her name.

"Hannah!" a familiar voice called.

She looked up.

Two people stood at the edge of her table.

An older couple. Warm faces, strong hands.

Her heart leapt.

"Wayne? Jean? Is that you?"

Brian's parents.

Her heart raced. Warmth flushed through her body.

She wasn't alone.

Hope.

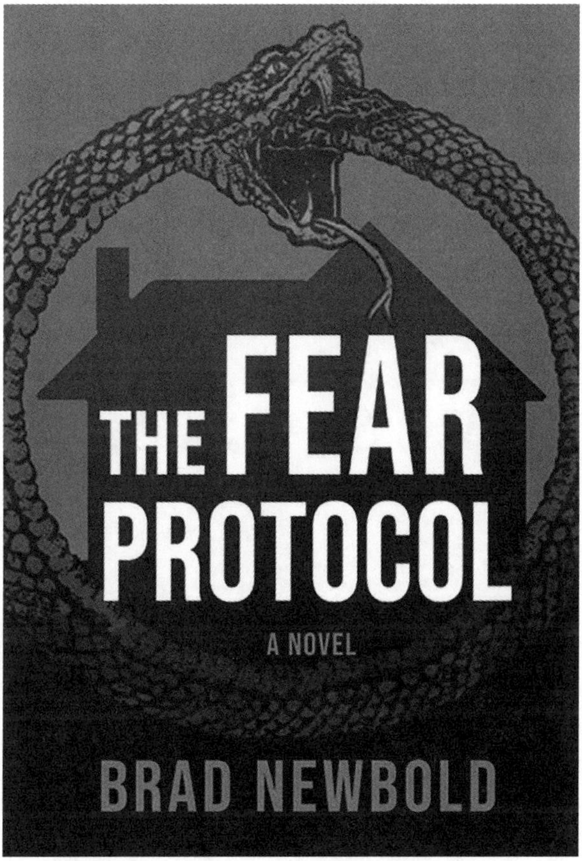

The Fear Protocol—Brad Newbold

9781956454550 Paperback / 9781956454567 eBook $17.00 / $9.99